Luke and Catherine met online via the BBC Writers Forum and decided to write this novel together as Luke wanted to see if he could write from a female perspective and Catherine from a male viewpoint. *Heading South* was completed in rapid time via email and telephone conversations, though as Luke tragically died in October 2006, aged just 34, the two authors never met in person.

HEADING SOUTH

Successful artist Cassie lives her life through her pets — her very own cast of 'Winnie the Pooh'. She's passionate about her animals — but can't help thinking she's missing out on something. That something comes in male-shaped packages . . . Good-humoured Nick, hapless and impulsive, is still reeling from being dumped by his fiancée. Thanks in part to a prank by Nick's mate — together with a black furry bundle of puppy named Rooney (after Wayne) — the lives of the two gradually come together, though neither can quite believe the reality. Can their relationship survive being plagued by ex-girlfriends, posh admirers, pets passing away and friends going into labour?

LUKE BITMEAD AND
CATHERINE RICHARDS

HEADING
SOUTH

Complete and Unabridged

ULVERSCROFT
Leicester

First published in Great Britain in 2007 by
Legend Press Ltd
London

First Large Print Edition
published 2008
by arrangement with
Legend Press Ltd
London

British Library CIP Data

Bitmead, Luke
    Heading south.—Large print ed.—
    Ulverscroft large print series: romance
    1. Love stories 2. Humorous stories
    3. Large type books
    I. Title II. Richards, Catherine
    823.9′2 [F]

    ISBN 978–1–84782–132–4

Published by
F. A. Thorpe (Publishing)
Anstey, Leicestershire

Set by Words & Graphics Ltd.
Anstey, Leicestershire
Printed and bound in Great Britain by
T. J. International Ltd., Padstow, Cornwall

This book is printed on acid-free paper

In memory of Luke, whose talent, wit, drive and smile will be greatly missed but always remembered by everyone who met him.

1

Cassie

Even in the snoozy Cotswold countryside, the mid-morning air isn't entirely filled with melodious bird song and the soporific mooing of cattle. Sometimes an impostor makes its presence felt.

'Caaaaassssssiiiiiiiieeeeee!'

Oh bugger.

Just as my dream man is leaning in for our first electric kiss, something else needs my attention.

'What?!'

'I'm sorry, Richard. I'll only be a second. Why don't you pour us some more of Tesco's finest and I'll be back before you've burped up the first few bubbles?'

'Cassie!' The voice comes again.

Could that be another man after my attentions? Phew! What a morning!

I haul myself out of the flowerbed where, back in the real world, I've been planting a red rhododendron, and dust off my knees.

'There's something on the girly wig!'

'Don't worry!'

This had better be a full-on disaster, I think, as I hoick up my too-tight-therefore-unbuttoned trousers. My daydream was so real I was actually getting drunk on it.

'Why don't you come and help me here, so I can see what you're doing?' I call out.

Silence.

'Wiggy,' I say a little more sharply, as the rhododendron collapses on its side. 'Wiggy!' My call receives no reply. 'Oh . . . f . . . iddle.'

I round the corner of the cottage onto a semicircle of crazy paving. It should have been normal paving but D.I.Y. was never my strong point. I call it D.D.I.Y. — don't do it yourself.

'Wiggy!'

Because of the dazzling sunlight, the scene that confronts me takes several seconds to become clear.

Underneath the whirly gig (or girly wig as Wiggy calls the clothes carousel) is a small bundle with something moving inside. The clothes still clinging on are thrashing about like spinnakers in high wind.

I approach with caution, crouching down like the tourists you see rushing from helicopters after a five-minute spin over The Grand Canyon or Rio de Janeiro, or the many other places I haven't been with my dream lover but would like to visit.

2

'Wiggy!'

'Here,' says a small, frightened voice.

'Are you ok?'

I reach down into the heap and dig about for the reassuring warmth of a childish form. Finding it, I fumble for a hand and pull Wiggy free from what must have seemed an alarming avalanche of bed linen, teddies, nighties and a tablecloth (had a slight disaster with a glass of red wine on Saturday night).

I sit her on one of the whitewashed garden chairs and, giving her a rub on the head, turn my attention to the carousel. The sound it was emitting has greatly reduced but it still appears to be half-filled with crêpe paper being rustled by a large kindergarten group.

I pull the washing apart, revealing the pheasant I adopted after he suffered a broken wing.

'You stupid, stupid bird, Eeyore.'

I grab him roughly and place him on the ground. 'How did you get in there?'

He gives me an indignant roll of his eyes as if to say, 'How do you think?' Then, with a stroppy flap of his wings, he scurries off into the hedge to brood.

Wiggy's now smiling brightly and waggling her feet like paddles under the chair. 'He's a silly bird, isn't he, Auntie Cassie?' she giggles.

My two cats, Piglet and Roo, are

play-fighting under her, twisting and rolling like leaves in the wind. I stoop down, stroking both cats and, now at Wiggy's eye level, ask her if she'd like some lunch. (I've bought alphabet spaghetti especially.)

'Can I have an avocado?' Wiggy chirrups.

'Sure,' I say, a little taken aback at her sophistication.

'With some French dressing and some chives?'

'If that's what you want.'

I take her hand and lead her through the French windows into the kitchen, my mind already wandering back to my earlier daydream.

How perfect this quiet country living would be with just a tiny bit less babysitting and a smidgen more sex.

Nick

As I wake-up I experience two sensations in quick succession. The first is a pleasant vibration around my groin. The second is like the pain of being kicked in the bollocks, only transferred to my head. The rest of my body feels like it's been in a road traffic accident.

I eventually persuade my hand to reach down and wrestle my buzzing mobile from

4

the pocket of my jeans.

'Nick Ratcliffe,' I croak into the handset. The mouth isn't so good either: a dry, desiccated wasteland, vaguely tasting of stale lager.

'Nick, it's Debbie.'

My sister's voice twitters anxiously down the phone. What kind of girly crisis has she managed to get herself into this time?

'Nick . . . are you there, Nick?'

I groan to confirm I'm still alive.

'Nick, Scotty didn't come home last night. I can't get him on his mobile and I've no idea where he is and . . . '

Oh God! She's sobbing, and sobbing means I'm going to do whatever it is she's about to ask me. What is it about a crying woman that makes a bloke drop everything and go running?

'Ok. I'll get dressed and come over.'

It's only a small lie but it seems to pacify her. I can't get dressed because I'm already dressed.

'No, don't worry, I'll come to you.'

'See you in a bit then.' I hang up.

I must have just crawled straight into bed when I got in, whatever time that was. Perhaps a shower will help.

I roll off the bed into an undignified heap. I have to use the corner of my chest-of-drawers to haul myself up. At least I managed to take my trainers off before I passed out.

I shuffle down the hall and into the bathroom, trying to decide whether I need to be sick or whether . . .

'Eurchhhh!' My foot touches something warm and soft on the floor of the bathroom.

I turn my bleary eyes downwards and see what appears to be the decapitated body of a man wearing nothing but an England away shirt.

My head swims. I try to work out exactly who might have put it there and what happened to his head.

The answer slowly comes to me. I'd recognise that arse anywhere. Anyone who has ever driven behind a coach taking Owls supporters to an away game would recognise that arse.

I prod the body tentatively with my foot. I get a pained grunting noise in response.

'Scotty, get your head out of my laundry basket and get some clothes on, will you? Deb's looking for you.'

Cassie

I watch Wiggy squeeze out a large blob of gouache onto my pine kitchen table and then raise a mucky paw to her mouth.

6

'No, don't eat it, sweetie.' Her multi-coloured fingers make their way to her lips. 'Mummy will not be pleased if you go home with a tummy-ache.'

She's already enjoyed two avocados, half a packet of (low fat, please) crisps and a satsuma.

As I scrub her hands for the second time in an hour, Jilly arrives to pick her up.

'Thanks so much again for looking after her.' She plonks herself down on a kitchen chair and gives an exhausted sigh. 'What a morning!'

'So how are things at Corruptly & Dork?' I ask.

'I need lunchtime alcohol! This woman looking round the barn conversion wants her husband to come and view it later this afternoon. Can't say no really but, if she doesn't buy this one, I'm going to tell her to find another agent. You know the kind of thing.' Jilly puts on a superior voice, ''The kitchen's a bit pokey. How many acres does the house come with? Ghastly wallpaper, that'll have to go. Carpet's a bit frayed.' She comments on everything, looks at the place three times and then says, 'No, it simply won't do. I'm not living in a hovel.' I've nearly punched her several times.'

I tut sympathetically and pour her a glass of Rioja. She glugs it back in one and gasps, 'Thanks Cass, you're a saint.'

'Much to do this afternoon?' I sit myself down, putting my elbows on the table.

'Christ yes. I'm cooking for Jeff and a few of his clients tonight. Suddenly got a terrible feeling I've left the beef in the deep freeze, so I'll have to buy another joint. Then I've got three more viewings to get through . . .'

'You're a miracle on legs.'

'I'm a mess.' She looks at her watch. 'Oh Christ, Cass, I've really got to run. We'll catch up another time, ok?'

She gathers up Wiggy and bolts out the door. I wave as she backs out at action-movie speed and careers off down the lane, shouting at Wiggy to put her seatbelt on.

I wander back into my little garden and gather up the debris a lunchtime spent with a child has caused. Wiggy is so exhausting I really don't know how Jilly copes. Let alone working too. I do worry about her. It can't be healthy living life at her speed, though I do help out with Wiggy whenever I can. It relieves her of some of the pressure, but it leaves me drained. I've made a mental note that if I decide to have kids to adopt a little person aged eight, so they have at least basic independence. I bet Jilly wished she'd done that too.

As I gather up the wrappers and discarded morsels of food, I think about the work I must crack on with this afternoon. I have a portrait to present on Tuesday and it's nowhere near complete.

Dumping everything in the kitchen, I scamper up the stairs and cross the tiny landing to my second bedroom, converted by an easel and a rubbish tip of paint tubes into a 'studio'. The light is good up here. It comes slanting in through the dormer window and fills the room with an attractive glow, perfect for painting.

At school, art was the only subject I was any good at. I couldn't add or subtract, I couldn't speak French and I didn't see the point of English literature, although I've always read loads of romantic trash.

My latest commission is for Mrs Ponsonby, a landed gentry type from Lower Slaughter. I'm painting one of her prize stallions, a handsome fella called Mr Tipsy. The day I went to photograph him was a nightmare. Not only would he not stand still, but something unspeakable happened between his legs while I was doing a close-up of his hindquarters. I'm not sure I will ever fully recover from the shock, or the memory of Mrs Ponsonby shouting, 'Oh Mr Tipsy, I know she's a pretty little thing, but really!'

I squint critically at the painting. I'm relieved to conclude it's going ok. It is definitely a horse, not a hippo, or a wildebeest. No way do I want to go back for more photos.

'It's not bad, is it Tigger?'

My mallard is perched on the paint-splattered stool, blinking at the canvas.

'What do you think?'

He turns his brown, dappled head in my direction and quacks.

'Hmm. Me too,' I agree. 'You've got to budge now, honey. I need to get on.'

Nick

I've never managed to work out how Scotty made the transition from being my best mate to being my brother-in-law. We were in the same class all the way through school. Pubs, football matches and holidays followed. Then suddenly, out of the blue, he started shagging my sister. I seem to remember he did very graciously ask my permission, but only after he'd already been doing it for a month. Next thing I know, she's got him down the aisle and he's a bloody relative.

I look across at him now as he sits on my sofa in the pair of boxers I've just lent him. Not an edifying sight. Either they've shrunk, or he's a lot fatter than I am.

'Sorry about puking in your washing, mate.

10

I could have sworn it was the bog.' He swigs from the mug of tea I've just made him and goes back to reading the paper.

'It's alright.' I shoot an ironic smile at him. It isn't alright, but I don't feel well enough to argue about it yet. The excruciating headache has started to ease off, but I still feel rough.

'Aren't you supposed to be at work or something?' he asks, not looking up from the paper. He seems incredibly chirpy for someone who drank half a brewery last night.

'No. Got sacked, didn't I?'

'What?'

'The wedding on Saturday got out of control. The best man lunged in for a snog with one of the bridesmaids. She told him to piss off. The groom intervened, then another bloke. End result: me breaking up the scrap in the hotel car park and getting smacked onto the pavement. I got a grazed cheek out of it, so I hit the best man and he complained to my boss.'

'Oh. Bad luck, mate.'

The news doesn't seem to have an impact on him. Perhaps I shouldn't give a toss either. I never planned to work in conference and banqueting; it just happened. Organising other people's weddings is the pits. Don't ever let anyone tell you they're happy occasions. They invariably end up in fights,

11

arguments and customer complaints.

Scotty folds the newspaper. 'We were bloody robbed!' He gestures at the picture of England's players despondent after a late defeat.

Coming from an ardent Owls supporter that's quite a statement. We should be used to watching our team lose.

I let my thoughts wander back to last night. Both of us sitting in the pub, fists clenched, waiting for that last free kick. The tension . . .

The memory is violently interrupted by the terrifying sound of screeching brakes followed by an almighty crash. An enormous set of ladders smash through the bay window onto the floor of my living room, spraying us with glass.

'What the fuck?'

We both race for the front door.

Outside there's a white transit van parked where my front garden wall used to be. It has charged over the pavement, obliterated the garden gnome and come to rest at an angle. There's a remaining ladder left clinging to the roof rack.

Debs' fast crumpling face is lowered over the wheel.

'What the hell have you done to my van?' Scotty screams, rushing over to comfort his vehicle. I half expect him to wrap his arms around it and stroke the huge dent in the bonnet, or scoop up the water that's flooding from the radiator and pour it back in.

'Oh, my God!' Deb cries, already opening the driver's door. She jumps down to the ground and rushes back to the road where I suddenly spot a small, lifeless body.

There are tears running down her cheeks now. 'He just came out of nowhere. I tried not to hit him. Nick, what are we going to do?'

I wrap my arm around her shoulder to comfort her. I can feel her shaking.

'I've killed him, haven't I?' She buries her head in my chest, smearing snot and tears over my nice, clean t-shirt as she has done in times of distress ever since we were kids. I guess that's one of the many pleasures of being a big brother.

But Scotty isn't in the mood for cuddles and comforting. He seems oblivious to the medical emergency we have in front of us. He's just walking anxiously around his van, tutting. Still wearing nothing but my boxers.

Cassie

'Twitchy' in my home is called being 'Piglet's tail', which seems to have a life completely separate to its owner's. Many times I've watched Piglet's little face track his tail with

13

a mixture of alarm and horror. It flicks about like a miniature black hose that's had the water pressure turned up too high. That's how I am sometimes if I'm getting behind with things: I feel a bit 'Piglet's tail'.

I'm feeling like that now as I squeeze an autumnal selection of colours onto my palette and mix up a dark bay to work on Mr Tipsy's face. I've realised I'm going to have some difficulty here because the only shots I managed to get of his head make him look like a mad thing, with wall eyes and flared nostrils. I think Mrs Ponsonby is looking for something altogether more regal. I may have to nip down to the library to find a photo of a non-mad horse head to work from.

Once I start working I become so absorbed that time drifts away from me like a rapidly receding tide. It's mid-afternoon when the phone goes, jolting me out of my concentration with a sudden, shrill ring. I've been painting in a trance since Wiggy left.

In the hall I have one of those old phones with the 'brrring, brrring' bell and a dial for the numbers. It's not that I want to live in the past; it's simply that the phone was here when I moved in and I found no reason to change it.

I rush down the stairs and lift the black, chunky receiver.

'*Buenas dias!*' I say brightly. For some reason I think this is amusing. Don't ask me why. Perhaps I think it makes me look well travelled. Tee hee.

'Hello, mother,' I continue, less brightly. A call when I'm this absorbed in my work is not good. My mother is a terrific talker. Anything less than half-an-hour 'to catch up' is unacceptable. The trouble is 'catching up' is at best pedestrian, at worst darn right funeral. My mother describes each day since we have last spoken in minute and exacting detail. A rip in the left-hand glove of the marigolds, their black Labrador's general state of health, problems with the Aga — they're all terrifically newsworthy.

So imagine my surprise when my mother says, 'Darling, this is just a quick call because I'm awfully tired, but I just wanted to warn you that you'll be getting a call tomorrow from Andrew . . . Hang on a sec.'

I hang on listening to my mother shouting at my father, 'What was the name of the chap you met today?'

In the background I can hear my father rustle his paper and mutter, 'Andrew.'

'Yes, I know that, darling, but what's his surname? Hughes was it, Hewitt? Something like that . . .'

15

'Hendry,' my father calls back. 'Say hi to Cassie from me.'

My mother fiddles with the phone and relays the news.

'He's down from London for a week to play polo and he'd like a portrait of this spaniel he's bought for his parents. It's their thirty-fifth anniversary.'

'When does he want it by?' I make a mental note to tell Jilly I have no need for a webpage with parents who are this good at networking. She's been on at me to get one for ages.

My mother tells me a couple of weeks, which will just about be ok. I only have one other painting I'm working on (a much-loved cat) and that's not due for a month. My mother signs off telling me Bumbles is in tolerably good health, though his cataracts are getting worse, and to let her know what happens with Andrew Hughes, no Hewitt; 'No! Hendry,' my father calls out again.

'He's knee-weakeningly good-looking, by the way,' my mother gasps before signing off, 'and we think he's single.'

Well, that's preferable to being bum ugly and married, I think to myself, and skip off to the kitchen for a quick snack.

Nick

'Right, that should do the trick.' Scotty steps back to admire his handy work.

I give a half-hearted smile. I don't see why I should be too grateful. It was he and Debbie who turned up and wrecked my flat between them. It's been a stinking hot day — not the kind of weather where you want your windows boarded up.

'I'll come round and put a proper one in when the van's fixed,' Scotty tells me.

'And the front wall?'

'I'll send one of the lads round from the site tomorrow if there's any slack. If not, I'll pop round next weekend myself, shouldn't take long.'

I suppose having a builder for a brother-in-law does have its advantages. I wouldn't have got the flat looking as good as it does without his assistance.

'Ahh! I think he's wagging his little tail. Look!'

We both look over to Debs who is maternally stroking the little black bundle of fluff that she mowed down this morning; the bundle that is now wearing a plaster cast on his front-right leg and one of those plastic buckets around his head.

'Never mind sweetie. Uncle Nick will look

after you,' she cooes in a nauseating tone as she stands up and grabs her handbag off the sofa. Suddenly, her words rearrange themselves inside my head and click into coherence.

'I think you'll find Uncle Nick has already stumped up the money for a large vet's bill and been conned into buying him a nice new bed on the way home, even though it wasn't him that ran the poor little bugger down in the first place.'

'He can't come home with us, Nick. I've just had all the carpets shampooed. Besides, he must be from around this area. It'll be easier for you to track his owner down.'

I don't know why I bother to argue with Deb. I can't ever recall winning.

'What if I don't track his owner down?'

'Course you will.' Scotty goes over and gives the fluff ball an affectionate tickle.

'They'll not want to be without you for long, will they mate?'

'Alright.' I know I'm giving in. I always do and it's probably best not to prolong the agony. 'He can stay here for a week and then he's off to the pound.' I sound decisive.

Debs' mouth falls open and a distraught wail echoes around my living room. 'You can't send him to the pound, you evil sod! How can you be so awful?'

'You take him home if you're so keen then.'

'I can't, you know I can't. What will we do with him while we're both at work? At least now you'll be in to look after him.'

The sound is suddenly sucked out of the room and an awkward silence is pumped in to fill the void.

'Thanks for reminding me.'

If being insensitive were an Olympic sport, my sister would be heading the Great British team.

'Come on love, time to head home.' Good old Scotty, always reliable. 'See ya later Rooney, mate.' He gives the fur ball another tickle before ushering Debs out of the room and towards the front door.

I survey the day's carnage. One big plywood monstrosity for a window, one dog with a broken leg, a coffee table with severe ladder impact damage and a dustpan full of broken glass left neatly at the corner of my new laminate floor.

Why do builders always do that? They make the effort to sweep up but they never get as far as tipping the sweepings into a dustbin, do they? I suppose I'd better do it myself.

I pick it up and plod out to the small backyard that plays host to the wheelie bins.

'You got it all fixed then?'

I turn to see Mrs Timmons' head bobbing over the top of the fence. 'I think we're just about water-tight.' I smile back. She's a bit of a nosey old duck, but harmless enough. Just a lonely old lady.

'I was wondering, while you're here.' She gives me the full show of grinning dentures. 'I'm off to my sister's next weekend. I wondered if you could just keep an eye on the place while I'm gone. That's if you've got nothing planned.'

I can answer that question with certainty.

'No, I've not got anything planned for this weekend, Mrs T.'

'You're a good boy.' She returns my smile, waves and ducks back behind the fence.

I sigh and tip the broken glass into the bin, and then it all hits me again really hard.

I was supposed to be getting married.

I close the dustbin lid with a slam and in a fit of anger give it a good kick. I throw the shovel onto the ground and then stomp off back into the flat.

2

Cassie

Several days later, I'm happy to say I've delivered the portrait of Mr Tipsy to Mrs P and she was delighted.

'You've captured his handsome face wonderfully,' she said. 'It couldn't be anyone else.'

I neglected to mention, having given up with the rubbish photos I had of his proud visage, that I'd simply copied a similar looking horse's head from a library book entitled, *Four-Legged Front Runners*. The head she was admiring was that of Red Rum. Still, if the client is happy, I am too. And so it was with a lively spring in my step that I set out with Pooh to The Tunnel House pub in Tarlton to meet the extremely smooth-sounding Andrew Hendry.

Pooh is my bright Border Terrier. I called him Pooh to continue The Hundred Acre Wood theme and also because when I take him walking, I like saying it. I call it in a sing-song way so it has two syllables more like 'poowhoo' and for some reason it makes me smile. On these social occasions I'm very happy for him to chaperone me. Not only is he a good judge of character, he's also a good talking point. Should the conversation die a death he will lie down, turn in a circle and jump up, all on command. He's clever enough to know it's silly, but he does it anyway. And I love him for it.

I'm hoping my meeting with Andrew won't require Pooh's intervention. He sounded like a good talker on the phone, but sometimes people clam up when they meet me in the flesh. Dazzled, no doubt, by my beauty!

I've resolved to keep the conversation friendly but businesslike. This way neither of us should get too nervous, even if the hint of chemistry I felt talking to him proves itself to be overwhelming.

Going up the gravel track to the pub, set next to the river on the Bathurst Estate, I find myself getting butterflies. I've been single for ages now and I'd love a bit of male company. I need space and tranquillity as an artist, but sex doesn't have to be completely factored out of the equation. A man who lives in London would be ideal. Space during the week. Sex at the weekend. Perfect.

I stop halfway up the gravel track in a bow-shaped lay-by and check my reflection in the rear-view mirror.

For someone who usually bums about at

home in a state of total sartorial meltdown, I've made a big effort for this meeting. I've applied a spot of mascara to the lashes above my large greenish eyes (my best feature apparently) and a smear of lip-gloss. This dual action, I hope, will draw attention away from my rather blobby nose and freckly cheeks. I washed my hair this morning and dried it straight. (My brown locks are naturally a kinky mess. Usually I tie them back in a chaotic ponytail to keep them out of my eyes, which is as fantastically unglamorous as it is effective.)

I've chosen what I'm wearing with careful consideration, too. I'm in my white cotton summer dress, which comes down to just above my ankles and sympathetically hides my fat calves. It also plunges low at the neckline to reveal a cleavage Jilly envies, though she hasn't seen me with my bra off, where everything drops a good two inches and looks far less pert. The central panel of this dress also performs the miracle of holding my stomach in, which, like a square of boiling ravioli, sometimes bulges more than it should. (And does, of course, today.)

On my feet I'm wearing some tan clogs I bought in Kensington Market. They're not what most girls would wear with a summer dress, but I am an artist so I should be allowed some concessions. My tan handbag matches them so at least I'm coordinated.

Satisfied with my appearance, I spray on a hint of Issey Myaki, drive up to the Fifteenth-Century pub, buy myself a white wine spritzer and take an outdoor table next to the river. Marvellous!

Sadly this turns out to be a mistake.

Though it is a glorious sunny day and a shame to be inside, the wind is charging through the trees like a hunt at full tilt. My beautiful, straightened hair is having great fun tangling itself round my face and generally behaving like the tail of a kite.

On the brink of collecting my drink and heading for the interior, a navy blue BMW pulls up and a tall, blond-haired man gets out. He is followed by a very springy spaniel.

Too late now. I haven't even got time to bolt to the ladies to check my hair.

'Hello there,' I call out as Andrew heads towards the Cotswold stone porch, making his way to the bar.

He turns and looks at me, a smile spreading over his face. He approaches with a long, sporty walk.

'You must be Cassie.'

I swoon as he gets nearer (but think I manage to cover it). His hair is cut short and is not so much blond as straw mixed with sand. His face is broad and honest. His upper lip is the shape of Cupid's bow. He has fine cheekbones and a lovely twinkle in his hazel eyes. And his body, well . . . dressed in a shirt with the sleeves rolled up and blue jeans, all I could think was Corrrrr!!! (Or perhaps cripes!)

When I come out of my reverie he's petting Pooh and introducing him to the spaniel in question, Digger. Thank God they seem to get along, and after the usual distasteful smelling rituals they lie down next to each other comparing tongues. I think dogs do this to cool off but it may be a blokey 'mine's bigger than yours' moment. I feel good for Pooh, and proud, for even though he is the smaller dog, his seems the larger. Well done, Pooh. One up already!

I turn and look Andrew straight in the eye. 'So, what size do you want me to do?' And then realising how foolish this sounds, add, 'The portrait, I mean.'

Andrew's eyes twinkle a little more brightly as he sits on the bench next to me.

'What size do you prefer?' He winks.

We both understand he's not being serious and burst out laughing.

'Let me just get us both a drink and we'll chat it over,' he says.

It seems like it's going to be a fun afternoon . . .

Nick

Welcome to the wacky world of the unemployed. I've just spent the last few millennia searching for jobs on the internet. And what is there available for the 28-year-old male with no references and a third-class degree in leisure and tourism? Answer: sod all.

I've been doing this longer than is good for my mental health. And what's worse, every time I log off the internet the phone rings. Debbie told Scotty he's got to take me out to stop me brooding.

I should be grateful someone remembered that tonight should have been the last night before my wedding. But I really don't feel like going out. I just want to be left alone.

I throw the squeaky lamb chop across the room again for Rooney to fetch. He's looking livelier now and has adapted well to his plaster cast and bucket. He also likes pork scratchings. Can't be a bad bloke.

I pour another large JD and resign myself to getting slowly and miserably pissed. Alone.

I've searched all the jobs fifty-billion times now and there's nothing but bar work and call centre 'career opportunities'. Perhaps I should get a paper round.

I'm feeling melancholy now. Just the right

frame of mind for melting my brain with whisky and descending into a bottomless pit of despair. And then for some stupid reason I click on Friends Reunited. That just sends me over the edge.

I don't need to read the entries. All the girls I went to school with have written something like, 'I'm married to a lovely bloke now and we have hundreds of little children'. So, no use to me then. And the blokes? Well, they're all living in London with flashy jobs, having escaped this dump years ago.

Yep. It's working. I'm really start to feel the misery take hold now. It's rising up my chest and making me feel like I could go out and bite the heads off small animals.

I scrawl up and down the page aimlessly. I can't even be bothered to click on the picture that someone has posted of me and Scotty dressed as big foam vegetables for the school fun run.

Hang on. They've changed the format. There's something called an inbox at the top and I've got a message in mine. I click on it, feeling a surge of excitement.

Pete Towser! The third musketeer. (The teachers didn't have much imagination at our school when it came to ascribing nicknames to slightly notorious groups of lads.) I wonder if he's contacted Scotty as well.

Ha! As I suspected: living in London, cushy job, married (well cohabiting), kids ... he wonders if I want to go and stay with him for a weekend to catch up.

I don't think so. The last thing I need right now is to be surrounded by people playing happy families.

I push the button and turn off the computer. I know it'll take ages to load up next time, telling me I didn't shut it down properly but I don't care. I don't care if the bloody thing never loads up again. I don't give a shit about anything anymore.

I walk over and unplug the phone from the wall, pick up the attractive-looking bottle of JD and head for the bedroom. There's something wholesomely tragic about drinking whisky in an empty bed straight from the bottle, don't you think?

I sit down on the bed and kick off my trainers. I can see my scabby face in the mirror — the mirror Danielle and I chose together in Ikea. The one I used to catch glimpses of her naked body in when we were shagging.

Perhaps it's just as well I'm not getting married tomorrow. Even if we'd done all the photos in profile I don't think I could have got through the day without picking at my grazed face. It itches like hell.

I take the packet of Bensons that I bought earlier out of my top pocket, feeling the cellophane crinkle as I peel it off. I haven't had a fag for two years. Danielle and I gave up together.

I lie back on the bed, sucking in the taste of moist tobacco before I light it.

Suddenly I feel a presence beside me on the bed.

'Hello mate.' I ruffle Rooney's fur as he nuzzles his bucket against my leg. 'We make a sorry old pair, don't we?'

I take a good swig from my bottle. I'm feeling good and miserable now. I try and imagine that I can beam it out. That I can transmit my misery to her, wherever she is now. I feel it surging through my body and fighting its way out into the world like some fledgling bird I'm going to send on a mission. I want her to know just how bad I feel.

If only I thought she'd care.

Cassie

The following morning I find myself in a state of high tension. Gouache is going everywhere, the portrait of Digger looks more like a JCB than Digger the dog and either Piglet or Roo has scratched my picture of the cat (right through the canvas), thereby forcing me to restart the whole project.

There's only one person in the world who can rescue me from this sort of mental torture . . . my wonderful sister, Daisy. I phone her and we arrange lunch.

'Sorry!' I coo loudly as I arrive at The New Inn twenty-minutes after the allotted time.

Daisy is already sitting at one of the round outdoor tables on a raised stone dais, looking like she doesn't have a care in the world.

I trot up the steps and sit down.

I left home at one to meet Daisy. There was no need for makeup or posh clothes this time. Any old kit would do.

We'd arranged to meet at one, but I knew she'd be late. Besides, the New Inn is only a fifteen-minute drive away so how late could I be?

Well, plenty late was the answer.

Daisy has ordered a bottle of white wine and is pouring me a glass. I grab it from her and take a long gulp.

'Sorry,' I say again when I've got my breath back. 'Got stuck behind a combine harvester, would you believe? You wouldn't think it was possible in this day and age, would you? Even I can't understand it.'

'I got stuck behind one the other day actually.' Daisy leans in and scrunches her nose. 'Happens all the time.'

'You haven't been here long, have you?' I ask her.

Daisy looks at her watch, a rubbishy Timex she's had since she was about eight, and says, 'Two minutes. No. Three.'

I sigh with relief.

'Thank God. I thought this would be the one day you'd turn up early and I'd have kept you waiting for hours.'

'That's never likely to happen,' Daisy shrugs. 'You know I'm far too disorganised to get anywhere on time.'

I nod, loving my sister for her laidback approach to life.

Daisy is quite a lot older than me at thirty-five, but she looks about the same age. I guess our features are similar, but her looks have had a little extra fairy dust sprinkled over them. Her nose is cuter, her skin is smoother, her legs a little longer. The only thing she doesn't usually beat me on is her hair, which normally looks as if it's attached to a girl who's recently been involved in a four-hour shagathon. Wonderfully, she doesn't care, and simply ties it back and still looks stunning. I imagine how proud her boyfriend must be of her.

'How are things with Guy?'

Daisy gives a mischievous little smile.

'I know it sounds awful. But better than ever.'

I clap my hands quickly to show my approval. I like Guy. He doesn't take himself too seriously.

'And no trouble from the dastardly ex-husband then?'

'No more than you'd expect.'

Peter was all about making money. Oh, and having affairs.

'So what's this lunch all about?' Daisy asks as the smart, very young waiter gives us the menus and puts up the parasol to protect us from the unusually harsh sun.

Good ole sis. She knows this isn't a crisis-free moment.

I gaze momentarily at the creeper on the pub wall and admire the large Georgian windows. Then I lean in and say, 'I've met someone I really fancy.'

'I thought so,' Daisy smiles. 'And?'

'Well, I've only met him once, but he's completely gorgeous. I'm painting a spaniel for him —'

'So you have the excuse to see him a few more times.'

'Yes, the trouble is, the painting's not going great.'

'Hmm.'

'It doesn't look like a dog.'

'What does it look like?'

'Hard to say. A woolly mammoth perhaps, or a sabre tooth tiger. Something never seen in our recent history anyway.'

Daisy laughs and takes another sip of her wine.

'But you're a great painter. Can't you fix it?'

I tell her I've tried three times, starting from scratch to get it right, and it simply is not taking shape.

'I think it's the pressure, Doodle.' (Nickname from childhood. I couldn't say Daisy.) 'Every time I pick up a brush I think of him and how good I want this portrait to be and I just start to quiver and it all goes wrong.'

'Hmm. You have got it badly.'

'What should I do?'

Daisy suggests convincing him that animal portraits have gone right out of style and that he should settle for a nice, tastefully framed photo. Possibly in black-and-white.

I disagree, order the chilli prawns from the attentive waiter, and think about sulking for a bit.

Doodle winks at me.

'Cheer up. Let's forget about the painting. Tell me all about him. That'll be more fun.'

So as we eat I relay what I know of Andrew's life. It doesn't take long.

'Brilliant. He's at an age where he's not shy to commit. He's fit. He's financially secure. Go for it!' Now it's Daisy's turn to clap her hands. 'Can I have another prawn? I'll pay the bill.'

I push the plate over to her with a smile.

'Thanks, Doodle. If it all goes wrong now I can blame you.'

When we've thanked the waiter, we kiss goodbye and I drive my little Renault home, feeling reassured and much less panicky.

Nick

Something wet smears itself against my face. The scraping sound of plastic against pillow, and the heavy, foul breath that is accompanying the wet sensation, leads me to think it might be Rooney's breakfast time.

I'm trying to pluck up the courage to open my eyes but I know it's going to hurt. There's a distinct feeling of déjà vu around: two monster hangovers in a week.

Is that a good or a bad thing?

It's got to be bad. I seem to be turning into a lonely, alcoholic saddo, not a sociable party animal.

That'll be my lack of ambition again. That nasty, vile, horrible lack of ambition that drove away the most beautiful woman I've ever touched.

It's funny, isn't it? You watch all these TV programmes and chick-flicks brimming with girls trying to find a bloke who they can cajole into marriage. The media would have us believe there's a world out there packed with ticking body clocks desperate for us to fertilise their eggs.

So what do I do? I throw myself in feet first. I'm up for it all: mortgage, marriage, kids.

'You're not serious!'

I can hear her words screeching through my head again.

'Why not? That's what married couples do, isn't it? Have kids?'

'For God's sake, Nick! Where did that come from? You've never mentioned it before.'

'Well . . . I just assumed-'

'Well, you assumed wrong. I've just got my career off the ground and you want me to stop just so you can clutter up the place with snivelling little mini-mes?'

That hurt. You think you've finally found the one: the woman you'd kiss Neil Warnock's backside for (probably) and she turns round and looks at you like you've just admitted to battering a seal to death, just because you offer to father her children.

I use the corner of the duvet to wipe my eyes. I promised myself I wouldn't do this again. I swore I'd wasted my last tear on that bitch. But I keep seeing her face in front of me, smiling and saying she loves me. Lying cow!

I was supposed to be getting my suit on now. I'd rehearsed it all in my head so many times. Scotty would be here, pretending he'd lost the rings and winding me up about the stories he was going to put into his speech. And in just a couple of hours' time I would be there in that church, looking into her eyes and promising that I'd love her forever.

And do you know what the really shitty thing is? I think I will.

Cassie

Why am I hopping about in my back garden like a mad bunny on heat?

I'm collecting up the teeny bits of Digger's photo from various disparate locations. I discovered it had blown out the window of my studio a minute after composing myself to continue the portrait.

I find a segment in Tigger's beak. A chunk on the lawn. A little balled-up section being skittered about by the overjoyed Piglet and Roo.

I kneel down and survey the carnage. Eeyore walks unsteadily up to me and gives me a solemn look.

'I know Eeyore,' I wail. 'I'm in the poo.'

And up bobs my little terrier all ready to play.

I laugh, but with more bitterness than mirth until Pooh licks my face and starts sniffling round my nose. Then I can't help giggling and letting all the tension out of me.

'Oh get off me!' I cry out. 'Get off!'

The neighbours must think I have a highly-sexed boyfriend with all the rough and tumble going on. Chance would be a fine thing!

I confess I have to take a very deep breath before phoning Andrew Hendry later that night. Just the thought of his voice makes my heart flit, so it is with a quivering hand that I laboriously dial his number on the old, black telephone. The ring-tone seems to continue uninterrupted for an eternity and I am about to hang up when a breathless, panicky voice comes on the line.

'Hello.' He sounds far less charming than at our meeting.

Oh cripes, I think. He's expecting the bailiffs round. He's not the dream man. He's in all kinds of debt and in all sorts of bother with the law.

'Andrew . . . Hendry . . . ' I'm unsure if I can call him by only his Christian name. Is this too informal?

'Yes, speaking.' He's more composed now. His breath has levelled off from Olympic sprinter to gentle jogger.

Disappointed he hasn't recognised my voice, I plough on.

'It's Cassie Oldham.' I adopt the most casual voice I can but I think it comes out sounding lofty.

'Ah, Cassie. To what do I owe this pleasure?'

He sounds like he's never met me, or is putting me at a great distance.

'It's about the portrait of Digger.'

'Ah yes, how's it coming along?'

'Great, great. I'm really, really, really, really, REALLY pleased with it.'

'Brilliant.'

'Although, I'd like to take a few more photos of him, if I may.'

'Why's that?'

'Well, I'm a perfectionist, I suppose. I haven't quite got his tail yet and I don't have any decent photos of it.' I cringe. Why did I blurt that out? He must think I'm mad.

Andrew laughs, or splutters.

'Well, yes. Why not? I'm back in London but you're welcome to come here. I'm free tomorrow night, in fact. Digger's still with me and he'd love to see you. Yes,' he continues, seeming to warm to his theme, 'yes, come on up. After you've taken the photos, we could go for dinner.'

'Really?' I speak with incredulity and then immediately regret it. 'I mean, really?' I say much less incredulously and perhaps a little patronisingly. 'Yes, that would suit me.'

When the conversation is over I pop the phone back on its holder and scream into the kitchen shouting, 'Yes!' at the top of my voice.

Piglet and Roo, who'd been quietly dozing in their basket by the oven, both wake with a jolt, as does Pooh who's by the fire in the little drawing room. Tigger quacks in the garden and I may have imagined it but I'm convinced Christopher Robin neighs in the back-field.

I gather Pooh up in my arms, who is now barking excitedly, and give him a kiss on the top of his coarse hairy head.

'He's invited me for dinner Poowhooo. He wouldn't do that if he didn't like me, would he?'

Suddenly the world is again a joy to inhabit and I dance Pooh out into the star-lit garden and roll around on the lawn with him while he yaps excitedly. It's all good, clean fun until Eeyore bustles up and nips him on the bum with his sharp beak and a low-grade fight ensues between dog and bird with bird losing more feathers than dog loses fur.

As a light goes on in a neighbouring cottage I hustle Pooh inside and flick Eeyore back into the hedge with a deft touch of my toe hooked between his wiry legs. The cats are shocked by my return into the cottage and give me a kind of 'do be quiet or we'll scratch another painting' look and, having soaked it up, I turn out the kitchen light with a whispered and apologetic, 'Night all,' and head for bed. Happy but somewhat chastened by my pets' social and moral rectitude.

If only I could be like them, I think as I snuggle in my duvet. Content, well looked after, cute and, on the whole, terrifically well-behaved.

3

Nick

The joys of dog ownership! Rooney decided to leave the travelling public of Sheffield a present right in the middle of the bus station. I'd taken him three times around the bloody park this morning before we set off. How can such a small dog generate such a huge amount of shit? Fortunately, a passing crisp bag served as a makeshift poop-a-scoop. I'd have left it but for the congregation of tutting old women who caught him in the act.

I just hope we get through two hours on the train without any disasters.

I look at the ticket: one adult to London. Pete's going to meet me at the other end. At least I hope he is. With a large holdall over my shoulder, a disabled dog under one arm and his bed under the other, negotiating public transport has been difficult enough. And that's when I know where I'm going.

Rooney seems to have made a few friends. (He's probably feeling more outgoing now he's ditched the bucket.) Two little lads are tickling his tummy and inviting him to sit

41

next to them on the train. Their mum seems quite taken with him too.

If I had one of my limbs set in plaster, would that make me more appealing to the opposite sex? I could just make one of my ears flop over at a different angle to the other one or grow a layer of black fur, I suppose.

The little guy certainly has pulling power. I've never had so many women crouching at my feet as I've had these past few days.

Even I have to admit he's too cute to be taken to the pound. I'm obviously going soft in my old age.

When I look up from the tickle fest, I see the nose of a train crawling out from the huge dark arches that flank the station. I'm surprised to find myself feeling a little excited.

I wasn't sure about this whole London thing. It was Scotty's well-developed powers of persuasion that eventually did it.

'It's got to be better than sitting at home pulling your plonker, hasn't it?' were his actual words. Pete had sent him an email too but he can't leave the site at the moment.

'Come on Rooney, mate. You'll have to catch up with your fan club later.'

I scoop him up off the platform as the train arrives in front of us. I don't know who looks more disappointed, him or his team of belly ticklers.

Their mum smiles warmly at me as we all shuffle towards the train, though she doesn't speak. I know why. I still look like the elephant man. Although most of the little peripheral scabs have dropped off my battle scar, I'm still left with the Frostie-sized ones. I could pass it off as a shotgun wound. With that and the broken limb, I could give the impression I'd foiled a post office robbery or a gang raid. That would have definite chick pulling potential.

Alternatively, I could hint that it's a really infectious skin disease. That would mean a seat to myself on the train.

I haven't been to London for a while. I used to go to the art galleries with Danielle. I thought it was a bit poncy at first but I got into it after a while.

Scotty ripped the piss. Said I was always on the lookout for posh skirt. He sang that Pulp song about common people to us when we first started going out. The song plays in my mind now as I search for my seat.

Why is it that dogs have to travel in the smokers' carriage? As far as I'm aware, Rooney hasn't got a sixty-a-day habit. There was definitely no sign of a smoker's cough when he was chasing his new Frisbee around the park this morning.

Which is more than can be said for me. I

keep saying I'm not going to buy fags anymore. But I just can't be bothered to stop. Perhaps if I smoke myself into an early grave she'll be sorry. I'll leave her a note scrawled on a Rizla packet telling her how she drove me to it.

I light one up and turn my most repulsive scab towards the aisle so that anyone still searching for a seat is deterred. This is a turf war. Me and Rooney are having this table. The thought of having to exchange banal conversation with someone I don't know fills me with dread. I'm getting quite used to my own company. And I've decided I like it.

Rooney's defending his patch manfully as well. I've dumped the holdall on the seat opposite and plonked him and his bed on top. He seems happy there, not too traumatised by the travelling experience.

The muffled voice of the train driver welcomes us aboard and tells us that this service will terminate in about two hours at London St. Pancras. It always makes me laugh when they say that. I get this mental picture of flashing lights and alarm bells ringing on the run-up to the station before the train finally blows itself into zillions of little pieces.

I hang my fag off my bottom lip for a moment and reach over to my bag. I can just tug open the zip of the end pocket from here and pull out one of those emergency cans of Stella I packed. It's early in the day, but they need drinking before they get too warm, don't they?

'Cheers mate!' I raise the can in Rooney's direction, but he isn't really looking. I think he's nodded off already. I'll do the same later.

Cassie

My cottage has a biggish back garden but at the front it's like the proverbial postage stamp.

Behind a low, dry stone wall is a path and a couple of flowerbeds parenthesised with two strips of impossible-to-mow lawn. I am out here with the long-handled shears doing my utmost with the grass when Jilly arrives.

She turns her Volvo into the parking area in front of my home (it should be gravel but it's all weeds and thistles now) and hollers 'Hello,' at me as she rises gracefully above the level of the wall, replete in large wicker sunhat, flowery River Island summer dress and flaunting a bottle of Champagne.

'Hi.'

Pooh looks up from his scuffling under the willow tree that hangs over from next door.

'Can you give me a hand with the food?' Jilly walks past me into the house with just the Champagne. 'It's in a hamper on the back seat.'

I look down at Pooh who is looking unusually attentive and loving.

'Fetch.' I point at the car.

He raises a doggy eyebrow.

'Fetch, Pooh.'

He tilts his head to one side.

'Go on. Get the hamper.'

Pooh bucks up on his hind legs and whimpers. He's trying to understand, but he just can't, poor love.

I try once more and Pooh barks. Now he's angry. He's saying, 'You know I can't speak. You know I can't understand. Now stop taking the piss.'

I swoop down and gather him up in my arms and give him a big kiss.

'I love you, you silly little dog. Do you love me?'

Pooh barks and lets his tongue loll out of his mouth.

'I'll take that as a yes.' I pop him back on the path from where he launches himself into the house and through the side door to the back garden. Why? I have no idea. That's the beauty of animals.

Back in the kitchen with the hamper I've

just managed to lug inside, holding it with both hands and aiding its forward motion with one knee, I find Jilly pouring two glasses.

She passes me one and winks.

'What are we celebrating?'

Jilly smiles. 'That old witch bought the barn conversion. For the sodding asking price!'

'That's great.' We chink glasses and take a sip. 'And what is Wiggy doing in the back of the Volvo?'

'Sulking.'

'Yes, but why?'

'Why do you think?' Jilly sits down. 'I refused to buy her some computer game or other.'

'Aged four?'

'Well, that's not the problem, darling. You know how in favour I am of children using technology. She surfs the net.'

'I thought people surfed the sea.'

Jilly smiles patronisingly. 'Sometimes I envy you your life.' Her tone is wistful.

'Can I have a drink, Auntie Cassie?' I hear Wiggy ask from the kitchen door. She's standing there looking adorable, with bunches, a little pair of denim dungarees and a red cloche hat.

'Are you going to behave?' Jilly's tone is stern.

47

Wiggy nods, twiddling her hands in front of her.

'What do you say?'

'Sorry, Mummy,' she says, and then, overcome with regret and emotion, runs on her stubby little legs into the lap of her mother and bursts into hysterical tears.

'She'll be alright in a minute.' Jilly pats her on the back and winks at me. 'You know how they are. Difficult age.'

I nod sagely and set about unpacking the food. Jilly has brought enough to feed the Trojan army. She thinks I don't eat properly so she'll leave it all behind for me to pick at.

Once we're set up under the parasol in the garden, Wiggy's tears now dried (Jilly: 'Their powers of recuperation are incredible! One minute the world's about to end, the next they've found Nirvana.'), we fiddle about with the food and gossip.

Wiggy amuses herself by throwing an old tennis ball for Pooh (who's loving the attention) and intermittently asking for titbits of food.

'Can I have a little more taramasalata, Mummy?' or, 'Is there any more guacamole?'

'She's incredibly sophisticated for four.' My eyes are wide with wonder. 'You're not 'hot housing' her are you?'

'Oh God forbid, no. Honestly, all she reads

48

are cookbooks. I'm amazed. I was a thicko all the way through school and Jeff wasn't top of his class or anything. But Wiggy's as bright as a freshly-shined doorknob. The game she wanted was *Chess Champions* or something. I'm all for her learning, I just don't want to spoil her.'

'Very wise.'

'Well, you can learn by all my mistakes.' Jilly leans in as she talks. 'So tell me about this man you've met. You'll need one of those before you start filling your garden with cries of grief and joy.'

I tell Jilly all I know, which again doesn't take long and leaves her looking terribly unsatisfied, or should that be dissatisfied?

'We'll have to meet up when you get back from London. You'll have more info by then. Wiggy, take your hand out of Pooh's mouth. He's friendly, but he might bite by mistake. He's a dog not a human. Wiggy! Wiggy!'

But now, I fear Pooh's friendly jaws have closed on the tasty little hand and Wiggy has plopped onto her backside in shock, and is about to . . . yup, there she goes with those unstoppable tears.

'Excuse me for a mo.' Jilly rolls her eyes. 'I just need to go and calm my daughter's second nervous breakdown of the day. Lesson one: you can't always get what you want. Lesson two: the world is sometimes a cruel place.'

And with that, she struggles up and walks over to Wiggy who is still in dreadful torment.

Pooh comes jogging up to me with his tongue out, unaware he's done anything wrong.

Nick

I lean back in the garden chair and let the warm evening sun wash over me.

Pete takes a drink from his glass before placing it back on the table in front of us.

'Go steady Harry, remember he's got a bad leg.'

I don't think Harry's heard a word his dad has said. But it doesn't seem like Rooney is that bothered.

Pete watches and smiles as the scampering mass of boy and dog race around the lawn. 'I'll probably get him a little dog when we get the bigger place.'

Carrine lets out a derisory snort. 'Yes Pete, *when* we get the bigger place.'

I laugh along with them both. I made the right decision to come down here. I thought I might be intruding with four of us crammed into a tiny flat, but they seem pleased to have me here and it's good to catch up.

I look across at Carrine in the patio chair

next to me. There's something inherently beautiful about a pregnant woman. They seem even rounder and softer and more squeezable than they normally do. Makes you want to snuggle up to them and nuzzle your face into all those warm curves.

It occurs to me that I ought not to be thinking thoughts like that about my mate's wife. (Well, she's not his wife really but they've been together so long now she might as well be.)

I gaze at her rounded tummy and try to imagine where exactly the baby is and what it's doing in there. They say they can hear stuff, don't they?

I look down quickly at the floor. She's caught me staring. Fortunately, she doesn't seem to mind. In fact she seems to know instinctively what I'm thinking. She holds out her hand towards me and gestures towards mine. I let her take it and place it gently against her bump.

It's the most amazing thing I've ever experienced. I can feel the baby moving.

'Bloody typical that is!' Pete stands up to retrieve the football that's just skidded under his chair. 'You invite him down to stay, he's been in the house for one afternoon and he's already feeling my missus' bump.'

Carrine gives him a withering glance. Why

is it that French people can do that so much better than anyone else? Not that she sounds very French anymore. Only the odd inflection gives it away.

Pete's done well for himself. Ten years ago we were all sat in the pub and he announced that he was off to France to train with one of the country's top chefs. I remember saying to Scotty that he'd be back within six months. He'd never stuck to anything. But he proved me wrong. Five years ago he resurfaced here in London with a beautiful French girl, a job in a swanky London hotel and little Harry on the way.

That's the only other time I've ever met her. He brought her back to Sheffield briefly and introduced us all before they settled down here. I've never seen her not pregnant. She'd be beautiful anyway. As she sits there the warm evening sun picks out chestnut highlights in her cascade of thick brown hair. She looks like one of those pre-Raphaelite paintings. Oh God. I'm doing it again.

'So, what do you want to do tomorrow then Nicholas, me old mate?' Pete asks as he picks up Harry from the small square of lawn and carries him upside down towards the table.

'Daddy, stop it!' His squeal is filled with laughter.

I shrug. 'I don't know.'

'Well, I'm on breakfasts tomorrow so we've got most of the day to play with. Are you coming love or are you putting your feet up?'

'I think I'll let you boys go out and enjoy yourselves.' As Carrine smiles she looks even more beautiful. (No, stop it Nick. Stop it now.) 'Besides, I need to stay near a lavatory at the moment. Bump, she keeps jumping on my bladder.'

'What about Harry?' I attempt to be considerate. 'Where would he like to go?'

'I want to see the diggers,' Harry calls out excitedly from his inverted position.

Pete and Carrine roll their eyes.

Cassie

I am standing in the Turbine Hall of Tate Modern for the first time in my life and I am incredibly impressed with it. I almost forget to obsess about Andrew and the wonderful digger we had last night. Sorry, dinner. (I think my brain really has dissolved in the acid-strength pool of lust I find myself in.)

I recently saw pictures of *The Weather Project* by Olafur Biassons and was spectacularly impressed by his 'sunset' installation. It bathed the Turbine Hall in a wonderful orange/red/yellow light suffused with autumnal shades, that even as an artist I wouldn't attempt to describe.

The Tate Modern used to be Bankside Power Station, but wandering slowly round the space, I can't believe it was ever anything but a gallery. I'm so staggered by what the architects have achieved that I can't close my mouth — and this coming from an artist who is not a fan of 'modern art'.

I gaze up at the balcony to view a giant sculpture. It's a vast eight-legged creature, like a spider but with long legs similar to a tripod's. I immediately feel that I need to go and stand beneath it, to be involved with it.

I join the queue of people rising up the escalator and reach the first floor where I have to turn left into the glass-fronted area, then take some stairs back down to the mezzanine where the sculpture stands.

Approaching it I realise how slender the legs are, like vines or emaciated human legs stripped of their skin. The body soars above me. I have to lean my head right back to see the top. When I progress beneath the bronzed, sinewy legs I look straight up at the creature's body. There in a sack rendered to look like a portcullis are five or six perfectly white eggs.

Somehow I knew this ugly but fascinating

sculpture would have a redeeming feature. Some religions believe the egg represents the soul. Something that is preserved. Good. Worth keeping. Eggs also represent new beginnings. New life and hope. I smile as I take a few paces forward to see the eggs from a different angle.

'Real beauty can create real ugliness,' I hear a voice mutter near me. It has a cynical edge. A weariness that I find depressing. I turn to face a man whose eyes are still fixed on the organic sack that looks like a metal cage.

'But ugliness can create beauty,' I find myself whispering. I do not want to make contact and start a conversation. I simply want him to hear what I've said, to give him some optimism, some hope, like those eggs contain.

The man turns to face me and his eyes look straight into mine. He doesn't look like the sort of man to appreciate art. But a second later I can see a vulnerability. I feel a prickly sensation on my skin and my breath catches in my throat. I look down at the ground, feeling embarrassed at having looked him so deep in the eyes. But when I recover from the intimate moment, I look up again, hoping for another glimpse. I look to my left, along the bridge. There's no one there. My eyes search the escalator and the people milling about below. He's vanished. Perhaps he was embarrassed, like me.

Disappointed, I spend the rest of the morning wandering around the gallery in a daze, thinking of those eyes, those eggs. Both oval. Both meaningful. I think of power: the power of the sculptures, the power of words, the power the old station used to pump out to light our lives, and my mind is so full of these terrifically intellectual thoughts that I neglect to look where I'm going and manage to knock a small child to his knees as my thigh brushes past his blond head.

'I'm awfully sorry,' I say to the little boy's mother as he inevitably worsens my guilt by pulling an anguished expression that would have impressed even Wiggy (who is a master of the look) and bursting into torrents of tears.

'Well, you could look where you're going,' the mother snaps rather haughtily.

'I was having an intellectual moment!' I blurt, immediately regretting it. 'I really am so sorry.'

I apologise to the little lad too, who is now clinging to his mother's leg, his lower lip still quivering. Mortified, I bomb off as quickly as gallery decorum will allow, heading for the exit. When I get there, flustered and lacking any kind of real composure, one of the security guards stops me. He seems like a friendly old soul, beautifully attired in his uniform, but I just want to get out of here. He reaches into his suit pocket and hands me a business card.

'A young gentleman wanted me to give you this.'

'You sure?'

'I am. He pointed you out.'

Still edgy, I take the proffered rectangle of cardboard, slip it into my little handbag, thank the guard and continue on out, not really daring to look anywhere but straight ahead until I'm on the tube back to Paddington station to take the lunchtime train home.

Back in the Cotswolds I take Pooh for a bounding walk (him not me) around the lanes and fields, forget all about the card I've been given and try to recall the night I spent with AH.

It doesn't take long before I'm smiling about it all over again and any nastiness/intellectualism I'd felt in the gallery disappears like smoke fading up into the atmosphere.

Nick

When I asked a four-year-old where he wanted to go for the day I never anticipated that he'd bring me here.

'It's Carrine's fault,' Pete had grumbled. 'Any normal kid would want to go to a theme park or something.'

I can feel Harry bobbing about excitedly as he holds my hand, both of us staring at the huge diggers and lorries that are rumbling across the flat screen in front of us. This is probably the tenth time we've watched this film today but Harry doesn't seem to be tiring. In fact he's almost salivating. Who'd think a kid would go mental for a video of something called 'The Spiral Jetty' being built?

I'd felt anxious about coming here. The last time I visited the Tate Modern I was with Danielle. It was a really good day out. So good I proposed to her when we got home.

A lot of the exhibits are different now. Having Harry and Pete here makes it feel different too. Harry and I are actually having quite a good lads' day out, despite Pete's chuntering.

'Come on mate, let's take Uncle Nick to look at something else.'

Harry looks temporarily disappointed.

'Uncle Nick hasn't been to London for ages so it would be bad manners not to let him have a look around.'

I can see Harry pondering for a moment.

It's a bit of a fib but maybe we've all had enough of jetty building for one afternoon.

'Come on. I'll take you to the café and buy you a milkshake.'

My offer seems to go down well and Harry beams his little grin at me.

★ ★ ★

'Wow. This is a big room.' Harry stares above him, taking in the huge distance between us and the ceiling.

'Can you stay with Uncle Nick for a minute while I nip outside?' Pete waves his mobile at me to indicate he needs to make a phone call. Harry gives an affirmative, although he's so busy contemplating the ceiling I'm not sure he's heard. 'I've got to check the orders have come in. Our supplier cocked up last week and it's one of the new lads in charge today.'

'That's fine.'

'Have you got a piece of paper on you, mate?' he asks, checking his pockets. 'Just in case I have to take their number down.'

I pass him one of my old business cards. 'Nicholas Ratcliffe: Conference and Banqueting Manager' doesn't actually exist anymore, does he?

He winks at me and tests out the

59

retractable biro he's just plucked from somewhere and trots off through the crowd of people.

'It's a big spider.' Harry pulls me towards the enormous piece of sculpture.

I let go of his hand so that he can wander up and have a closer look. I can hear two men having a really deep and meaningful conversation behind me. One says something about beauty creating ugliness. I've no idea what he's wittering on about. You get a lot of people who are up themselves at art galleries. I just stick to deciding whether I like it or I don't.

Then I hear the voice of a woman say something from just beside me but I don't quite catch what it is. I get the feeling she thought I spoke first. I turn to look at her, but immediately look away when I realise how attractive she is and that I have nothing to say.

God, I feel a complete tit. I don't mind art galleries but I still have no idea what I'm doing half the time. I look to Harry for some support. Perhaps if I get him involved, I'll be able to strike up a conversation. Shit. Where is he? My heart leaps into my mouth. He was there, right in front of me. He can't have gone far! I spin round and round, trying to take in every face in the room. He must be in here somewhere. I breathe out at last. He's a few feet behind me with Pete.

'You alright mate?'

'Yeah, I'm fine. I just thought I'd lost him for a moment there.'

'Nah!' Pete doesn't seem to be angry about my lack of vigilance. 'Come on mate. Let's go and get that milkshake before Uncle Nick forgets it's his round.'

★ ★ ★

I look across at Harry slurping away at his big glass of strawberry milkshake and take a large suck at the straw of my chocolate one. Well . . . when in Rome, as they say.

'So who was that bird you were staring at when I came back?' Pete looks at me mischievously.

For a moment I don't follow him at all. 'Oh that one. She just passed comment on the sculpture.'

'Well, is that what they're calling it these days?' Pete laughs heartily. He's always laughed like that: like it comes right up from his toes and then booms out of his mouth. He doesn't do it very often, a wry smirk usually suffices.

I don't reply. That would be like a red rag to a bull. I just give him an ironic smile and

61

carry on sucking at my milkshake.

'So, you weren't checking her out then?' He's still as persistent as he always was.

'As if,' I stay in ironic mode.

'You can't hang around brooding all your life, mate. You gotta get right back on that bike and start pedalling.'

I know what he's trying to do and I appreciate it but I really don't need to be hurried into the dating scene again. Bachelor-hood is looking more tolerable by the day.

'You don't really fancy her then?'

This is getting annoying now but I humour him. 'I don't know. I hardly even saw her.'

'Oh.' He tries to look put out, but within nanoseconds his face erupts into a sinister grin. I've seen that look before far too many times.

'What have you done?'

'Well, I thought I'd help you out a bit.' He's laughing again now. This is bad.

'What?'

'You'll find out some day.'

My whole body groans. He really hasn't changed at all.

4

Cassie

From the new batch of Digger photos, I carefully select one and place it in an envelope. Folding down the flap I put it in my desk drawer, promising myself I will work from it later. Then I pick up my net, sling my camera over my shoulder, round up half the menagerie and head off to the bluebell wood.

It's too glorious a day to be stuck inside fiddling about with gouache!

We wander slowly for the mile or so, Pooh prancing around my ankles, bounding off purposefully then zigzagging back, his nose on permanent alert for some hidden treasure in the wild verges. I twiddle with the net that's flung over my shoulder and listen to the slop, slop sound my Wellington boots make as they stir up the dust on the ruined tarmac.

I imagine that I look just like Christopher Robin trudging out to Hundred Acre Woods for another day of fun and adventure. I smile to myself and think what a (relatively) carefree existence I do lead, and at this moment how happy I am.

I rub the real Christopher Robin's white nose and he curls his lip at me. The rest of him is dapple grey. His mane and tail are as shaggy as a fireside rug. He looks like a pony version of a Seventies' porn star, but I love him.

I lead him on a rope attached to his new red halter. As he clip-clops along I make sure Tigger is not about to slide in a graceless and ego-bruising manner from Christopher Robin's back. For a mallard, Tigger is now a proficient equestrian and only quacks and flaps his wings frantically when he breaks into a lolloping trot. I don't consider Tigger a wimp in this matter as I do exactly the same, except I quack a lot louder.

'You ok there?'

Tigger rearranges his webbed feet on Christopher Robin's broad back but doesn't reply to my question. He concentrates on what lies ahead with a watchful rigour worthy of a lookout. He's in no danger of being swept off by a low branch or twig, however. Christopher Robin is short even for a Shetland. I can almost fling my leg over him and still have both feet on the grass.

It takes us twenty minutes to reach the bluebell wood. Even though I come here often, my mouth still drops open at the sight of it. In the shade of lime-trunked trees and rustling leaves lies a bed of luminescent purple-blue flowers that seem to glow in the semi-dusk created by the canopy above.

And this is not the only treat we've come for. The bluebell wood is home to a wide variety of butterflies, a passion from my youth that was recently rekindled by some nature programme or other on BBC2.

So, having tied Christopher Robin to the gatepost with Pooh for company, I head into the wood along one of its very narrow paths with the one companion I can't leave behind, Tigger.

My mallard is wonderfully loyal and I love it that he follows me around whenever he gets the chance, but sometimes I wish I could just tie him up, this afternoon being one such occasion. Butterfly-catching is tricky enough without having a duck waddling behind you and then attempting flight when it can't keep up. I wish I'd left him at home but he looked so jealous when he saw me heading out with the others that I had to pop him on Christopher Robin. Besides he'd waddled and half-flown all the way to the side-gate of the field so I felt I owed him a favour.

'Just don't quack when I spot something.' I raise my butterfly net in mock seriousness.

Tigger looks up at me unabashed. And quacks.

I shake my head and continue down the path, as stealthily as is possible, with the net cocked, ready to capture anything that flies within range. It isn't long before I spot something fluttering in among the bluebells. It's hovering near a tree just within reach of my net. My hands firm their grip on the long bamboo rod and I hold my breath as I time my swing.

I must admit I wasn't much of an athlete at school. I didn't run or do any sport that involved much mobility for fear of making my calves more muscular than they already were. This limited me somewhat, so I ended up horse riding, with the occasional swimming and tennis stint thrown in.

The tennis comes in particularly handy for the hand-eye coordination required to swing a net.

Swwwooooosh! I bring it down as straight as a car park barrier, only twice as fast. No three-times as fast. Or perhaps even more.

Tigger quacks and flutters his wings. I'm so pleased he hasn't given the game away I remind myself to give him a kiss on the beak before he shuffles off to bed tonight.

I advance up the length of the bamboo rod like a woman in a tug-of-war winding in the rope, only more gently. I was once in a tug-of-war. It took place at the Lechlade Fete and spanned a narrow section of the Thames. A second after we were told to 'HEAVE' I took an early bath in the icy cold water. Needless to say, I have never attempted tug-of-war since.

I peer into the hazy world of the green netting. There is something delicious fluttering in there. My heart leaps a little and I stroke Tigger's head as he comes up to view my success, quacking excitedly.

'Sssh. You'll frighten the poor thing.'

This is the moment in butterfly-catching I'm a little nervous about. I wouldn't say I feel guilty, but I don't feel wonderful about it either. For in order to get my photo of this handsome, frail creature I must first alarm it. Leaving the netting carefully over the butterfly, happily noticing that it's stopped flapping, I reach into my camera bag and pull out a six-inch nail.

Don't panic. I'm not going to harpoon it.

Next, I smear a little honey on the nail's broad head and carefully move my hand under the net and push it firmly into the ground. The theory is the butterfly is now relaxed and, urged on by the smell of honey, will alight on the nail where it will stick. This enables me to take the net away for a moment and photograph it. Brilliant! And I thought it all up by myself! I also have some dental floss, which when stretched tight and eased under the butterfly's legs, will free it back into the wild unharmed. I tell you, Enid Blighton would be proud. (Bet she wishes she'd thought of this for The Famous Five.)

While the butterfly works out how to perch on the nail, I get my camera to the ready, switching the photo option to Macro. You won't be surprised at this, but Jilly wants me to get a digital camera. I'm not being swayed. I like mine. It weighs a ton, it's clumsy when changing lenses, but I will not be parted from it. My parents bought it for my 18th birthday so it also has sentimental value.

'Come on, my beauty,' I coo at the butterfly. It seems to be stirring now I've positioned the netting for it to have a decent flight path. 'Up we come.' Tigger's beaky face is agog. He's fascinated by this fragile miracle of nature, but I'm so nervous he'll try and eat it that I shoo him away.

With a flutter of his wings he recedes a few feet and, as if drawn up off the long grass by the air turbulence, the little blue butterfly alights on the nail.

'Bingo,' I whisper and make ready for the unveiling.

Nick

'So there's some poor woman wandering round London with Nick's business card thinking . . . ' Carrine stops mid-sentence and looks exasperatedly at Pete who is still sniggering. 'You stupid man! We have a visitor and that is how you treat him?'

I feel the score is evened as Carrine gives Pete a harder than playful cuff around the ear.

'Look at that! Husband abuse!'

'If you were my husband, you would be better behaved!' Carrine picks up the plates from the patio table and disappears back into the flat.

I exchange a laddish smile with Pete before we both collapse back into infantile laughter.

'Have you checked your voicemail yet, mate?'

'Like she's going to ring some psycho who goes around leaving his business card with the security staff at art galleries.'

'Daddy, Uncle Nick, look what Rooney's doing!'

We look over to the lawn where the next Barbara Woodhouse has managed to train my dog to roll over on command.

Bloody typical. I can't even stop him jumping on the sofa; I give him to a four-year-old for a day or two and he's become a bloody circus act.

'Can we take Rooney for a walk tomorrow?' A pair of heart-melting blue eyes look at us hopefully.

'You'll have to ask Uncle Nick about that, mate. We've got to go and see if our new house is ready but Uncle Nick might have other plans.'

I feel a ball being volleyed into my end of the court. Not that I mind; I haven't got any plans. In fact, I didn't expect to be here.

'Can you and Rooney come and look at our new house Uncle Nick, please!'

The 'please' is one of those long emphasised ones that cute kids always use — the ones that make you feel like the biggest ogre on the planet if your next word is 'no'.

'I don't know if your dad wants me to come.' I do a shimmy to the side and go for the defensive lob. Pete can make the call. The last thing I want to do is intrude. I've put them to enough trouble by taking over their sofa for the last couple of days.

'The more the merrier!' Pete responds with a wink.

Cassie

'Catching a butterfly is nothing like catching a man,' Jilly scoffs when I dare to posit this

70

theory over our second bottle of wine of the evening.

We're sitting at my kitchen table, which is still littered in papers from the weekend, coffee cups and half-burnt candles. Piglet is on my lap. Jilly is stroking Roo. Tigger, my butterfly-catching companion, is asleep on my bare feet.

'Well, obviously the man is a little bigger. Possibly heavier. But you still have to be stealthy. The net must come down swiftly. You have to offer a little honey . . . '

I laugh indulgently at my own metaphor, even though I don't really mean it.

I have never been the type to try and 'snare' a man. I like things to happen naturally and, if they don't, well they don't. It's not like I don't have company, what with all the animals and great friends and family. (Though of course I'm not sure they'd be any use beyond a cuddle.) And even though I'm not a full-on emancipated girl, I do believe in independence and freedom. I don't like to be crowded or jostled into someone else's life. Though it'd be nice to know someone is out there thinking about me . . . yes, that would be lovely.

'You still haven't told me much about your dinner with Andrew,' Jilly moans when she's stopped laughing at my joke.

71

'No.' I give her a mysterious smile.

'Did it end in a kiss? Just tell me that before you start, otherwise I think I might burst.'

'Burst away! I'm saving the juicy bits till last.'

Jilly seems to inflate a few pressure points before relaxing again and pouring us both more wine.

'Go on then,' her eyes sparkle. 'Give it to me.'

★　★　★

The train got me into Paddington exactly when it said it would, which was a relief because I'd been having visions of combine harvesters on the track or the wrong kind of straw or something.

I had forty-five minutes to find his flat in Eaton Row, not far from Sloane Square. I made it and was immediately impressed that his street was cobbled and very quiet. Just like the country. How lovely.

I knocked on his door at 7.12pm. Perfect timing.

He answered, sweeping me in before I had a chance to get a good look at him. But I knew one thing straight away, he smelt delectable. Not being an expert on men's aftershaves I couldn't tell you what it was, but I'd have a stab at Givenchy or Polo or something like that. Doesn't matter, it made the impression I'm sure he was hoping it would.

His living room was upstairs and his flat had three floors.

'The kitchen's downstairs,' he said, 'and there's bedrooms and whatnot on the other floors.' He poured me a gin and tonic (his suggestion) and sat in a comfy-looking armchair nearest the plump sofa I was sitting on. As he stretched his legs out our feet almost touched and I nearly squealed, but I managed to contain myself.

'So,' he said, arching an eyebrow at me. 'Your journey up here was ok, I hope? It can be such a frightful bugger. All that mucking about with cars and trains. I hate it.'

I smiled knowingly and nodded. 'I did ok. How was your day?'

I know, I know! Naff question, but it just slipped out. Luckily (because Andrew needed to look out of the window pensively to answer it), I was able to admire his noble profile and swoon quietly.

While I goggled, he rambled and I admit I wasn't paying much attention to his little speech. I was transfixed by his arms, naked up to the short sleeves of a burgundy polo shirt, and they looked even more muscular than before. Further down I couldn't help notice the swell of his muscular thighs straining to escape his beige cotton trousers. Phew!

'So then, after that, I thought I may as well head home,' came a voice from the heavenly body. It speaks too!

'Hmmm,' I acknowledged, but I hadn't heard a thing. There was a long pause where I realised I was expected to start something off, so I covered with, 'Hadn't I better photograph Digger? Then I can, you know, relax a bit more.'

AH agreed and showed me downstairs to where the dog lay in his basket, catching a quick trip to the land of nod. He woke the poor thing commendably gently. If I'd been lying there in that cosy-looking padded basket, blissfully unaware of the world turning around me, I had no doubt that I'd have woken up in a good mood.

Andrew stroked his head gently. He whispered, 'Diggers, Diggers,' and I tried to supplant that tone and my name to a Saturday morning where we're both in bed together, slightly hungover, and he's rousing me for a bout of gentle, tender lovemaking . . .

'Cassers . . . Cassers . . . '

It didn't work brilliantly, but it did the trick. I entered a brief reverie, only swimming up from it when Digger rose unsteadily in his bed.

He looked terribly cute with his bleary eyes and snuffly nose. He had a good smell of both our feet (he's getting used to me already!), then a drink from his bowl labelled, helpfully, 'water'. As he couldn't read, I didn't see how this did him any good. But I guess it was better than a bowl labelled 'Turps' or 'White Spirit'.

While all this was going on, and as Andrew was rubbing Digger's head fairly forcefully (not sure if I'd like that on a Saturday morning, if I'm honest), I had a quick scan of the quartz-surfaced kitchen. It was all immaculate, which was a shame because I was looking for some hints into Andrew's life. Some family photos, perhaps, some empty bottles of wine, a pair of running shoes by the bin (that would have been bad, but then at least I would have known he was an avid jogger). But there was nothing. I was thrilled and disappointed at the same time. My worst nightmare had not descended on me. The entire flat was not wallpapered in pictures of ex-girlfriends in hundreds of exotic locations. It didn't stink of Chanel Number 5. And Digger wasn't following me around with his nose stuck to my bum. So that was a relief . . .

But for there to be no hints at anything more than I already knew about him was most . . . unrewarding.

'Tell you what.' I had a flash of inspiration. 'Could I just nip to the loo while Digger wakes up? Don't want to be crossing my legs during the photo session, do I?'

Andrew told me to go ahead and pointed up the stairs.

'Great,' I took the climb like a high-hurdler high on Pro-Plus.

On the landing there was a bedroom to the right and bathroom to the left. I so desperately wanted to snoop in the bedroom but with these old places I just knew the floorboards would creak and I'd be caught trying to get under the bed or something, so I abandoned the idea.

I did, however, strain around the door to have a peak. It was very tidy and there was a photo on the far bedside table. I couldn't quite make it out. It was of three people, which was reasonably reassuring. Not just him and the supermodel girlfriend, then.

But a minute later as I was sitting on the loo tinkling away (as I was up there, I thought I might as well go), scanning yet another barren room for clues, I had a sudden and all-consuming paranoid flash.

No, the photo wasn't of him and the supermodel, with slim calves, a stomach like a tea tray and super-straight hair. It was of him, the supermodel and his sister, who was also a supermodel — when she wasn't saving the whale and helping out in orphanages in Uganda, while running her global golf course design business from her mobile computer. What are they called? Typetop or something. Or is it Mobtop? Or Moptop? Agh! My brain was collapsing in on itself under the duress of trying to impress.

On the loo, I nearly burst into tears. I was never going to be good enough for this man, so I should just do the job I came to do, shoot Digger (well, you know what I mean), say the portrait would be ready some time in the next half-century and then bugger off.

Hoicking my knickers up, the plan became concrete. This was what I should do. No point in embarrassing myself. An animal must always hunt for a similar or weaker prey. Would I, the timid hamster, be able to catch and overpower the sleek, confident bobcat? No. And I'd be a fool to try.

Dabbing my hands dry on the towel (nice and soft . . . Lenor?), not from peeing on them but having washed them thank you, I marched downstairs and right off the bat said, 'You know I've just realised I've left the lasagne in the oven. A few quick snaps of the dog and I should push off.'

Andrew looked genuinely downcast at this brusque comment.

'Don't you have neighbours?' he said when he'd regained some composure.

We were back in the living room now and he was pouring two more G&Ts.

'I do.' I suddenly felt like an incredible fool.

'Could they turn the oven off for you?'

'Would you like them to?' I demanded huffily.

'Yes, of course.' Andrew seemed unsettled. 'I've booked us a table at Quaglinos. I even made up the spare bed if you are too tired to travel home. Look Cassie,' he said, coming nearer and giving me my drink and some fiercely provocative eye contact, 'Surely there must be someone who can help you out. Besides won't the lasagne be burnt by now? Don't you have an oven that turns itself off in this type of situation?'

Not terribly likely. We don't all cook in Quartz comfort, fiddling with the dials on our six-ring ovens.

'It probably does turn itself off.' I tried to sound cool. 'But I'd better just check. Do you mind if I use your phone?'

'Go ahead. It's right here.'

I was dismayed to find that 'right here' really was right here — a drinks table next to the sofa that I was standing in front of.

'Brilliant.' I wondered who the hell I could phone and ask the pointless question to. I considered Jilly but she'd just whoop with laughter, so I chose my mother.

I dialled the number with trembling fingers, willing Andrew to go back into the kitchen. Sadly Digger had arrived and he was now sitting back in his chair, all of three feet away, rubbing Digger's chops.

'Hello David,' (first name I could think of. Had to be male to create some kind of false rivalry). I rubbed the back of my neck frenziedly, hoping that the unattractive nerve rash I get wasn't coming up too vividly.

'Hello?' My mother was clearly confused but not completely bamboozled.

'I was wondering if you could nip round to mine and turn the oven off,' I blurted. 'I've been a terrible noggin and left it roaring away.'

'Cassie. Is that you, dear?'

'Oh that's brilliant of you. I owe you one. Probably see you tomorrow then, thanks a million. Bye.'

I hung up the phone and then, still feeling flustered but relieved, perched back on the sofa and gulped back half my drink in one go.

'So you can come to dinner then?' said Andrew charmingly.

'Looks that way. Stroke of luck. David was supposed to be going out with his broking buddies tonight, but he was in. Phew.'

'Great. Who does he work for?'

'Ah . . . yes, he's just moved, actually . . . '

And then a stroke of luck! The phone rang. Blimey, close call. I frantically considered possible changes of conversation while Andrew was busy. He got up out of his seat in a cool, languid fashion and wafted the phone to his ear.

'Hello? Yes. Yes of course. Just one moment.'

He put the hand over the receiver and thrust the phone towards me.

'It's for you,' he said. 'I think it's your mother.'

I smiled sweetly and nearly passed out.

Bugger! 1471. How did she get to know about that?

Nick

I climb out of the back of the car and feel the heat of the sun on my face. It's another scorcher but we're ok. Pete's Saab has aircon.

We've just spent the last hour or so driving around Gloucestershire. It's a pretty place:

lots of cottages and streams, patchwork fields and plenty of wildlife. We even saw a deer bounding along in one of the fields near the tree-lined perimeter.

I can see why Pete and Carrine want to move here. I've always found the hustle and bustle of London quite amiable but I suppose living there and bringing up a family is slightly different to being a tourist.

'Yeeaaahhhh!' That's the sound of Rooney and Harry leaving the car at high velocity to go and play in the back garden. At least it was described as a back garden on the way here; I think I'd put it in the field bracket but it's all relative, isn't it?

'What do you think then?' Pete asks, leaning against the open car door and suavely removing his shades like some pretentious movie star.

I'm impressed. It's covered in scaffolding and surrounded by battered-looking skips but you can see this is one impressive patch.

'Come on, I'll show you around.' He smiles at me and leads me towards the first of the two buildings.

'Welcome to the new Chez Towser.' His voice is full of pride as he steps over the threshold into what will be the hallway.

I don't begrudge him a moment of it. He and Carrine have worked hard for what they've got and I'm sure I'd be just the same. Though it makes my pokey little pad back in Sheffield look even more substandard.

We walk through into what will be the lounge — a huge airy room with large French windows at one end and another large window at the other. Outside, Carrine is talking animatedly to a flustered looking man in a suit.

'Poor bugger!' Pete chortles.

I laugh.

'Our site manager,' he explains. 'She's a bloody perfectionist when she's designing houses for other people, but this one . . . '

'She's done a good job.' I feel it's time to express my admiration. Even with bare walls and wires sticking out everywhere it's obvious that this house is going to be something else.

'You wouldn't believe it, mate. The lengths she's gone to just to get the right door handles is unbelievable.' Pete shakes his head. 'I've learnt the best thing to do is let her get on with it. I keep telling her as long as the roof doesn't leak and we've got room for a fridge and a telly it'll be ok.'

The upstairs is no less impressive. 'Three bathrooms?'

'Yeah, I said it was probably overkill but I have to admit, having seen it, she knew what she was doing.'

I'm shown the guest room. That's en-suite too.

'Christ! It's massive!'

'Well, I suppose it's more of a granny flat really,' Pete explains. 'It's for when Carrine's family come and stay. Gives us all a bit of extra space.'

I walk over and have a quick glance out of the window. It looks out over the back garden where the football is now in full flow.

'And that's where Carrine's going to have her office.' Pete indicates a stone outbuilding at the far end of the garden. 'She can work from home most of the time and just go up to London when something needs sorting.'

I look around and take it all in. 'It's fantastic mate, it really is!'

'You haven't seen the best bit yet. Come on!' He leads the way rapidly down the stairs and back out of the front door. I sense more than a hint of excitement in his tone.

'Fucking hell!' Time for a low whistle to signify how impressed I am. I'm standing in the kitchen of Pete's new restaurant, surrounded by acres of stainless steel and pristine white tiles.

'Cracking, isn't it?'

I've never seen him look as pleased with himself, even when Wednesday were still in the Premiership and used to win trophies.

He leads me through swinging doors to what will be the restaurant. It's just a big cavern of freshly plastered walls but you can see the potential. This bit isn't a new building. It's an old pub they've renovated. It has the potential to be pretty swish. Carrine has obviously worked her architectural genius again.

'And the best bit is, I don't have far to go to work.'

It occurs to me that I ought to be feeling envious at this point, and I suppose there's one little corner of me that does, but what I actually feel is admiration. My mate, who was born a few weeks before me and lived two streets away for most of his life, has done all this. He's taken his chances and made the best of them.

I end up feeling so happy for him, I offer to buy him a pint if he shows me where the local is.

Cassie

I have a quiet day on Friday. Jilly didn't end up leaving until after midnight last night and I still hadn't got halfway through my story, so I was instructed to 'email' her the details. I've only recently had an internet connection installed and I have no clue how it works. I didn't even want one, but Jilly insisted.

'If you don't keep up, darling,' she is fond of telling me, 'you'll disappear like the honey you put in your herbal tea. You'll cease to exist. The outside world will rush past you like the 9.15 Charlbury to Paddington.'

Who cares? But I sit in front of my computer and have a go. What a nightmare! Different screens flashing up every five seconds, having to 'log on', 'log off', open this, close that . . . I thought technology was supposed to make life easier!

As far as I can tell, all it does is run up your phone bill. I have to phone Jilly six times for help before I finally manage to get it right.

By the time I've organised the whole shebang, I've completely run out of enthusiasm for the geeky chore so I just tell her the basics before 'logging off'.

Anyway, how much can you say about dinner and cheeky flirting? I don't have the energy for long descriptions. I'm too exhausted obsessing over: if he'll call/when he'll call/what he'll say/what I'll say/if I should invite him down to the country . . .

To take my mind off things I study the photos of 'Norman' the butterfly. Don't ask me why I called him Norman, I think it's something to do with a new-found respect for the North of England . . . or watching Sean Bean struggle manfully with his desire in *Lady Chatterley's Lover*, which I saw a repeat of on TV recently. Cripes, what a hunk! The North . . . I should go, I think, with babes like that trudging about.

My other TV totty *du jour* is Richard Madeley, who I was fantasising about in the garden the other morning. I know! I have still yet to fathom how this crush crept up on me (but I have a feeling it happened at a stealthy pace, very late at night). I have become so addicted to his boyish enthusiasm and requests for people to phone in for virtually any reason under the sun, I have taken to recording their afternoon show so I can watch it first thing, back in their old *This Morning* slot. Somehow it seems too indulgent to watch it in the afternoon, which is my more productive work time. (Though sometimes I do; I can't resist it!)

Today's show is filled with the usual random line-up of conversational topics from vasectomies to holiday locations and Richard's doing his usual great anchor job and trailing pretty much every feature with the words, 'Now, have you ever wondered . . . ?'

Well, as you're asking Richard, yes I have!

I tear myself away to look up what kind of butterfly I'd found in my *Boy's Own Book of*

Butterflies. Daddy always wanted a boy, poor lamb. He had to make do with two girls. At least we were tomboyish as kids. We did our best at cowboys and Indians.

I flick through the well-worn pages until I find a picture that matches up.

Norman is a Large Blue butterfly. He's very rare. I'm just taking a few moments gazing at him, my heart swelling with pride, when I hear a knock at the door. Funny, I think, I'm not expecting any visitors . . .

Nick

Harry has somehow managed to get Rooney's retractable lead wound round and round his legs several times and is lying helpless on the ground having his face affectionately licked. Pete is doing his big, hearty laugh with Carrine and me joining in.

Everyone who is sat outside the pub near us is having a quiet giggle. Perhaps if I don't find a job when I get home I can hire Rooney out as a children's entertainer.

Carrine heaves herself up to go and untangle the mess. I don't think Harry's too bothered. He'd probably be quite happy there all afternoon.

'Come on child, let's go and get those

hands washed before our meal gets here.' She passes Rooney's lead back to me before leading his victim, slightly glistening from all the dog slobber but none the worse for wear, off to the toilets.

I tie the end of the lead to the leg of the table and throw Rooney one of my cheese and onion crisps.

'It is beautiful here,' I remark to Pete before having a refreshing swig of cold lager.

His expression softens and he looks a bit dreamy. Not a look I usually associate with Pete. 'Yeah.' He takes a gulp from his pint. 'I think we'll be alright. London's great for grown-ups but it'll be better for the kids here, more space and fresh air.'

'I'm chuffed for you, mate.' I feel lager-induced back-slapping coming on here, which is worrying as we're only on our second pint.

'I'm looking forward to being my own boss as well. I just need a top-notch restaurant manager to sort out that side of things when I'm away.'

I take another sip of drink and stop abruptly mid-swallow as I realise he's looking straight at me.

'Don't look like that. You could do it standing on your head, you know you could.'

A strange feeling comes over me. I'm

chuffed he's even considered me but at the same time I can't help feeling like a charity case.

'Mate, I used to run a restaurant in a poxy chain hotel in Sheffield. It's a bit different to something swanky down here.'

'Bollocks!' He sniffs and takes another swig of lager. 'You can take bookings and shout at waiters, can't you? Besides, I need someone I can trust as it's my own set-up.'

I don't know what to say. I knew he'd been skirting round something all morning but it never occurred to me that it'd be this. It's all clicking into place now. The invite to stay, the trip out here; the sly old bugger has had it all planned from the word go.

'Anyway,' he helps himself to a crisp, 'you don't have to decide now. We don't open until the end of August so you've got a few weeks to mull it over.'

Cassie

I open my front door, look out, see no one and I'm about to shut up shop when I hear a sad little voice from around waist high.

'Hello, Auntie Cassie.'

My eyes drift south until they alight on Wiggy. She's standing pigeon-toed, head bowed in front of me, her fingers going like knitting needles. I immediately sense there's something wrong and usher her into the kitchen, the crowd of animals parting at our feet.

I pour her a glass of pineapple juice, hoping that's exotic enough, and pop it on the table in front of where she's sitting, legs dangling limp above the flagstone floor.

I sit on the wooden chair next to her and ask what's wrong.

Wiggy doesn't say anything. She places both hands palm down on the table, either side of the glass of juice and raises her head slightly to look at me.

There are tears rolling down her cheeks, gathering like a transparent goatee on her chin and then falling onto her smart white shirtfront.

'Shouldn't you be at school?'

Wiggy nods her head sadly.

She started pre-school last September. After a fun start, Jilly informed me she was being bullied by some of the older children and she'd had to talk to her form mistress.

She was teased for being a swot because her reading age was years ahead of the other pupils'.

Wiggy, trying to be stoic, wrings her hands together more tightly, but eventually the floodgates open and she's soon crying into my lap. I stroke her blonde hair and say soothing words, but I almost feel like crying myself, saddened by the way some horrors can treat little people.

When she's got rid of the first flush of emotion she can finally speak and her first strangled words are, 'I hate it. I don't want to go back. Ever, ever, ever.'

I don't know what to say. I'm hardly in a position to grant her wish, so I just sit her on my lap and hug her, listening to her and trying to absorb some of her pain. I've never seen the poor thing so miserable, not even Piglet or Roo purring in sympathy around our feet can cheer her up.

In desperation, I pop her on the living room sofa, get Pooh to sit next to her and be all cute and cuddly while I phone Jilly.

Jilly is in the middle of showing a house when I get hold of her, but her reaction is instant.

'Right, I'm coming straight over. I'm taking her out of that fucking school once and for all. Sorry,' I hear her say to the shocked house viewers, 'family crisis.'

She arrives in half-an-hour. Wiggy is still on the sofa staring at the ceiling. I've been in the kitchen so I'm in range if she decided she needed to speak to me. Tigger, clearly aware something is wrong, flaps up onto my lap and quacks sympathetically.

'Where is she?' Jilly asks as she bustles into the kitchen.

'I put her on the sofa. She's quietened down a bit.'

Jilly walks straight through into the living room and sits next to Wiggy on the sofa. She takes her hand and smiles at her, talking to her gently.

'Do you want to go home?'

Wiggy nods and I can see the tears begin to come again.

'Do you want to tell me what happened?'

Wiggy shakes her head and puts her arms up for a hug.

Jilly moves forward and comforts her.

'Don't make me go back, Mummy,' Wiggy wails. 'Please, please, please.'

'You don't have to go back, darling. Of course you don't. Just hang on one minute while I phone Daddy and we'll sort this mess out.'

She gets out her mobile and dials. 'Jeff. Family crisis, darling. I want you home right now . . . ' There's a short pause. 'What time can you be here? An hour. Fine . . . Why? Because we're going down to the school to give a few little boys a clip round the ear.' And with that Jilly hangs up.

She lifts Wiggy off the sofa and carries her into the kitchen.

'Thanks Cass, darling,' she says to me as she walks through. 'I'll call you later, ok?'

I open the front door for her and tell them both to take good care.

I watch as Jilly reverses her Volvo at controlled speed from my driveway. When I see she's safely away I go back upstairs.

I look at the photo of my 'endangered' Large Blue butterfly and wonder briefly why life has to be so cruel to its most beautiful inhabitants.

Nick

If you were standing with me now, here on the platform of St Pancras Station you would see a sight that'd turn even the hardest of hearts into a warm puddle of sentimental mush.

Sitting in front of me, on one of the seats, is a little boy in his number nine England shirt crying as if someone has told him the world is about to end. Next to him is a mournful-looking black dog whimpering and licking the tears off his shirt as they fall.

'Can't Rooney stay a bit longer?' Harry manages to heave out the words between sobs.

'We've been through this, mate,' Pete says casually, seemingly unaffected by the scene of woe before us. 'Uncle Nick's got to go back to Sheffield.'

I'm not managing to be quite as stoical. If that train doesn't get here soon I think I'm going to cry myself.

'We've got to go, mate,' I try to explain. 'Rooney needs to see the vet about his poorly leg and I've got to . . . well, I've got to find a job.'

'You can come and cook in Daddy's new restaurant,' Harry suggests. 'Then we can all live together in our new house and I can look after Rooney when you're busy.'

I look sharply at Pete who holds his hands up to indicate that he'd not engineered that one. I kick myself for thinking it. Even Pete wouldn't manipulate his own kid like that. He may be devious at times but he wouldn't go that far.

I feel a lump start to form in my throat. A pair of teary blue eyes look at me intently.

'The 10:49 service to Edinburgh calling at Peterborough, Newark, Derby, Sheffield, Durham and Newcastle has now arrived at platform 3.' Saved by the bell. Well, the tannoy anyway.

'Bye bye, Rooney.'

I allow the grief-stricken pair one last

cuddle and exchange of snot, slobber and anything else that you care to mention and then tuck the unhappy bundle of fur under my arm.

'We'll come and visit when you're in your new house, I promise.' I try one last attempt to pacify him but it doesn't seem to slow down the tears. The loud howling noise he's now making indicates I've probably made things worse so I decide to leave well alone.

'You see that you do, mate.' Pete gives my free hand a manly shake. 'Otherwise we'll never get any peace. Thanks for buying him the shirt. I'm sure he'll appreciate it when he's got over this trauma.'

He returns my smile before helping me hoist my enormous bag over my shoulder.

'Goodbye Harry,' I add, before starting to heave myself, dog, bed and holdall towards the platform.

'Woof!' Rooney adds, rather glumly, from under my arm.

★ ★ ★

I treat myself to a taxi home at the other end. I'm completely shagged and I've had enough of public transport for one day.

I pay the driver and stuff my wallet into the back pocket of my jeans before trying to remember where I put my door key. I can see Scotty's been busy while I've been away. I now have a fully restored front garden wall and a window you can see out of.

I put the key in the lock, but it won't turn. The bloody thing's already open. I'll fucking kill Scotty when I see him. Not that I've got much worth nicking. It's the principle of the matter.

I dump my bag heavily just inside the door and unclip Rooney from his lead.

'Hello,' a voice greets me, making me jump out of my skin. It takes me a while to bring the room back into focus and realise where it's coming from and who it is.

'Danielle!'

There's a lump in my throat again but a different sort this time. My first instinct is to rush over to her, hold her, nuzzle my face into her hair. But I stop myself and wind the defence shield up to full power.

'Hi.'

She looks at me with a coy smile as if she's just got back late from the shops or something.

'What are you doing here?' I make no attempt to disguise the suspicion in my voice.

'I just thought I'd pop in and see how you are,' she offers.

The anger rises inside me like bile. 'Bollocks!'

She seems put out by my hostility.

'Alright.' Her tone turns to confessional. 'I've come to tell you I'm moving. I've got a job in Birmingham and I'm moving down there in a few weeks. I just thought you might like to know.'

'Why . . . why the fuck does it matter to me anymore?' I can feel myself spitting the words out. Smug bitch. So that's her game. It's a 'look how well I'm doing without you' visit. 'And for fuck's sake, don't you dare say anything along the lines of hoping we can still be friends, or I'll puke.'

She looks at me wistfully and I can just detect the faintest hint of tears starting to form.

'I just thought . . . ' Her voice trails off and there they are, trickling down her pretty little cheeks in tiny little rivulets.

'You can stop that!' I sit down on the sofa and look at her impassively. 'If you think turning on the waterworks is going to make me say, 'There, there darling, I'll be your friend,' you can forget it. It doesn't work anymore! See!'

'You bastard!' She chokes out the insult like a melodramatic actress.

I've had enough now. I can feel it all bubbling up to the surface. All these weeks of chasing it round in my head, wondering what

I did wrong; it's all slipping into place now. It wasn't me that was in the wrong. It was her.

'Is that the best you can do?' I ask, looking straight at her. 'You come round here just so you can rub my nose in it and watch me beg you to come back one more time. Then, when you don't get what you want, I'm a bastard.'

She's bordering on hysterical now, but I don't care. I even stand up to face her. She's had this coming for weeks and I'm going to make sure she gets it.

'What's the matter?' I ask, as the next wave of tears is forced out. 'Sorry, were you expecting doormat Nick? The one who spent five years running around to the rhythm of your clicking fingers. Well sorry babe, he doesn't live here anymore. He had his heart ripped out by some selfish bitch who decided she'd rather have a high-powered job than have his children.'

She attempts a look of hurt. 'So, that's what you really think of me?'

'Yep!' I answer coldly. 'Door's that way, sweetheart. Close it on your way out.'

She drops her keys dramatically on the coffee table and flounces out of the front door, slamming it loudly behind her.

This should be the point where I collapse back on the sofa, regret what I just said and have a good cry myself. I'm amazed to find that I don't. I feel better than I have in a long time. My hands are shaking but I feel ok. Lighter somehow.

The phone rings and I vault athletically over the coffee table to answer it.

'Nick Ratcliffe . . . yeah, hello Harry, mate . . . yes me and Rooney got home safely . . . yes that's him barking at you in the background . . . do us a favour would you mate, put your dad on for a minute . . . '

Cassie

I phone Jilly in the evening to find out how things went at the school.

'She's out of there,' she tells me. 'It's our fault. We just haven't realised how gifted she is so we're looking for a fast-track school for her. Somewhere she'll feel like all the other little people.'

'And Wiggy's feeling better is she?'

'Much. She's playing chess with Jeff at the moment. I'm not sure who's winning but Jeff is slugging back the whisky and rubbing his forehead which is always a worrying sign.'

'Crikey. Who'd have thought you two would have given birth to a genius?'

'God, I know! Perhaps two wrongs do make a right!'

We both laugh at this, but I can tell Jilly's tired after an emotionally exhausting day so I decide to let her go to collapse on the sofa.

'Oh wait!' she speaks again just as I'm hanging up. 'Have you heard from Andrew?'

I haven't. Damn! And I tell her so.

'Bastard,' she groans and asks me to keep her informed.

I promise I will and before replacing the receiver tell her to give Wiggy a kiss from me.

In comparison, I suppose Andrew not phoning is hardly what you'd call a crisis. But I do feel a pang of loneliness when I consider how their family has crunched into gear, closed ranks and got things sorted. It strikes me that I have no one in my life I can really rely on. Daisy's great and supportive but she's rarely at hand and, when she is, she's as scatty as a kitten. My mother is mad and my father is lovely but usually on a different planet . . .

It'd have to be Jilly. But what if she has a family crisis going on when I'm in need myself? It really is high time I get myself into a proper, secure relationship with a decent man. One I can look to the future with and perhaps even think about playing happy families.

I fancy Andrew, but there are nagging doubts over his suitability. For a start, he lives in London. There's no way I can move my animals there and nor do I want to. I love the country too much. Over dinner he'd said there was no way he could relocate. So . . . is there any point?

Feeling pretty deflated at this sudden realisation, I drag myself into the study and flop on the sofa, only just missing Tigger's sleeping beak.

'Sorry, honey.' His eyes bulge open. 'It's only me.'

I flick the television on and idly channel surf (the four I've got). Everyone else I know now seems to have about five-thousand channels. I have no idea where they get them all from but sometimes I'm jealous. With no Sean Bean and no Richard I opt for a nature programme. It's a study of the Great Barrier Reef and I find it relaxing but not altogether gripping.

Bored, I empty out all the crap from my handbag to give it a good clean. If a handbag is a girl's best friend, then it must be looked after properly and I've been sadly neglecting mine recently. It bulges, straining at the zipper, not unlike a pair of jeans I bought last summer at an ambitious size ten.

You know sometimes you start a job and then immediately wish you hadn't?

Well, this turns out to be one such

occasion. My handbag is no ordinary bag. It's a Tardis. The volume of rubbish that spills out of it is three-times what it can actually hold.

I never wear much makeup, usually because I can't find any, and now I can see why. It's all in my flipping handbag! Lip liner, mascara, blusher, a pot of Body Shop cherry-flavoured lip balm, a comb (not that it ever does me any good), articles I've ripped out of papers, receipts, telephone numbers I've scribbled down. Yes, Jilly told me if I actually used the mobile she gave me I could simply punch the numbers in, but where would be the fun in that? It would be so sterile. A piece of paper and someone's grubby handwriting on it gives you a time and a place and some character to go with the number. I like it. I do. And I'm sticking with it, 'old-fashioned' or not.

As the detritus mounts up, even Tigger seems to give me a disdainful look, his eyes moving a little closer together and narrowing at me.

'Don't you get on your high horse with me, matey,' I tell him, thinking that he wouldn't be able to get that high on Christopher Robin anyway. 'What have you got hidden in your feathers, hey?' I give his wings a bit of a ruffle, which I can tell he really doesn't appreciate. In fact he hops off the saggy sofa and waddles into the kitchen, his tail feathers parting in a 'V' sign as he goes. I'm not too bothered he's gone. Now I have more space to make the four piles I wanted:

- Stuff to chuck
- Interesting things to keep (but not in the bag)
- Makeup
- Bare essentials to leave in the bag

I spread the bumf out like a picnic and begin to sort my way through. The makeup is easy; that gets done in no time. Then comes the stuff to throw out, which is more tricky because it involves its inverse — stuff to keep.

I get through all the bits of paper in a few minutes. I then come across two business cards that present me with a question. One I was aware I had in my possession, the other definitely not. The one from AH I put carefully in my 'keep' pile, the other I study for some time. I don't recognise the name, or the company. Did I meet someone recently who wanted me to do their pet's portrait? Had I been to a party where I was given it by some hot young stud? Obviously the memory isn't great, but I'm sure I would remember someone giving me their card. Especially a bloke . . . it might mean a possible date.

I umm and ahh for a while, but decide I really have to be strict with myself and get rid of all this muck cluttering up my life, and fling it on the 'chuck' pile with all the receipts and sweet wrappers. By the chore's end, my bag is gratifyingly half its previous size and weight. If only I could do something as simple and painless with my stomach.

Feeling I'd really achieved something I stick the crap in the pedal bin in the kitchen, give Pooh a dig in the ribs, shout 'Walkies,' and stride out to the side door where I put my trainers on. Pooh follows with the Frisbee in his mouth. His tail wags from side-to-side like one of those old metronomes. My piano teacher used to have one tick-tocking on the upright iron grand during my lessons. I hated it. I'm sure it wasn't in time. Then again, neither is Pooh.

5

Nick

'Don't cry, Deb,' I give my sister a hug.

'I'm sorry.' She buries her face in my shoulder. 'It's your good news and I'm spoiling it.'

'I'll still be there for you sis, I promise!'

I hold her tightly to let her know I mean it. I guessed she'd probably react like this.

'I'm sorry.' She pulls herself away from me and finds herself a tissue. 'I'm really pleased for you, Nick, I am. I'm just going to miss you.'

I give her a chance to wipe her nose and then pull her close for another cuddle. I'm going to miss her too. She might be a bit dizzy but she's still my sister. We've always looked out for each other, especially since Mum died.

We never had a dad (or not one that either of us can remember) so Debs and Scotty are all the family I've got, apart from distant cousins, aunties and uncles who we never see.

'We'll have to go out and have a celebration before you go.' She looks up into my face with a brave smile. 'You, me and Scotty.'

'Course we will.'

'Go round all the old haunts.'

'Come on, sit down. I'll make you a cup of tea,' I offer, releasing her from my grip.

She smiles meekly and does as she's told.

I pluck cups and teabags from various cupboards. They're still in the same place they were when we all lived here: Debs, Mum and me. It was just Debs and me for a while but then Scotty moved in and I moved out.

That sounds awful, doesn't it? I didn't mean it like that. I wasn't pushed out. The two of them asked me to stay on several occasions but it seemed the right thing to do to move out. I was ready for my own pad. Things were getting more serious with Danielle and . . . well . . . Debs and Scotty needed their space too. There's only so many times you can lie awake at night listening to your best mate shag your sister.

I'm glad it worked out like that. The idea that the two people in the world that I care most about are together, looking after each other, is rather comforting. I don't think it would be quite as easy to leave if things hadn't worked out that way.

Scotty might try and put himself across as a bit of a rough but I know he loves her as much as I do. And he wouldn't let anything happen to her. He's a good bloke when you look behind the laddish façade.

Cassie

Apparently there are 57 species of butterfly in Great Britain and a further six that visit us regularly from abroad. How sweet of them. Presumably they come on package tours, cameras at the ready, with plenty of Euros that they find they can't spend anywhere. Most of these butterflies come from Northern Europe and don't stay for long.

Just imagine starting life as a sleeping bag on legs and ending it flitting from flower to flower with wondrous wings and gorgeous skinny legs. If I could be anything else in this world, I would be a butterfly. I would. I love them.

This evening I have painted my rare Large Blue and it looks incredibly striking, not only because I made it so big, 4ftx4ft, but also because I managed to capture its luminous quality just right. I have temporarily hung it on the wall of my downstairs loo so, should Andrew ever bother to come down here, he will have something interesting to look at while he has his pee. He may even realise how dowdy his own loo is.

The bugger still hasn't called me and consequently the portrait of Digger, in stark contrast to the Large Blue, looks terrible. It's dull, lacklustre and full of worry, hormonal upheaval and distrust. Just like me. Every time I pick up the brush and look at Digger's face in the photo, all I can see is Andrew raising a half-empty G&T at another woman in his flat and saying, 'Cheers,' before rambling on about some boring meeting he'd had that day.

Why am I so lacking in confidence? I often wonder. I mean my legs aren't that fat, my hair isn't that out-of-control, I'm not hideously ugly or terribly reconstructed by plastic surgery, like some celebrities whose faces look like they've come straight out of a mould.

I'm not totally thick, either. Admittedly I did screw up my GCSEs rather badly and didn't go on to take 'A' Levels but I do distinctly remember being one of the very few people in form five who knew that Canberra and not Sydney is the capital of Australia. Or is it the other way round? Never mind, I knew it then and then was when it counted, in front of all those other children.

In order to ponder my insecurities and perhaps come up with a resolution, I tuck up my animals first and then myself into bed for an early night. I am snuggled deep in my 12-tog duvet, bedside light on, cuddly toy Pooh nestled by my neck, writing a list of all my achievements since I can remember.

I get up to age 11 and my 50-metre swimming badge when my eyelids suddenly feel as heavy as a night of Russian poetry readings. My notepad, with a picture of Piglet and Pooh holding hands and Piglet saying, 'Pooh,' and Pooh saying, 'Yes Piglet,' and Piglet replying, 'Nothing . . . I just wanted to be sure of you . . . ' slips out of my grasp. I can feel myself descending into a sleep that begins with that thought. That's all I want. Just someone I can be sure of . . . Just someone I can be sure of . . .

And as I dream all kinds of things go through my head. Butterflies (in the air and in the stomach), animals frolicking about, Andrew's apartment with no pictures, all the paintings I've done recently, the huge, dark spider in the Tate coming towards me to suck me out of the night, out of this feeling and . . .

Suddenly I wake up and sit bolt upright in bed. I switch on the light and wonder for a moment if I'm going mad. My heart is racing, the picture in my mind is still there — the eyes of the guy I saw in The Tate. I rush downstairs, pull the top off the pedal bin and rustle inside until I come up with the business card I'd thrown away.

I read the front of it again. Nick . . . could it be him? Could that be the guy who gave his card to the security guard to give to me? I put it on the kitchen table and go back to bed. This is something that needs thinking about more clearly in the morning, after a good night's sleep.

Nick

I push the front door with my foot and start to shuffle myself and the three huge cardboard boxes that I'm carrying into the living room. I can hear the phone ringing but there's not a lot I can do about it at the moment.

I drop my bulky cargo at the end of the coffee table and then go to pick up the receiver. 'Hello.'

'You coming over to watch the match?' Scotty's voice speaks to me nonchalantly from the other end of the line. It doesn't take Einstein to work out what's going on here. My sister is obviously the instigator of this phone call.

'Tell Debs I'll do her a swap. I'll come over and keep you entertained if she comes and packs up my flat for me.'

'Had to ask, mate. Wouldn't have got any peace until I did.'

I smirk to myself. Why Debs always makes Scotty ring up when she wants me to go round there, I'll never know. It's one of those female traits I'll never get to grips with. They always have to turn a perfectly straightforward situation into something laced with subtexts and conspiracy theories.

'Tell her I'll call round and see her tomorrow, if I get a chance.'

'Will do mate.'

I replace the handset and refocus on the task in hand. This is a logistical nightmare of the worst kind. Three days to pack a whole flat. When I said to Pete I could start straight away, I didn't think he'd take it literally.

Soon that feeling starts. The one where you know you're going to avoid the job at any cost. Why does that happen? The more you need to get on with something, the less inclined you feel to do it. I'm sure that's why they used to give you homework at school, to prepare you for work avoidance in adult life.

I feel my hand reaching for the TV remote. Nope. That would be rewarding myself for being lazy. If I'm not going to do any packing, at least I need to do something first that'll make me feel virtuous.

★ ★ ★

I push the little white button and hear the doorbell ring. For some reason I feel tentative about this. We've never really done social calls.

'Ooooh, hello.' Mrs Timmons seems reasonably pleased to see me when she eventually opens the door. 'It's alright Gladys. It's only young Nick from next door. What can I do for you, duck?'

'Well,' I feel my brain shuffling all the relevant information around in an attempt to find a starting point. 'I just wanted you to know I'm moving out at the end of the week.'

She opens her mouth wide and gives me a look of exaggerated disbelief. 'Well, you'd better come in for a cuppa before you go.'

I accept the invitation graciously, although it wasn't quite what I'd planned. I was only popping round to deliver the news while I thought of some other way to waste my evening.

Mrs T escorts me into the living room to where another, rather larger, old lady is sitting in one of the armchairs, munching on a large slice of sponge cake.

'Gladys, have you met young Nick from next-door?'

'I can't say that I have.' A row of dentures,

112

coated in jam and cake, grin at me as I shuffle in from the kitchen.

'Nice to meet you,' I lie, averting my gaze from the mouth which, still open, is stirring round another bite of cake like a cement mixer. Watching the process is making me feel queasy.

I'm ushered to sit down on the settee next to a character that I do know.

'Look Tommy. Nick's come to see you. You like Nick, don't you?'

I eye Tommy suspiciously as Mrs T heads back to the kitchen. Yes, I know Tommy. I once volunteered to look after him for a week while Mrs T was in hospital. Never again.

I always thought budgies were sweet fluffy little things that just hopped about their cage chirruping a bit, but not this one. He's a mean, green killing machine under that soft feathery exterior.

I have recollections of a grumpy, petulant little creature who managed to escape from his cage every time I went to sort out the seed or the water. He crapped over every level surface in the flat and then pecked my hands to ribbons when I eventually caught him under a towel and tried to wrestle him back into his wire prison.

He stops head-butting his mirror for a moment and shuffles over to the nearer end of his cage to give me an evil stare. Thankfully the cage door is closed, so I feel reasonably safe.

'Here you are, duck.' Mrs T returns to the room with three mugs of tea and a plate of chocolate digestives. I pick up my mug and blow the surface of the tea gently, to cool it.

'Thanks very much.'

'I've put you a nip of something in there.' She smiles at me warmly as she sits down in the armchair next to her friend. 'We always have a nip in ours at this time, don't we Glad? Makes you sleep better.'

'Aye, it does that,' Gladys agrees before reaching across and loading three of the digestives onto the plate where her sponge cake used to be.

'So, where you off to in such a hurry, young 'un?'

'I'm going to Gloucestershire to work in my friend's restaurant,' I tell her, and notice how real it's all starting to feel now.

'That's down south somewhere, isn't it?'

'Yes, near Cirencester,' I inform her before taking a small sip from my tea and wincing slightly as I realise that it's actually a mug full of whisky with a hint of tea. Christ! She's not kidding; I will sleep after this.

'You ever been down south, Glad?'

'No. My George did though, when he

114

worked for t'cooperation. Went to Basing-stoke twice. Didn't like it though. Said they were all poofs down there. He were right an' all. Look at some of the nancies on TV.'

I don't know quite whether to laugh or be appalled.

'You'll be much missed, young 'un.' Mrs T sounds almost affectionate in her remark. 'It's been nice having decent neighbours after that last lot.'

'Aye. You don't appreciate good neighbours until you've 'ad to put up with bad 'uns.' Gladys speaks with authority before stuffing in what must be her fifth digestive.

I snigger internally, maybe it's the whisky but the whole conversation is just starting to seem a bit surreal.

'I've got a young couple next to me. Terrible they are. You can hear 'em all night . . . you know . . . at it.'

I have to bite my lip now. I'm definitely in danger of laughing. I have this rather gross image in my head of Gladys in her nightie, a glass pressed to the wall and a slice of sponge cake on the bedside table. Jesus, this tea must be about 60% proof. I have to keep sipping it to stop myself laughing.

'No consideration.' Mrs T now joins in the denouncement. 'You were never like that when you had your lady-friend living with

115

you, were you Nick? No. I have to confess, I only ever heard you once or twice.'

At this point I start to choke on the mouthful of tea I've just taken. I'm not sure whether I'm laughing or letting out a cry of embarrassed disbelief. Either way I end up blowing half the tea down my nose while two old ladies slap me hard on the back and cluck around me like ageing hens.

The evening doesn't get any better when I get back to the flat and, instead of packing, I flick the TV on for the rest of the football.

Cassie

I'm sure every creature in the world has good and bad nights' sleep. Even tortoises must sometimes blink in the middle of their hibernation and go, 'Cripes, I think I forgot to polish my shell,' or some such concern.

I am the kind of creature who generally sleeps well. I think I have as much sleep as I need. Why do I think this? Because I don't push my body to do what it isn't interested in. I go to bed when I feel tired and I get up when I wake up. In this way I'm very like my cats Piglet and Roo.

When animals get sick they don't soldier on with the nine-till-five. They don't say, 'I

116

just have to fax the details of the transfer off today otherwise the whole deal will go Pete Tong.' (I know what 'Pete Tong' means, by the way, but I don't know who he is. Am I embarrassing myself with a lack of knowledge of Eastern leaders here?) They have more sense than humans and that's why I love them so dearly, cats that is, not Eastern leaders.

However, I am human and have not entirely managed to filter out the influence of the world so I am less able to stick to a relaxed sleep pattern if my mind is disturbing me with strange thoughts.

And so it was, having wisped down to the kitchen to ferret about in the bin in the middle of the night, I wake early, still plagued by a strange sensation in my stomach, not unlike mild indigestion. I am going to have to phone Daisy about this, I can tell. But before I bother her at six in the morning, I blow in Pooh's ear to wake him and take him out onto the lanes around my cottage for a pensive traipse along the roads.

It is a cool, dewy morning and the sky is unmarked by clouds. The birds, who start their version of *Pop Idol* at 5am, are still going for it over an hour later with their varied range of vocal talent. Pooh, who usually bobs about like a cork on choppy seas during these early morning jaunts, is strangely low-key. He slinks along the verges with only a passing interest in smells, and his tail refuses to wag. Perhaps he's got a bitch or two on his mind. Not that I've noticed him getting much recently.

As Pooh seems like he's pining for his basket, I cut short our walk. We double-back to the cottage where I prepare the other animals' breakfasts. I scatter some grain about in the hedge for Eeyore to find, give Tigger some bread and water, put some KiteKat down for Piglet and Roo and a splash of milk in a saucer. Then I wander down to the end of the garden to the five-bar gate with a clutch of carrots.

'Helllooo!' Christopher Robin trots up, his nostrils snorting steamily as he arrives. The cute little thing can't get his head over the gate, though he will strain pretty hard (his eyes going all white) if there is a carrot dangling above it.

I don't want to tease him today, so I yank open the gate and enter the field to stroke him as he eats.

His coat is so deliciously warm that I hug his neck as he munches. He doesn't seem to mind. He knows I have my soppy moments and sometimes need his attention as much as he needs mine.

As he, too, seems in a tame mood this morning, I clamber onto his back and we trudge across the field. The next field is oil seed rape and glows luminous yellow in the morning light. Three grey rabbits bomb out of the hedgerows as we approach and birds rustle in the trees. I smile at the whole scene, feeling wiser to nature's plan now I've seen her magic at work.

There is a path out there for all of us. All we need to do is find it.

★   ★   ★

When I return to the cottage there is someone on my path I would rather not see . . .

'Morning, love. Where have you been? Up all night partying?'

The smart navy-blue uniform with red piping and the duffel bag with the Royal Mail logo imprinted on it should not be draped on a man who is so 'alive' and 'flirty' at this time in the morning.

He's no young pup, either. Well into his fifties, he's tubby, balding, has teeth like badly lined up sweetcorn and breath even Pooh would be ashamed of.

'Just been for a walk.' I smile.

He looks me up and down or, more

precisely, he stares at my chest, trying to see a hint of bare flesh between the two sides of my collarless shirt.

Then he stands there flicking through the letters, enjoying his moment of power.

'This is for you.' He hands me an electric bill. 'Bad luck, love.'

'Thank you.'

'And . . . this one looks a bit more promising. Hand-written, local postmark. Hope you don't have another man on the go, do you?'

'How could I cheat on you?' I force myself to say.

He gives me the letter and shuffles again. He probably hasn't got anything else to give me, but he wants to hang around.

'So when are you going to make an honest man of me then?' He fiddles with the elastic band around his bundle of envelopes. 'I've got them queuing up, you know. You wouldn't want to miss your chance, would you?'

'I'm sure you have!' I beam as I sidle past him, having to put one foot on the flowerbed to make my way to the door. 'You take care,' I finish and then call sharply to Pooh, letting him scuttle between my legs before I close the door.

I don't usually like to be rude to people, but I can see with this chap that if I hang around chatting he will actually ask me out and then try to stick his tongue in my mouth, which I really don't think I could handle, however polite my parents have brought me up to be. Eurrrgh. Just the thought!

At the kitchen table I open the handwritten envelope, which I already know is not from some distant prince asking for my hand in marriage, but from my mother.

I slide out a card, its front depicting a country scene (horse ploughing field, Robin perched on gate post) and open it up.

Darling, hope you are ok. Remember if the pressure of running your own business, keeping all those animals and living alone ever gets too much for you, you are more than welcome back at home.

With love, M. and Daddy xx

I smile and stand the card on the table. My mother can be very sweet sometimes. Clearly she is worried about the mysterious phone call she received from me when I was in London. I told her it was a practical joke but she wouldn't believe a word of it. I may have to go round for Sunday lunch or something in the near future to prove a space shuttle has not left earth with me in it.

Sighing at the thought, I get up and put the

electricity bill unopened by the bread bin. I will save it for a moment when I can be bothered to pay it. No need to know the bad news before then.

Just as I am about to ponder the mystery of the unknown business card while lying on my back on the sofa, I hear someone knocking on my front door.

I groan. This is a favourite trick of my postie who will often withhold one letter so he can return to bother me again (no doubt hoping I will have to leap out of the shower to answer his knock, giving him more of an opportunity to see some bare flesh).

'Yes!' I snap as I open the door and immediately wish I'd moderated my annoyance as there standing in front of me is not the rotund, navy-blue suited full figure of the postman, but my dashing Andrew, looking rather shocked.

'Oh. Sorry. Have I come at a bad time?'

My first thought is, 'You couldn't have come at a worse time. I look like an absolute horror. I'm wearing threadbare clothes, I haven't showered, I smell, I have a spot on my chin . . . ' But I manage to say, 'Well, it is a little unexpected, but no. It's nice to see you.'

I let him in and ask him what he's doing in The Cotswolds.

'I'm playing polo again.' He gives my

kitchen the once over. 'Nice place you've got here,' he continues. 'Very . . . '

I hope he doesn't say Bohemian, which is the polite way of saying it looks like I live in a kindergarten.

'Very . . . Bohemian.'

Bugger.

'Thanks,' I beam. 'Would you like a cup of coffee?'

With shaking hands I prepare the mugs of coffee before excusing myself to the loo (he must think I'm incontinent by now) where I frantically wet the palms of my hands and attempt to straighten my hair. It's no use though. I actually make it worse, by plastering some of it to the right side of my head while the other side remains distinctly bouffant.

As I'm about to brace myself to go back to the kitchen, I hear Andrew's voice (a little quieter than normal), presumably speaking into his mobile.

I pin my ear up to the thin door and listen, my eyes bulging.

'Yes, tonight is fine,' he's saying. 'No, darling, I'll be back in plenty of time; I won't let you down. Ok, great. Love you, big kiss. Bye.'

I clench my teeth as I feel the blood drain from my face.

I knew it! He is a scoundrel. He's probably got thousands of women on the go.

That's why he keeps his flat so photo-free. He's never sure who's coming round next!

I remain in the bathroom a few minutes longer to compose myself. Be polite, I tell myself, but no more. Don't accept any invitations. Stay calm.

I walk back into the kitchen and sit down, putting my hands round the warm coffee mug for comfort.

'So how's the portrait going?' Andrew beams. 'Photos a great help, are they?'

I had foolishly admitted over our dinner in London that Digger's portrait had not been working out too well.

'Making much better progress, thanks,' I lie. He still looks like a small grisly bear crouching low.

'Can I see it?'

'No. Don't want to spoil the final unveiling, do we?'

'Suppose not,' Andrew agrees. 'Well, I just thought I'd pop in and see how you were. You must come up to London again some time.'

'Yes, I will.'

'Great.' Andrew gulps back the last of his coffee and stands up, giving me a brisk kiss on the cheek.

'Right.' He strides for the door. 'Off to

Cirencester Park for a few Chukkas.'

Yes, I think as he disappears up the lane in his BMW, I bet you've chucked a few in your time.

I shut the door and immediately pick up the phone to call Daisy. After I've outlined my distress and my need to see her, she responds, 'Yes, actually Guy and I were going to phone you anyway. We were wondering if you wanted to join us for lunch on Saturday. Do you want to meet us in the Tunnel House?'

Ooooh. I think. Is this symbolic? The same pub I met Andrew in . . .

'Ok,' I say. 'See you there.'

Nick

I reach out and turn off the alarm clock. Not because I have any intention of getting out of bed but because I can't stand listening to the music any longer. I know, I know, I should be getting up and finishing off the packing but it's nice, warm and comfortable here under the duvet. It's my last morning in this bed. It's going to Deb and Scotty's spare bedroom later today, along with my sofa and all the other big bits of furniture. I'll be kipping on a camping mat on the floor tonight.

I lay flat on my back and look up at the ceiling.

I wondered whether I'd be having second thoughts by now. But it's all happened in such a rush I haven't had time to. I'm actually starting to get excited about it. It feels like a big adventure.

The positive thinking does the trick and spurs me on to get out of bed. After a hot shower, I'm ready to face the final bout of packing. Not much left to do now, just throwing things into boxes once I've finished using them. The living room is pretty well sorted. The bathroom just has the basic grooming kit and a solitary bog-roll clinging to the holder. Then there's the bedroom.

To get my strength up, I have breakfast standing in the empty kitchen. Toast, fruit pastels and a bottle of Stella. Tea's out as I stupidly packed the kettle and I can't remember where and, as I don't see the point in doing more shopping, I'm just eating and drinking what's here. Not very healthy I know but I'll nip out and buy a salad sandwich or something for lunch.

Fortunately I didn't pack the bottle opener. I hold it in my hand for a moment as a thought scrolls across my mind. Danielle bought it for me when I got promoted (the opener, not the lager). She said I needed a proper one as the cheap rubbish I kept buying always broke. Just like a blacksmith needs a good hammer or a carpenter needs a good saw, if you're serving wine, you need a good corkscrew.

I'm tempted to chuck it. Just because I know it'd piss her off. That would be silly though. It's a good one and it's served me well. Made in Sheffield of the finest steel, just like me. I've probably got a few more bottles of wine to open before I retire so I stuff it into the pocket of my jeans.

Bottle now open, I trek back into the bedroom to begin the final onslaught. One half of the fitted wardrobe is empty. Danielle did a thorough job when she went. Just my half to sort out.

The clothes are easy. I simply pull them off their hangers and stuff them into the suitcase I've got ready.

I then turn my attention to a small shoebox that's sitting at the bottom. I'd forgotten I'd put it there. I'm about to take it through to the living room to be packed inside a tea chest when I pause for a moment.

I lift the lid and cast my eyes over the contents. There's all sorts of bits in there. I pick up the gold band lying on top of the other stuff: my mum's wedding ring. I often wondered why she still wore it. My dad walked out on her only a few months after Debs was born. Disappeared and never came back. As far as I know he never bothered to divorce her. She still wore the ring until her dying day and kept the name Ratcliffe. She never explained why but I got the impression she thought that was the proper way to do things. I guess her generation behaved differently.

I let my fingers wander through the pieces of paper and card in the box. Eventually I pluck out a photograph. It's of me standing with my mum and Deb on my graduation day: cap, gown, the lot. I felt like a complete prat in all that get-up, but my mum loved it. No one in our family had ever been to university before. It gave my mum something to crow about.

I can still remember the excited look on her face as we were reunited after the ceremony and the huge hug she gave me.

She died a few months later. She was diagnosed with terminal breast cancer, and there was nothing they could do. We just had to watch her gradually get worse until one day she wasn't there anymore.

She had this photo by her bed in the hospital. Occasionally she'd point it out to the nurses and tell them just how proud she was of Deb and me. It was embarrassing at the time but I'm glad I heard her say it.

I wonder if she'd still be proud of me now. I guess it's up to me to make sure she would be.

Cassie

This time I ensure I arrive in plenty of time to meet my sister. I know she's good-natured but no one likes to be let down twice in a row. Besides, I've been waiting two days to speak to her, so I don't want to waste a moment.

I sit in the lounge bar of the pub to avoid getting my hair blown all over the river. It's a peculiar place, this. There are postcards of bare-breasted girls at the bar, photo montages of drunk students from the agricultural college which show a shocking amount of bare bum, stacks of magazines and rumpled sofas and armchairs littered about. Take away the pictures and I could be almost sitting in my own living room. I feel right at home and Pooh is even allowed to join me, although there is a sign that clearly says 'NO DOGS ALLOWED'.

'Ignore that,' the friendly landlord had said when I first brought Pooh here and inquired as to whether I had to leave him outside.

'That's only to please Health and Safety.'

I thought at first he may just have been making an exception for me because it was raining outside, but then I saw his two great Labradors appear from the hatch in the bar and realised he really was a dog person. We have since become (in a customer/landlord fashion) good friends.

'Watcha Pooh,' he says as we come through the low door and approach the bar, which is tiny and fronted by two dentist chairs. 'Caught any rabbits recently?'

Pooh wags his tail and gives a little bark as if to say 'yes'. He's just showing off, though. He's caught bugger all in ages. Some days I wonder if he's even capable of catching his tail anymore. He really seems to be slowing up in his old age. Today he seems particularly sluggish.

I perch on one of the dentist chairs and tell Pooh to sit quietly beside me. It's one thing taking advantage of a landlord's tolerant attitude to our little four-legged friends, quite another letting your animal run riot, barking and baring his teeth at anyone who has the cheek to wander through the door.

Pooh is very obedient here. I think he senses his privilege and doesn't want to ruin a good thing. Besides, I feed him crisps if he's quiet and he gets a little kick if he isn't.

Which would you choose? Oh yes. He's not silly, my little Pooh. There's something rattling around in that little head.

I'm halfway through a glass of house white by the time Daisy and Guy arrive. They look terribly healthy and cheery, like they've just had some really great sex. I feel a sudden pang of jealousy. I've had a bit of a crush on all Daisy's boyfriends, perhaps because they've all been that bit older and more 'worldly'. And Guy is no exception.

He isn't what you'd call classically good-looking but he does have lovely eyes, a pretty good body (though it looks like he's put on a bit of weight since I last saw him) and a vulnerability that makes you want to give him a big hug every time you see him (which I normally do).

He had a problem with the booze a while back, but Daisy helped pull him through. He still likes a good drink but he's learnt where his limits are. After a night out, he no longer finds himself crawling home or into the nearest bus shelter.

'Hi, guys.' I hop off the dentist's chair, hugging them both and ordering the drinks.

'You're looking very sexy.' Guy winks at me as we walk into the tiny dining room, its ceiling hung with racing passes and its little fire lit even though it's summer. 'Have you been getting some action?'

'Well, that's what we're here to talk about,' says Daisy. 'My little sister is going to tell all. Aren't you?'

I nod, feeling I am about to undergo a tough exam, which I manage to put off until after we've eaten. Then Daisy pounces.

'So, do you want to know the gossip about Andrew Hendry?'

This throws me off-course. 'I thought I was supposed to be telling you the gossip?'

Daisy looks at Guy who is wiping his mouth on a red paper napkin. He's just wolfed down a huge steak and kidney pie with chips, followed by Daisy's chips, washed down with three pints. That'll be where the extra weight is coming from then.

'Well . . . Guy, why don't you tell her?'

Guy puts his napkin down in a scrunched-up ball, runs his forefinger and thumb around his lower lip and says, 'I know the guy. Well, that's not true actually, my brother does.'

'Which brother?'

'Jack.'

'The one you don't like?'

'I don't like either of them particularly but, yes, Jack is a particular arsehole.'

I ruminate on this for a second. This doesn't sound promising. It's all starting to go wrong with Andrew.

'Why are you swearing, by the way?' I ask to give me more ruminating time. 'Didn't you give up?'

'Yes, I did, but the only point in quitting something is to take it up again, isn't it? Besides I only swear about special people. The ones who really deserve it.'

'Oh, so does Andrew deserve it?'

'Well, if he's a friend of Jack's I wouldn't say it looks good.'

'And?'

'And nothing, really. I met him once when he came down and stayed at my parents' place for the weekend. I could find out more if you want; I could ask Jack about him.'

'Ok.' I mean, what harm can it do? I may as well confirm that he's a complete womanising bastard.

'I do remember he was pretty good at croquet and was very competitive. Apart from that, he seemed ok. In fact, the worst feature I could spot about him was his friendship with Jack.'

I nod sagely, while fumbling in my hand-bag.

'I wanted to show you guys this.' I dig out the mysterious business card and put it on the table.

Daisy picks it up and reads the details it divulges, her lips moving as she does so.

(Daisy was also 'unacademic' at school, but her energy and enthusiasm meant she'd always find something she'd be good at, namely her catering business.) Then she passes it to Guy who does the same.

'Wow. A cheaply-printed business card. Fascinating.'

I tut and explain that I have no idea who it's from, but think that a man left it for me at the Tate Modern.

'Oooooh,' Daisy squeals, putting her hair up into a high ponytail as if readying herself for some serious business. 'A mystery. I love mysteries.' She snatches the card off Guy and looks at it again.

'He's from Yorkshire. What do we know about Yorkshire? Mmm . . . '

'They like their beer, don't they?' Guy comments. 'Whippets. Flat caps. Silly accents. Blokes are all big and brawny and up for a fight. The girls are all loud, plastered in makeup and covered in babies.'

I can't help myself frowning a little at this. I have absolutely no idea what people are like up north, but I'm sure Guy's being rather stereotypical.

'What do you think?' I ask Daisy.

'I'm not sure I could point it out on the map. Do they like Cornish pasties there?'

'I think that's Cornwall, isn't it Guy?'

Guy doesn't reply. He simply shakes his head in disbelief.

'Oh wait!' Daisy seems to have spotted some new detail. 'There's something written on the back. She brings it closer to her face and peers at it. 'Oh golly, the handwriting's awful. No wait! Hang on! It says, 'Can I be your Tigger?' '

I grab the card off Daisy and squint at the very small handwriting. She's right. That's exactly what it says. Guy has a look and agrees.

'Must be someone who knows you. I mean Winnie the Pooh is popular but not everyone likes him.'

'I think you should phone him,' Daisy giggles. 'What harm can it do?'

'Can't do that. I'm far too shy.'

Guy has another look at the card.

'It's got an email address. Why don't we send him one from here? Come on, it'll be fun. He might even reply right now!'

'Go on Cass,' Daisy wills me on. 'It's not every day a mystery man wanders into your life.'

I pull a bit of a face and think for a moment. My romantic choice this summer is between Andrew, who may well be a serial womaniser, or the postie. Eek! My own little Sean Bean could be quite fun. And if it's the

135

same man, he did have lovely eyes.

'Ok, why not?' A wave of excitement crashes over me.

'Good girl.' Guy leans over and guides me on his phone. 'What's the worst that can happen? Either you don't get a reply or you get a reply that you don't want to reply to.'

'That's a lot of replies!' Daisy cries. 'Come on. Let's do it.'

For several minutes we chatter over what we should send, though I don't seem to get much choice as I can't work out how to write it.

What we end up with is:

Hi! Have a feeling we exchanged a look at the Tate Modern. I already have a Tigger but could do with another Piglet.

'What's that supposed to mean?' I ask as Guy hits the send button.

'It's only for fun,' Daisy informs me. 'It doesn't mean anything. You must let us know if you get a reply, though. Wow! This could be such a laugh.'

Nick

It's 2am and I'm drunk. The clubs of Sheffield are turning out and throngs of people are spilling onto the streets. I cross the road, trying to take it all in as I wait for Debs and Scotty to catch me up.

I look at the dark, imposing building that I've just exited. The place is responsible for most of my spectacular under-achievements in the world of academia.

'Bright lad, but could have done better.' The mantra of my 28 years so far.

I have a feeling in my gut tonight. A surge of energy that's about to burst out and make the whole world come alive. I feel a new mantra on the way and it all starts tomorrow.

'We're going to walk round to the station and get a taxi.' Debs says when she and Scotty finally emerge from the club.

'I think I'll walk.' I make an executive decision. I don't feel like rushing home tonight. I just want to savour the evening for a little longer.

'See you tomorrow then, mate.' Scotty pats my arm a little harder than is necessary.

'Yeah. See you tomorrow.' I smile before giving Debs a hug and watching the two of them disappear off into a swarm of pissed but happy people.

As I set off in the opposite direction, the feeling of excitement and anticipation is still there in my stomach. I thought I'd end up morbidly sentimental tonight, but I'm not. I look around at all the buildings that make up this city, the city that's been my home for as long as I've existed. It's changed a lot over the years. Bits have been knocked down, built up and filled in. Steelworks and rolling mills have been flattened and replaced with stadiums, shopping centres and snaking tramlines.

There are still things that are the same. I raise my middle finger at Bramall Lane, the same way I have done every time I've ever passed it. Don't get me wrong, I'm a proud Yorkshire lad and always will be, but it feels like this city has been sucking the lifeblood out of me for the last few years. I need to get out for a change of scene. I should have done something different years ago, like Pete did.

When I eventually reach home, I pat the bonnet of my new purchase. Nothing flash, just a second-hand Polo, but it'll get me down to Gloucestershire tomorrow and will be ample for running around doing all the little jobs Pete's got lined up for me. I'm quite excited about it. I've never had a car of my own. I used to borrow Mum's when I lived at home and I'd spent the last few years zipping about in Danielle's girly vehicle.

I step inside the flat and Rooney gambols across the room to greet me, doing an undignified skid across the laminate floor. His tail is wagging furiously and, maybe it's just the drink, but he seems to have an excited glint in his eye too.

I contemplate going to bed for a moment but know I won't sleep yet. It's like being a kid again the night before you go on holiday. I'm starving as well.

I wander into the kitchen and look around, pondering the possibilities. Everything but the very bare essentials is packed into boxes, ready to be loaded into Scotty's van tomorrow. We're travelling down in convoy. The 'Three Musketeers' will finally be reunited.

I eventually decide on toast and turn on the grill.

I know, I'll get on the internet and print off those directions too. Save me a job in the morning. Well, in a few hours. I suppose it is the morning really — nearly 3am now and only about 12 hours to go before we set off on the epic journey. I can't be bothered to unpack a plate so I bring my toast and place it down on the desk beside the PC which I'd decided I'd pack at the last minute in case I get any final emails from Pete.

I log onto my hotmail address just in case. Oh. Plenty of stuff in the inbox. Ken, my ex-colleague, has finally managed to hack into my work account and forward all the stuff to me. What a top bloke! Most of it's crap though. People fussing about their wine order or whether the tablecloths will clash with the bridesmaids. I raise my index finger flamboyantly and bring it down time after time on the delete button, filing those particular messages in the 'some bugger else's problem' folder. There are a couple of things from my friends so I reply with my new contact details. And there's an email from someone called Cassie.

I mull this over for a nanosecond or two. Do I know anyone called Cassie?

Rather a bizarre message anyway.

My finger hovers over the delete key once more and if I was sober I would press it. But I'm not sober, so I type in a facetious reply and then log onto the AA website for the directions.

Cassie

Two days after my first experience with email and, after much coaching from Jilly, the 'www' has become an integral part of my daily regime.

My morning still starts with a nervous nose poking over the top of my duvet and my slitty eyes sneaking a peak at the Winnie the Pooh curtains to see if it's sunny (groan if it's not).

It still continues with a short shower, a minor freak-out over my appearance and then a cup of coffee. But where I would then have a bowl of Special K or, if I'm feeling skinny, Cocoa Pops, I now traipse up to my studio where I have relocated the computer (previously it was next to the sofa in the living room, on the floor, unplugged) and fiddle about with flashing screens and whirring noises.

After I've typed in a password to my msn email account (msn: an acronym for my safe niche? My sex needs? Hmm. Don't know, don't care). I have to wait a disturbingly long time for information to filter line-by-line onto the screen. Jilly says I need more 'ram' to speed things up. I have no idea what she's talking about. Is she trying to implicate I have no motivation? Well, I do. I'm fascinated to know if the mysterious Nick has got my email and, if so, if he's going to reply to it.

And so this fine morning finds me perched on a little wooden stool staring wide-eyed at the monitor, waiting for the pixies to do their thing. Jilly calls them pixels, but I'm sure she must have got this wrong. How can pixels deliver messages? Hmm. No idea. But pixies can. They do it with the fairies.

Finally, the screen is filled with a rather lovely sky-blue background and all sorts of information that I can't possibly take on

141

board at this time of the day. Skipping it all, I move my mouse (now here is a computer term I do understand — I have a little white one that I've painted a face on and have used some fibre optic strands as whiskers) until his nose is pointing at the word 'inbox'. I press his left eye twice in a double wink and the screen again goes into transition.

I sip my second coffee of the day as images again reappear. Finally, I get this: 'You have one new message'!!!! I click on the line, wait a second and then get, *Have you heard from him yet? Love Guy.*

Balls.

Feeling terribly let down and dejected, I finish my coffee, head downstairs and make myself a piece of toast. While it's shifting from white to brown in the toaster I put some Chum in Pooh's bowl and feed all the other animals as usual outside. When I get back in, Pooh, the lazy little thing, is still in his basket.

Somewhat irked because I wanted to take him for a walk, I consider rousing him from his doggy dreams, but decide against it. He seemed terribly tired yesterday and appears to need his rest.

So for companionship today I make do with Tigger. He's an eager and amiable buddy, but somewhat slow. Even with a much-curtailed walk it is over an hour before we return to the cottage. I imagine it would be easier if I could put him on a lead and he flew along with me but, humanised as he is, he seems to have forgotten how to get airborne. And besides, we would look ridiculous, wouldn't we?

The walk must have worn him out because the minute we get back to the kitchen, he curls up under the table and falls asleep. I wash my hands and prepare to tackle the day's painting. I have three portraits on the go at the moment: Digger, a rabbit called Percy and a hamster. So far, the hamster is a blob with two eyes. I'm not sure how I'm going to tackle the fur, but this morning is the morning to have a go.

'Come on Pooh,' I say as I'm about to go upstairs. 'Time for you to get up now, you lazy thing.'

Pooh remains steadfastly in his basket.

'Pooh.' I linger by the stairs, my hand on the banister. 'Come on. Come and help me with the hamster.'

Still there is no response.

Tutting, I walk back down the short corridor to the kitchen. Crouching next to his basket I tickle him under his chin. I immediately realise the reason he hasn't got up this morning. He's stone cold. Before the reality registers, I lie down on the cold flagstone floor, put my arms around his basket, trying to convince myself it's terribly cold in the kitchen and he is still alive, then burst into tears. I can't move from this position until well after midday when I phone the vet in Cirencester and ask if I can take him in for a post-mortem.

★   ★   ★

Something good always comes out of tragedy.

In the instance of Pooh's death, the positive that came of his passing was that I became closer to my father.

Unable to go to the vet's on my own, I phone home for moral support and it is my father, not my mother, who picks up. Once I have explained the situation, he immediately says he will come round to the cottage and take us into town.

'Your mother stayed at her friend Paula's last night. Another séance night, or something. She isn't back yet. I'll be with you in half-an-hour.'

When he arrives, smartly dressed in a blazer and chinos, his receding grey hair swept back off his forehead, I run out of the front door and throw myself into his arms, sobbing.

'Daddy. I can't believe he's gone. He's . . . '

And I can't speak anymore after this because the wracking sobs choke my voice.

My father leads me back into the cottage and goes into the kitchen where he examines the little body that used to be Pooh. He crouches down and strokes his head and when he straightens up I can see tears rolling down his cheeks.

'He was such a super little chap. I'm going to miss him bounding in through our front door and leaping onto my lap.'

My father puts his safe, strong arms around me and lays his wise head on top of mine. He bought me Pooh as a present for graduating from Goldsmiths with honours. I'd been pestering him for a dog my entire childhood.

'Now you're a woman,' he'd said, 'I think you're old enough to look after him.'

Pooh was a tiny little puppy back then and I absolutely fell in love with him the moment I held him. He was my best friend through those tricky early-twenties' years. He gave me the love and security I desperately wanted from boys but couldn't find. No matter how nasty a boy was to me, Pooh was always there with a friendly bark and a hearty face-lick to cheer me up. And he never complained no matter how many times I played *Rainy Days and Mondays* by the Carpenters after I'd been dumped. (Everyone else did.)

Of course at times he did piss me off. Crapping all over the show and getting growly with other dogs for no reason, but that's just nature, isn't it? No one's perfect but Pooh was as close to perfect as I wanted or needed.

'I'm going to miss him so terribly,' I say to my dad as he drives at a statesman pace along the leafy back road to Cirencester. My father keeps his eye on the worn tarmac, but he puts a hand on my knee and gives it a squeeze.

'We'll get through it together,' he says. 'You should maybe come and stay with us for a few days. Have some company for a bit.'

At the vet's my father hands Pooh over in the cardboard box he'd brought in the boot of his car.

The vet is very sweet and promises to have some results for me early the following week.

'It must be an awful blow,' he says kindly. 'You must grieve his passing like any member of the family.'

This doesn't help my trembling-lip state-of-mind but I manage to choke out a quick 'Thank you' before being led away like a widow by my father.

'You know,' he says on the drive back to his village (I had agreed to spend the afternoon with him and Mother), 'I cried when my parents' cat died and I think I was almost thirty at the time. It never gets any easier. But death is part of life. Pooh had a wonderful life; he died peacefully knowing he was loved.'

'Thanks, Dad,' I croak again and snivel for the rest of the journey.

When I get home in the evening I sit in the kitchen for two hours, staring at Pooh's empty basket, occasionally closing my eyes, expecting him to be there when I open them. When I am too tired to continue this soul-destroying activity I go upstairs, taking the painting of the Large Blue I was so proud of. I hang it on the wall in my studio and stare at it, imagining Pooh with little blue angel wings somewhere above me, and on impulse I dip a fine brush in some black gouache and paint:

For Pooh. You'll always be my best little friend. Love Cass xxxxx

Then I go to bed and lie there thinking of all the fun times we'd shared. I'd like to say the following morning I woke up feeling refreshed after a good night's sleep. I wish I could say I'd reached the conclusion my father had suggested — that Pooh had a great life and was now in a better place. A wondrous doggy heaven where every tree trunk smelt like the doggy equivalent of Mary

Archer and bones grew out of the ground like grass.

But that doesn't happen.

I wake early with a sense of emptiness that I simply cannot shake off. It takes me an hour to pluck up the courage to go down to the kitchen and not see Pooh there. When I do eventually go and make myself a coffee, I can't stay there looking at his empty basket so I quickly feed the rest of my brood and nip upstairs thinking that throwing myself into my work might take my mind off things.

Unable to paint real animals this morning, I have a go at the spider from the Tate. I pin one of the postcards I bought to a large canvas and crack on with it. I outline the legs in fine charcoal until I'm satisfied with what I've got, then spend ages mixing up a range of browns, greys and blacks I can use to define the muscles in those long legs. I imagine Pooh being cradled in one of those eggs and, rather than finding it upsetting, I'm actually amused by the idea and begin to paint in a more fluid, relaxed manner.

As I glide my brush across the canvas, the great legs taking shape, I think of the man with those intense eyes once more and suddenly realise I haven't checked my emails again.

After the usual rigmarole, I finally find my

'inbox'. I have two messages! I open the first. It reads, *Have you heard from him yet? Love Guy.*

Balls. Again.

I open the second mail. It takes a while for me to register who it's from and what it says, but once I've scanned it several times I'm sure I have it right. It's from a Nick Ratcliffe and it reads:

Not sure about Piglet. Think I'm more of a Pooh.
Who the hell are you?!
Nick

6

Nick

As I start to ease myself into consciousness I'm aware the world is different today. It's much quieter. It feels cleaner.

All I can hear is the sound of birdsong and someone gently snoring.

I've no idea what time it is. It feels early but it's light outside.

I sit up tentatively and blink a few times while I get my bearings.

The snoring is coming from a still unconscious Scotty, asleep at the other end of the caravan with a small black dog curled up on his chest.

Quietly, I get up from my sleeping quarters and tiptoe towards the door. I gently turn the catch and step outside. The dewy grass feels soothing against my bare feet and the air is moist, but fresh and clean. For miles around I can see nothing but green: rolling fields punctuated with little clumps of trees. The only contrast is the orange glow of the sun, which has just broken free of the horizon.

I wander a little further around the back of

the house and up to the fence at the end of the garden. Through the windows of Carrine's office I can see the boxes that are host to 28-years of assorted clutter: CDs, books, pots, pans, all the things that you collect as you go through life without even noticing it.

As I look over the fields I suddenly become conscious that I'm wearing nothing but a pair of boxers. I don't think anyone can see me. I do a quick 360-degree check. I can see a couple of cottage roofs poking out of the trees in the distance but I'm not overlooked by anyone else. I could run around the garden naked and no one would notice. I almost give in to the urge to do it but I resist. I settle for doing a couple of handstands and walking across the lawn on my hands.

Slightly out of breath, I head back towards the caravan, on the way glancing through the French windows into Pete and Carrine's living room. It's almost finished now. No dangling wires, just neatly plastered walls waiting for the painters and decorators that I've got to let in later today.

I reach into the caravan and pull a pair of jeans off the end of the bed. I tug them on and slip my feet into the trainers that are lying by the door. Once across the car park, I select a key from the huge bunch that Pete has entrusted me with and let myself into the restaurant. Here the walls are polished plaster. The floor is tiled and littered with furniture still wrapped in the plastic it was delivered in.

I walk to the far end and through the small door that already bears the warning sign 'Staff Only'. I creep up the small flight of stairs and into my office! I hold the door open and look around. I get a warm feeling inside as I picture how it's all going to be: a desk at either end, one for me and one for Pete. This time next week I'll be sitting in my black leather swivel chair, interviewing waiters and chasing up linen suppliers. And inside me there's a new determination like nothing I've ever felt before. I'm going to make this work. Not just for Pete but for me. I'm going to be the best bloody restaurant manager the world has ever seen.

★   ★   ★

In the afternoon, I wave as I watch Scotty's white Transit disappear off into the distance and I'm suddenly aware of how real all this is. I'm here now on my own with a house, a restaurant, a team of builders and various delivery personnel to deal with. The responsibilities don't end here either. I'm now off to Cirencester to sign Rooney up at the vet's.

Pete's given me detailed instructions on how to get there so I'm feeling confident, but it's still odd not knowing where anything is.

Scotty did manage to find us a pub to have lunch in before he went so the place maybe isn't too hard to navigate. That said, you could drive Scotty around with a bag over his head, drop him out of a helicopter and switch off the earth's magnetic field, and he'd still find the nearest pub. Boy's got a nose for it.

Anyway, I'm still full of the spirit of adventure so I load His Nibs into the car and then climb in myself.

★   ★   ★

We find the vet's without a great deal of trouble. Looks rather posh and that worries me slightly. I've just stopped to get some petrol on the way here and nearly died when I saw how much it was. The vet's bills were bad enough in Sheffield; Christ knows what they're going to be like here. 'You'd better look after yourself in future, mate,' I remark as I help him out of the car.

He doesn't seem too bothered. His tail's going like a windscreen wiper and his eyes are sparkling as usual. Obviously never sustained a major injury to the wallet or he'd have a bit more sympathy.

I turn the key in the car door. I couldn't afford one with a blipper thing, so I have to make do with central locking. I can just about hold my head up in public. Mind you, parking between a BMW Seven series and an XKR probably wasn't the best way to show it off. Encouragingly, I do notice an ordinary-looking Fiesta over in the corner. Perhaps there are some normal people around here after all.

As I push open the door and step inside, my worst fears are confirmed. The place is immaculately decorated. The photos on the walls are of people in tweedy jackets sipping Champagne, or horses covered in rosettes. It's better than most people's houses in here.

The one good point is that it's not busy. There's a couple with a cat in one of those plastic dungeon things and two other people but that's it.

'Can I help you?' The receptionist sounds as posh as she looks and I'm suddenly aware of how different I sound to everyone around here.

'Yes, I'd like to register my dog please.' I look down at Rooney, before placing on the desk all the record cards and stuff the vet back home gave me.

'I see.'

She smiles too politely for it to be reassuring.

'And could I take your name please?'

'Nick Ratcliffe.'

I start to feel even more uncomfortable as my voice echoes around the waiting room. I can feel myself putting on one of those slightly-posher-than-normal voices, like people use on the telephone before they've worked out who it is on the other end. Why I'm doing it I don't know; it's not as if . . .

My train of thought is abruptly halted as I feel the vet's surgery door swing open and crack me on my Achilles tendon. I've been leaning forward on the desk, my legs far out behind me. Teach me to look what I'm doing, won't it?

'Oh, I'm sorry,' I hear a ladylike voice say from underneath the large cream sunhat that's just walked in through the door. I think there's a girl under there, but it's hard to tell. All I can see is a duck tucked under her arm. 'The door's really hard to open.'

The girl puts the duck on the reception desk, gives a sigh and taps her fingers on the wooden surface.

Rooney, who had been sitting on my boots, is now up and sniffing round the girl's trouser leg. He doesn't seem to be doing any harm, so I leave him to it.

Then, of course, his nose has to travel a bit higher and the girl is suddenly squealing.

155

Bloody hell Rooney! You'll have to be a bit better behaved than this now we're down here; otherwise we'll be pissing people off before we even start.

Luckily the girl isn't screaming for help; she's pleased to see the little fella.

'Ah, you're gorgeous.' She bends down to rub his face and tickle him under his chin. All I can see now is the big sunhat, Rooney's windscreen wiper going like he's in a blizzard, and a very sexy arse. And I'm not talking about Rooney's.

'What's his name?' The voice tinkles out from under the sunhat again.

'Rooney.'

'That's an unusual name for a dog. How did you come up with that?'

Bloody hell. What planet has this woman just landed from?

'He's a footballer,' I decide to explain politely.

'Oh, I see . . . ' She pauses for a minute. 'How old is he?'

'Twenty-one.'

'That's impossible!'

'That's what they all say. He's a freak of nature.'

'I'll say! Border Terriers only usually live about ten or eleven years.'

It's only then I realise she's talking about

156

the dog. I can't stop myself laughing.

'What's so funny?' The girl asks as she straightens up and I see her face for the first time. She's dead pretty, this one. Nice eyes, cute little figure.

'I just thought you were talking about the footballer, that's all.'

'Oh,' the girl puts her hand over her mouth and giggles. 'Sorry, I don't know anything about the game. Tennis, maybe; football's not my thing.'

'Yeah, I kind of got that impression.'

And it's then that she looks at me for a fraction too long and I get the impression she thinks she knows me . . .

Cassie

'It's him!' I realise as I look up and hear the friendly sounding voice for the first time, and immediately look away again, embarrassed by the thoughts I've had about those eyes since the first time I saw them at Tate Modern. I'm so pleased I wore my large sunhat. It's perfect to hide under!

Busily stroking Tigger and frantically thinking of something to say, I blurt, 'So you're not from round here, are you? What are you, Scottish? No, no. Welsh?'

I hear that friendly laugh again. Not patronising or snotty, but warm and honest.

'I'm from Sheffield,' he replies.

Oh crikey, I'm thinking. This is fate. First London. Now here. Either that or he's a stalker.

'So, what are you doing all the way down here?' I ask, still examining Tigger with furious urgency and hoping I'm not blushing too beacon-like.

'Is . . . Roomy sick?'

'RooNey? No. I'm registering him; I've just moved down here.'

Oooooh. I want to look up at that face with those intense eyes but I can't.

'What's up with the duck?'

'Nothing.' It sounds foolish, but it's the truth. After Pooh, I've decided I need to have all my animals fully checked over. Tigger's the first. 'I mean, he's just here for a check-up.'

'Oh right. Funny thing to have as a pet, isn't it?'

'Well, it wasn't planned. It just kind of happened.'

Oh God, now Tigger sounds like a love child. Luckily the receptionist arrives back at the desk and the guy starts filling out forms for his dog, so the pressure to talk is off. I tell the girl I'm here for Tigger's appointment. She gives me a disc with a number on and asks me to sit down in the waiting room.

I gather Tigger up and sit on one of the plastic chairs. There are only two other people in the surgery. Both old women, both with those plastic pet carrying boxes you often see on the backseat of a car heading up the M4.

But I'm not interested in them. I want to talk to this man some more.

Using all the courage I can muster, I take off my sunhat and place it on the chair next to me. I feel terribly exposed, but I want to be seen. To hide my worry, I idly flick through a copy of *Country Life*, pretending to be deep into an article about crop rotation, or global warming, or global crop rotation.

When the man is finished at the desk, he comes and sits on the chair one away from me. I studiously ignore him until he says, 'You know, I was thinking. You don't know any good places where I can walk my dog, do you?'

And somehow from that, I find myself agreeing to have a drink with him the following evening in my little local. My head goes into a whirl. Suddenly, I can hardly wait to get home and phone Daisy. Perhaps Jilly is right. Mobile phones aren't only for emergencies . . . they're for high-octane gossip, too!

As the man gets up to leave, having

finished his form filling, he smiles down at me and says, 'What's the duck's name?'

'Tigger.'

'Ok.' A sudden thought seems to travel across his face. 'I'll see you guys tomorrow.'

'Bye.' I smile. And he's gone.

Nick

I push back from my new desk and spin round on my office chair, laughing as I turn. Everything is going great. We now have PCs and printers. The plumbers have just finished the bathrooms and the cutlery has arrived.

I feel a certain amount of pride as I unwrap it and read the words 'made in Sheffield' embossed on the knife blades. A little reminder of home.

There's a few weeks until we open but there's plenty to do. I have staff to recruit, a process that's been helped greatly by the installation of a proper telephone line (the mobile signal really is shit out here). I've got to supervise the delivery of all the furniture and I must go into Cirencester again later today to pick up a load of flyers and business cards.

I feel really proud that Pete's trusted me with all of this but, if I think about it too much, it scares me shitless. I've never been good at responsibility. Scotty can vouch for that. Any time I was put in charge at school it went pear-shaped. Soccer kit went missing. School discos didn't turn up. And one time, a bunch of frogs escaped from the biology lab. I'd forgotten to close the door after I'd been asked to clear up after the lesson. Little buggers ended up hopping into a French class. Ironic perhaps, but not appreciated. Needless to say Scotty never lets me forget these disasters, even though I'm more efficient than I used to be. Or maybe just better at delegating.

Pete'll be here in a couple of weeks, so I've just got to keep it all afloat until then. Shouldn't be a problem. I'm gaining confidence every day. Somehow it all seems to be coming together down here. Particularly now I've got a date.

I don't know what made me ask her out. Well I do actually: she's jaw-droppingly fit. Listen to me; I sound like a dirty old man. I suppose that's what several months of celibacy does for you. Or perhaps it's all this fresh country air.

I'm surprised I did it. I've spent the last five years in 'look but don't touch' mode and then it suddenly occurred to me that I could. That's not quite what I mean. I didn't rush up to her and grope her, though it was tempting. The date will be a laugh if nothing else. If she turns out to be ridiculously posh and up herself, I'll just keep sending her to the bar so I can admire the view.

Do you know what the really weird part is though? What made me ask her out more than the flirty eyes and curvy bum? It's this nagging feeling that I've seen her before somewhere . . .

I glance at my watch. There's still a few hours before I need to be at the pub, but I reckon I may as well freshen up and have a shave now. (This designer stubble is about to progress into something seriously less stylish and it'll give any razor cuts time to heal and the aftershave time to mellow.)

Functioning showers have arrived just in time. Having got myself within striking distance of some local totty, I would hate my chances to be compromised by poor standards of personal hygiene. Generally I don't think I'm too bad. (Sniffs pits in paranoid fashion.) I've had some basic washing facilities but it's not quite the same as giving yourself the head to foot treatment with the old Imperial Leather, is it?

I have one final spin on my chair and head off to find a towel.

Cassie

'No, that looks awful. Tragic!'

Jilly is sitting on one of my wooden kitchen chairs eating a little tray of sushi while I parade various outfits in front of her. My current ensemble comprises a full-length flowery skirt and a low-cut white ruffly blouse.

'You look like a Dutch barmaid.'

'Is that bad?'

'Frightful.'

'I thought boys liked that sort of thing.'

'They do! Which is precisely why you shouldn't wear it. Well, not on a first date. You want to look composed, attractive, possibly cute, but not like a slapper who eats men for supper.'

Tutting, I hurtle back upstairs and rummage through my wardrobe again.

I simply have nothing to wear. I can't remember the last time I went shopping. I'm not prepared for casual drinks. I can either go full-on smart, or milkmaid scruffy. There's no in-between.

Having finished her sushi, Jilly joins me upstairs, takes one look at the remaining candidates for the final election and shakes her head.

'I'm afraid Cheltenham is your only hope, sweetie.'

'I can't go to Cheltenham!' I cry. 'I don't know the shops; I don't know what I'm looking for . . . I'll get lost.'

'That's exactly why I'm taking you.' Jilly grabs my hand. 'Come on, if we go now, we'll be back before rush-hour.'

I'm still not that keen, but I'm powerless against Jilly's forceful nature.

'Come on. You'd be doing me a favour. I need to talk to you about something.'

'What?'

'I'll tell you on the way.'

We're already back downstairs and Jilly is gathering up her handbag when I say, 'Do you think I could have a second to put some clothes on?'

Jilly looks me up and down.

'You're right. Bra and pants are a bit casual.'

*   *   *

On the way to Cheltenham, Jilly says something that brings me out of my usual afternoon stupor like a hypnotist snapping their fingers.

'Jeff's having an affair. I'm convinced of it.'

My mouth hangs open for a full minute before I can say anything. And then what I say isn't especially helpful, 'Really?!'

'Yes.'

And after this affirmation I'm afraid my ability to speak totally leaves me. I just sit in the passenger seat of the Volvo, my chin resting on my lap, blinking like a confused owl. Or Owl in my AA Milne world.

It's not until we've parked up around the corner from Montpelier that I realise I'm going to have to do my best to convince her that he isn't. Which won't be easy because I don't know Jeff particularly well. The only times I've ever spoken to him have been at their garden parties so I'm hardly qualified to judge the state of their marriage, but I feel compelled to convince Jilly that she's wrong, just to make her feel better.

Throughout our jaunt around the shops, while I leap in and out of a wide variety of togs, I inform her that she's just stressed at the moment and is therefore making stuff up in her head.

'Jeff hasn't got time for an affair,' I point out, while hoisting myself into a pair of dark denim jeans.

Jilly stares at my waist as I struggle to do up the buttons.

'Try the twelve,' she utters in a matter-of-fact tone.

'But I'm a ten!'

'You're not.'

'I am!'

And just to prove it in front of all the staff and shoppers in River Island I suck my gut in, force the two sides of the trousers together and fasten.

'See!'

'Comfy?'

I nod and then turn puce. I get Jilly to help me undo them again.

'So you're a ten and Jeff's not having an affair,' she tells me cynically.

'Correct.' I pass her the size ten and grab the twelve. 'Only sometimes things don't appear as they seem.'

And with that I slink back into the dressing room.

Over coffee in a little café near The Everyman Theatre I realise I've done an ok job because Jilly turns to me and says, 'You're probably right. I could be imagining things.'

'You are,' I agree, agreeing with myself. This is wondrous. Perhaps I should be a relationship counsellor.

'To celebrate this wonderful realisation I'm going to buy you another couple of t-shirts. Come on. Drink up!'

I groan, taking a final slurp of my coffee. I've had enough of shopping for one afternoon. Being bought stuff isn't nearly as much fun as you might imagine.

Not for a giver anyway.

Nick

A strange, slimy man leans in towards me as I stand at the bar.

'I think you're in there.'

I try and smile politely but the overpowering stench of his breath makes me wince. Jesus, he could strip wallpaper with that.

'I've had my eye on her for a while but, you know how it is, so many women, so little time.'

I think about wishing him luck in finding one without a sense of smell but I resist. I don't want to start upsetting people before I've been here two minutes.

I force another smile and hobble back to where Cassie's sitting with the drinks.

I've already explained to her what happened in the bathroom this afternoon. I was so pleased with the deluxe-tiled interior that I mimed a penalty kick and ended up bending my big toe back on the edge of the glass screen. It killed, so I legged it into the shower cubicle and frantically twisted the taps to get some warm water on it. It was ice cold — I hadn't turned on the heater.

And just to top it all off, I gashed myself shaving and bled for a full half-hour into the sink. Thank God Scotty wasn't around. The words 'twat' and 'you' may well have been used . . .

Still, Cassie has been sympathetic, so it could all turn out to be a blessing in disguise.

'I think you've got an admirer.' I nod towards the king of halitosis.

'Oh, don't!' She looks bashful for a moment. 'That's my postman. He's always turning up at ridiculous times of the day to make letchy comments.'

'I might join him.'

I give her my smooth and dashing look. I haven't used it for a while so I think it's about time it had an airing. Yes, result! She's doing that coy, giggly thing that girls do when they're slightly tipsy and starting to fancy you. I can still do it then.

And she's not stuck up like I thought she'd be. She's just . . . well . . . lovely really. She tells me she's an artist but from what she says she also runs a zoo. I'm trying very hard to keep up with the long list of pets but I don't think I'll pass the end-of-date exam.

I don't know much else about her yet. We've been discussing the local attractions more than anything else. Can't take things too quickly, can I? I can hardly invite her back for coffee when I'm squatting on the floor of my mate's semi-built house, using a mattress I've dragged from a caravan as a bed. Not that I've ever had any intention of getting that far. A good laugh and some pleasant company would suit me fine. For now.

I feel a mood of decisiveness come upon me. Time for an old party trick.

I pick up the book of matches that is sitting in the ashtray on the table. I feel her eyes follow my movements.

'Right then.' I look into her sparkly eyes. 'Time to get to know each other properly.'

She doesn't answer. She just looks at me a little baffled.

'The trick is,' I pluck one of the matches from the book, 'to light the match and you're not allowed to let go until you've told your whole life story.'

'Seriously?' Her mouth opens in amazement. She's led a sheltered life this one.

'Heads or tails?' I ask her, selecting a pound coin from the small pile of change that I plonked on the table when I came back from the bar.

'Tails.'

I toss the coin. 'Tails it is. Do you want to go first or second?'

'Second.' She gives me a nervous smile.

'Right then.' I strike the match. 'Nick Ratcliffe, aged twenty-eight, born in Sheffield, South Yorkshire. One sister, mum died seven years ago, never knew my dad. Eight GCSEs, four 'A' levels and a degree, all fairly crap.

Girlfriends seven, two serious, engaged once, dumped a few months ago. Worked behind a hotel bar as a student, stayed there so long they turned me into the conference and banqueting manager. Got sacked, came down here, met you.' I blow out the match and drop it into the ashtray.

'Ok, I'll have a try.' She takes a deep breath, like she's about to do an Olympic sprint, then strikes the match. 'Ok, I'm twenty-six, I have a sister too, Daisy. Um. I've lived in the country all my life. Can't remember how many boyfriends I've had. Not because I'm a slapper. I haven't had that many at all, it's just I have a terrible memory and when they're gone, well that's that, isn't it and . . . um . . . Ouch . . . '

She drops the match on the carpet and shakes her hand.

'Let's have a look.' I take her hand to inspect the damage. 'I'm sorry, it was a silly game.'

'It's alright.' Fortunately the look on her face tells me she means it.

'Sorry. I'm not very good under pressure.'

I pull her hand gently towards me and softly uncurl her fingers. I can see there's no damage done. She's got lovely soft hands, delicate little fingers and smooth, supple skin. I know I shouldn't but I can't resist lifting her hand towards my lips and giving her fingers a kiss better.

She goes all swooney and giggly again.

I'm feeling pretty giggly myself. Or hammered. I didn't manage to eat before I came out and I've been knocking back the lager on an empty stomach. She probably thinks I'm a real lightweight.

I notice her glance at the clock behind the bar. 'I'm going to have to go soon,' she says. 'I'm afraid my menagerie will be pining for their supper.'

'That's ok.' It's nearly eleven anyway and I've got to be up early in the morning. 'We'll go after this one.'

'Are we going to do this again?'

It never fails to make me feel good, that question.

'Yes, if you like.' I make sure my tone is casual but I actually feel like standing on the table and punching the air in an animated fashion. I'm ready for this. I reach into my inside pocket and produce one of the crisp new business cards that I went and picked up this morning.

I lay it on the table in front of her and then notice she's laughing. It's a bit more than a tipsy giggle this time.

Now, I'm pretty sure my flies aren't undone and I haven't got lager froth stuck to my top lip or anything, so this is a little perplexing. I look at the card carefully. There's not a hideous spelling mistake on it.

She reaches inside her handbag and produces another business card and lays it on the table next to mine.

Right. Now I'm confused. There are two business cards on the table in front of me, both of them mine, one new, the other out-of-date.

'Where the hell did you get that?'

'You left it with the security guard at the Tate Modern.' Her eyes look at me all bright and shiny. 'I emailed you!'

Something happens in my head now, like when the wheels on a one-armed bandit stop spinning and clunk into place one-by-one. The déjà vu feeling slides away and all becomes clear. She must think I'm a complete numpty.

Time to tell her about Pete, I think.

★   ★   ★

We step out of the pub into the cool evening air. Oh my God! I've gone blind! No, I haven't. It's just they haven't invented streetlamps down here yet.

'You alright?' she asks, obviously noticing my reaction.

172

'Yeah. I'm just used to a certain amount of sulphur glow.'

I look across at her and feel something I haven't felt in a while. It's hard to describe what it is. It's a happy feeling. Not anything as serious as being in love but something a little more honourable than lust. A first-date-went-well glow, I suppose.

I decide to be gallant. 'Shall I walk you home?'

She's giving me the usual look that you get on first dates; the one that says, 'well, I like the idea but how do I know you're not going to batter me to death in some hedgerow and eat my liver?'

'Erm . . . '

'It's ok, if you don't want me to.'

'No, that would be nice, thanks.'

I contemplate the idea of putting my arm round her shoulders but decide against it. I don't want to make her feel uncomfortable so I opt for stuffing my hands into my pockets and shambling along beside her.

Eventually we reach a little cottage. I can't see that much detail in the gloom but it looks cosy.

'Goodnight then.' She looks up into my face.

To snog or not to snog, that is the question. Hmmmm.

I opt for giving her an affectionate peck on the cheek before watching her disappear down the little path to the front door, giving me a friendly wave before she closes it.

Cassie

When I arrive at the pub I feel more relaxed than I did an hour earlier, but only because I drank two-and-a-half glasses of Chablis before leaving the cottage.

Jilly had been a great friend buying me all these clothes ('No, I'm paying,' she kept saying. 'It's my treat'), but although I now have a hundred things to choose from, I find myself to be no better off. From no choice to too much choice is no improvement.

Still, I'm reasonably happy with the deep-blue denim jeans, the fitted red t-shirt and faithful clogs I've got on. With my hair tied-up in a high ponytail, I feel if not gorgeous then reasonably human.

Taking a long, deep breath at the door, I grasp the brass handle, turn it, and stride confidently into The Bug Bear and order a glass of wine. It's not too busy tonight. This is good. Nothing worse than a pub full of locals listening in on a first date conversation.

'You made it then,' says a familiar voice. A

voice whose accent I am beginning to become drawn to.

I turn and smile. Phew! He looks good tonight. He's shaved, put on a nice blue shirt and given his hair that rough look that's designed to look as if he hasn't bothered, but is teased to flatter his round but attractive face.

The landlord places the glass of Chardonnay on the bar and Nick's hand immediately comes over my shoulder, proffering a ten-pound note.

'I'll get that.'

How sweet!

'Thanks.' I take a sip.

'Let's go to a table. I don't imagine you like standing at the bar.'

Well, I don't mind really, but when meeting someone for a quiet drink, I do prefer to sit. Helps when trying to avoid postman with unwelcome deliveries too (smells and jokes mostly), who I spot lurking at the other end of the bar.

Once we're seated, Nick gives me a run-down on the differences he's noticed since moving south of the Watford Gap. Like he can't find crappy corner shops down here. And he can't find a surly milkman to deliver. Or a man in a worn boiler suit to bring him coal on the back of a donkey. I enjoy his light-hearted banter.

We then discuss the restaurant and I feel myself beginning to relax in his company, even though he tends to avoid eye contact. I find this frustrating. I want him to do it lots. I want to see what's there. To catch a glimpse of that look I saw in the Tate. And I want to see if he likes me. I'm not so bothered about the details of his life that he's giving me. They don't mean much.

I say a few dizzy things to try to ease the tension and, after a few drinks, we are giggling together. He even dares to look at me a few times, but I still don't think he realises who I am.

At one point he gives me his new business card (showing off!) and, feeling bold (well, pretty smashed really with all the wine), I put the business card he left for me in the gallery next to it. This should remind him, I think!

But for someone with so many 'A' levels he's dreadfully slow. He simply looks at one card, then the other.

Disappointed, I remind him that he left it for me at The Tate. Aha! The fog seems to clear. Those exams weren't all for nothing!

'Actually, I didn't,' he laughs. 'That was my friend, Pete.'

This comes as a relief. I'd be worried if he had left the card and then forgotten all about it. That would make him either a serial womaniser, or mad. And I don't fancy either.

After I've sipped some sparkling water to sober up, Nick tells me a bit more about his card-giving chum.

'He's got it all,' he concludes after a long soliloquy about family and career perfection.

'Don't worry, you can have all that too, one day, when you find the right girl,' I blurt out and suddenly realise I have been dreadfully over-familiar.

Nick tries to hide his blush but I can see I've made him uncomfortable.

'Sorry.' I try to correct the mess I've just made. 'What I mean is you seem to be such a nice guy. There must be loads of girls out there who'd be thrilled to be going out with you.'

He half laughs at this and looks down at his pint.

'Yeah, well. I haven't had them breaking down my door recently.'

I am so tempted to reach out and hold his hand, but I resist the temptation. I also want to say, 'I'll go out with you, if you want. If it'll make you happy. If you're nice to me . . . ' But I refrain from doing that too. I'm getting much better (mostly) at holding my tongue.

'Something'll turn up.' I give him what I hope is a friendly but also sexy smile.

'We'll have you set-up in no time.'

The next part of the evening I can't remember so well. What with the excitement, the wine, all the information he's given me to take onboard, I think my brain suffers from overload and begins to pack up on me.

Before I start to come across as dizzy I tell him I have to get home to feed the animals, even though I gave them supper before I came out.

He very sweetly offers to walk me home and I accept even though I'm slightly nervous of stumbling about in the dark and doing something very unladylike. Falling in a drainage ditch, for example, or walking into a tree.

We don't talk much on the way home. The cold, sobering air and the ample opportunities that walking close to a member of the opposite sex late at night present, serve to create a certain electricity between us.

By the time we reach the cottage, I am desperate for Nick to kiss me, but I don't do anything to show him. Nothing worse than lunging in for a snog and finding your lips on the side of the boy's ear as he shifts his head to kiss your cheek.

Instead, I just look up at him and give him the tiniest of smiles. He kisses me on the cheek and says, 'Goodnight'. I squeeze his hand, bomb up the path and fly into the cottage before the temptation to run after him and snog him becomes over-riding.

In bed I kick my legs about with excitement at how well the evening has gone. I detail in my mind all the moments when he smiled at me, the times he looked a little shy, the stuff he laughed at. And then I think how much I'm looking forward to seeing him again, and realise to my horror that we haven't actually lined up another date! Agh. I know if I'd had more energy I'd have obsessed about this for hours but, fortunately, exhausted with all the nervous tension and wine, I close my eyes and pretty much pass out.

7

Nick

'You're breaking up Debs. The signal's well dodgy here.' I shout into my mobile like it's going to make any difference. 'I'll go across to the office and ring you from there in a few minutes.'

I press 'end' and stuff my mobile into my pocket. I need a minute or two to prepare myself for the grilling I'm about to get. Rather stupidly I mentioned going to the pub last night with Cassie and now Debs wants every last detail.

Not that there are any details. She accused me of lying when I told her we haven't even kissed yet. Nice to know my little sister has such a high opinion of me.

I'm not usually that chivalrous. I've always been prone to throwing myself into things and then worry about the consequences later. That's how I was pre-Danielle, when I was younger. Maybe I need to take things steady. I'm not ready to have my heart broken again.

I stand with my hands on my hips,

contemplating my current dilemma. I'm in Carrine's office surrounded by boxes and one of them contains my CD player; now which one is it?

I've worked my way methodically though most of them and I'm down to the last three. I pull one towards me and open it up. Bingo. Full of CDs so the player can't be far away. I dig my way down to the bottom and find it. Marvellous. That should make the working day more bearable. More noisy at the very least. It's so quiet around here I keep thinking I've gone deaf. Apart from the occasional car trundling past on the road outside, you could go a whole day and hear nothing but birdsong.

I've nothing against birdsong, but I prefer something with bass and drums. Not crap like The Coors and Daniel Beddingfield. What the hell are they doing in here?

I make a hasty apology to *The Joshua Tree* and *Appetite for Destruction* for having cooped them up in the same box as that bilge. Obviously in her haste to get out of my life, Danielle left a few things behind. Shame it couldn't have been a few Led Zeppelin albums. No chance of that with her tinny pop taste.

My initial instinct is to take the CDs outside and introduce them to my fag lighter.

On the other hand, I've made a new resolution to be more mature. So, CD player and Jimi Hendrix collection in hand, I head off towards the restaurant office.

Once my sense of hearing is being gratifyingly assaulted I set to work finding an envelope. I know there's some in here somewhere. Ah yes, large brown box in the corner.

I slip Danielle's two horrendous examples of musical taste inside and scrawl my old address on the front. I've no idea where she's living now but as I haven't received any post for her recently, I presume she's had it all redirected.

I'm just about to seal the envelope, having suppressed the urge to include a petulant note, when I spot my new business cards on the desk.

I smirk to myself. Perhaps it's time Danielle saw that someone else is capable of getting themselves a decent new job. Wouldn't want her to think I was still moping about in Sheffield, waiting for her to show up and rub my nose in things again.

So I casually drop one in and head for the post office, the smirk on my face turning into a big grin. That should show her.

Cassie

When I wake the next morning, I lie in bed much later than usual, thinking of the previous night's date. I lie on my side in the foetal position running over various details in my mind, trying to work out if Nick really likes me, or if he's just interested in being friends. Or much worse, just a shag!

I've never been one for casual sex. Without emotion, the bump and grind seems rather pointless. Like stoking a fire before it's been lit.

I eventually get up and shower and, while I'm drying myself, realise what incredibly poor shape my bikini line is in. It's like something from a sheep-shearing contest. In Peru, where they base their livelihoods on knitting exotic woolly jumpers, I might be heralded as something of a cash cow. Back on home turf, however, I will doubtless fail to add interest to my account.

Alas, it is no longer the Seventies . . .

So I spend what seems like hours, knickers unceremoniously hoicked up tight against my crotch while I first trim and then shave the offensive areas. When I'm done, there's no stray hair, not a single one. What there is, however, is a couple of sideburns of red pimples, making me look like I've been the victim of a swarm of randy mosquitoes.

F . . . .iddle.

I was going to wax my top lip as well, but I don't think I'll bother now. Clearly, depilation is a dangerous business.

I traipse downstairs feeling pretty dejected and nip out of the side door to feed the animals, who give me accusing looks as I provide their breakfast — at lunchtime. The only plus point for the day so far is that it's searingly hot with a light, cool breeze. I turn my face up towards the sun and have a sudden brain wave. Wouldn't some UV rays clear up my rash?

Doctors say sunlight is good for pimples, so why shouldn't it work with shaving rash?

Deciding on the spot (so to speak) to give myself the day off to sunbathe, read and generally obsess about Nick and when I should phone him and what I should say when I do, I rush upstairs and change into my bikini.

I have to admit I have only ever felt comfortable in a bikini once and that was way back when I was sixteen. It was the summer I grew boobs. Having watched all my friends' chests develop from bee stings to ice cream scoops to ripe mangoes and beyond at the ages of thirteen or fourteen, my chest had remained resolutely like an ironing board with a couple of jelly tots stuck on it. There was only one girl in the fifth form I pitied more than myself. She was a girl called Claire. Her chest had started wonderfully promisingly but had rapidly gone out of control. She spent a month at the perfect ripe mango stage before continuing on and on until she ended up with a couple of Zeppelin stuck to her chest. Facing south. When anyone teased me about my boyish figure, Claire, bless her, would always offer me some of hers. I declined politely, but I often wonder about her now. Did those breasts ever stop expanding? I guess I'll never know.

But that summer was heaven. So distracted was I by the development that had suddenly taken place under my chin, I had no time at all to worry about any other body part. I'm sure I didn't look a great deal better, but I sure as hell thought I did.

Gazing into the mirror now, I am devastated by what looks back at me. My calves are like a rugger player's, my thighs have definitely got bigger, my stomach hints at early stage pregnancy and my upper arms aren't as toned as they were. The only areas I like are my knees, my lower arms and my breasts, which as they grew late are holding up remarkably well against the harsh yank of gravity. I can't even bear to look at the mess

I've created between my thighs.

Oh well, I think as I amble back down the stairs, everything will look far better with a bit of colour.

I must say, sunbathing is good for the soul. I've been lying out here for an hour now, listening to the birds sing, watching Eeyore scrabble about in the hedge, stroking Piglet who came to visit earlier and didn't have the energy to walk back inside. Yes. I must remember to do this more often. The sun shining on bare skin definitely lifts a dark mood.

I roll onto my front and open my book. After I've read ten pages, I feel pretty soporific and thirsty.

'Piglet,' I dig my black cat in the ribs until she opens a green eye. 'Piglet, be a honey and nip inside and get me a lime cordial would you?'

Piglet opens the other eye and meows at me.

'Thanks. Make sure the water's nice and cold.'

I rest my head on my hands and close my eyes for a second. When I open them again, I see Piglet is still by my side.

'Do you not understand English?' I ask.

Piglet starts purring as I stroke the top of her bony head.

'No?'

Piglet closes her eyes again.

'I guess you don't, do you? I really need to get a grip.'

Giving Piglet one last tickle under the chin, I head inside myself and fix my own drink. I also visit the downstairs loo to check how my skin's getting on under the glare of the sun.

Oooooh. Not bad! I have a vague hint of colour coming to my cheeks. If I press on, I might have a healthy glow by this evening. Encouraged, I go back outside and resettle on my sleeping bag (so much more comfortable than a towel), and make a mental list of all the things I fancy about Nick. I come up with:

- Greenish eyes
- Slightly flared nostrils
- Way he moves his wrists
- Deep, vaguely accented voice
- Hint of danger about him
- Vulnerability

And I continue in this vein until I drift into a deep reverie and then a bone-idle afternoon nap. When I wake I'm chilly as the sun is going down so I head inside to put on a pair of tracksuit bottoms and a sweat-top. I then settle in front of the six o'clock news before preparing a light supper.

By the time I'm done it's eight o'clock and

I feel incredibly tired again.

Perhaps it's all the emotional upheaval. Whatever, I scoot off to bed to continue my reading.

Nick

'It'll be great to have you here, at last.' I twirl the phone wire casually around my finger as I talk to Pete on the other end.

'I can't wait myself, mate.'

I can almost hear his grin down the phone. You can't blame him. He's worked damned hard to achieve his dream and now it's only weeks away.

I check through the list of jobs with him once more and then say my goodbyes.

As I place the receiver back in the cradle, a strange feeling swirls around inside me. It's mostly excitement. Pete's enthusiasm for this place is infectious and I guess there's quite a lot of me been poured into the project now. I'm feeling more proud by the day. If a bit lonely.

The good news is they're all moving in next weekend so I won't be on my own anymore. I offered to stay in the caravan but Pete and Carrine insisted that I have the granny flat for as long as I want it. They're letting me have it rent-free. How cool is that?

I haven't done a thing about selling my old flat yet, back in Sheffield. This all happened in such a rush I never got a chance to sort anything out. I just left the keys with Debs and Scotty and zoomed off down here to my new life, a life that seems to be suiting me just fine.

There's something else putting a smile on my face too — nothing to do with the restaurant. It's more to do with Cassie.

'You're in serious danger of becoming besotted Nicholas.'

I sit back in my chair and click the little button on my biro on and off as I ramble to myself.

She's lovely. I was relieved when Debs rang yesterday. Really, I was bursting to tell someone about her. Even if my sister does ask too many questions. My only regret is that I didn't pluck up the courage to kiss Cassie properly. I wanted to, oh God, I wanted to.

Why didn't I?

I don't know. I was vaguely aware of not wanting to come across as a . . . well . . . you know . . . just after one thing. It also felt strange, having someone new to kiss after all this time. It felt like being a fourteen-year-old again . . .

I'm just about to use the surplus of positive

vibes and enthusiasm to catapult myself into the list of jobs when the phone rings again.

Who the hell is it this time?

Cassie

On Saturday morning I get straight out of bed, rush downstairs, pick up the phone and ask Nick if he wants to come kite-flying with me one afternoon next week. I do it straight away so there is no opportunity to chicken out.

Even so, my hands shake a bit while I dial his number.

He seems a bit bemused at first but, after we've had a little chat, he suggests Tuesday (a day on which he hasn't got much to supervise in the afternoon).

'Come round to the cottage and then I'll drive us to Cirencester Park; we can have some fun there and, if you're not too bored of me after, I know this great little Thai restaurant we could go to.'

'Wow. You've got it all worked out then.' He sounds impressed.

'I do have some organisational skills. They're just a bit erratic, that's all.'

He says he'll be up for both kite-flying and a Thai meal.

'And thanks for inviting me. Be good to see you again.'

He then hangs up, saying he's got to make sure the bar goes in alright.

Hmm. Did he sound keen enough? He was very friendly and relaxed. That's not a good sign. He should have been a jibbering wreck. Oh no! Perhaps we are just becoming 'good friends'. What a hideous thought! In a state of neurotic distress I scamper back upstairs and hop straight into the shower.

Agh! The water on my skin is like razor blades. I look down to see a paunchy red expanse above my ravaged bikini line. Below, my thighs look like sticks of Brighton Rock. White on the inside and bright red on the outside.

I leap back out of the shower and run into the bedroom, fling open the wardrobe door and look in the full-length mirror. The image that greets me is of a wild-haired Glastonbury Festival freak who's overdone the luminous red body paint. Not to mention the muffins and acid tabs.

I scream like the kid in the *Home Alone* film and dash to the curtains, which I draw shut with a great yank. I take three deep breaths, put the bedside light on, place my towel over it, and again look in the mirror. In the almost pitch-darkness I look reasonably ok. For the date on Tuesday I will have to wear long sleeves, long skirt and plaster myself in foundation.

Yes, I think. I should get away with that. Provided I don't blister.

I spend the rest of the day applying witch hazel, calamine lotion, lemon juice and fake tan to try and soothe and cover my tanning disaster. By the evening I look like I've been pickled in carrot juice and I feel like I have a steam iron pressed to my nose, cheeks, legs, arms and back.

In the semi-darkness I lurk in my study, trying to paint but I soon give up as my arm hurts where the skin is stretched tight and Digger is again starting to look like a gorilla.

Nick

I've always loved the smell of fresh paint. I don't know why. I'm standing in Pete and Carrine's kitchen, the French windows flung open, drinking a mug of tea, smoking a fag and literally watching paint dry.

The decorators have just been in and added the final touches. The whole place is now coated in tasteful matt shades that reflect and bounce off the polished floorboards.

I feel like an intruder here now. It was ok

while there were bare plaster walls and the odd skirting board still to be nailed in place but this is now a finished house, apart from the absence of furniture. A huge, airy house with just me and a small black dog to rattle around inside it.

'Still, we won't be on our own for long, will we mate?' I give Rooney a quick ruffle before taking the tennis ball that he's kindly brought me and slinging it down the garden for him to chase.

He's after it like a rocket.

'Hey, don't burn off too much energy. Remember we're off kite-flying this afternoon!'

I laugh to myself as I say it. Dating around here is certainly different. I've never had a girl ask me to do that before, and I've had some strange requests over the years. Still, I'll try anything once. Especially if it means I get to redress the lack of snog issue.

I let myself assess that thought for a while. Kissing Cassie. It has the same warming effect on my soul as thinking about cute little puppies or Sheffield Wednesday winning something. I can't imagine it being anything but magic.

Listen to me. I sound like a right soppy sod in my old age. I'll be driving into Cirencester to help old ladies across the road next.

I take a last drag on what I've promised

myself will be my last cigarette (I've been saying that for weeks now), stub it out and drain my cup of tea.

Right. Now onto more manly pursuits: ironing.

I fucking hate ironing. I used to have a deal with Danielle when we lived together. I did all the washing-up and she did all the ironing. I used to deliberately buy dry-clean-only clothes so that I could pay someone else to straighten the creases out for me.

Sadly, there's a lot to do. I've put it off as long as is humanly possible. All my clothes have been packed away in boxes and suitcases for days now and I'm beginning to run out of things that look good with scrunches in. Perhaps I should invite Cassie on an ironing date. Hmmm, maybe not . . .

I climb the stairs like a condemned man feeling oppressed by a society that insists on uncrumpled clothes. Perhaps I ought to start a campaign to bring in creases.

As I reach the top of the stairs my attention is momentarily distracted from my fate as I see a car pull into the car park. My heart misses a beat. It couldn't be, could it?

I race down the stairs and fling open the front door. No, there's no mistaking it, it is her. She's walking towards me. She waves at me and grins.

I stand rooted to the spot.

She walks right up to me, her eyes smouldering with lust.

I pull her in to my body and kiss her like I've never kissed a woman before.

Cassie

The afternoon of my second date with Nick, I wait in the kitchen expecting his knock at the door for over an hour. When it doesn't come, I try phoning his mobile but it's switched off and all I get is his answer phone.

Loads of thoughts crowd into my head. At first they're lenient: he's forgotten; he's been held up by some disaster at the restaurant; his car has broken down somewhere. And then they become more severe: he's out getting drunk with his friend Pete; he doesn't want to see me; he noticed my fat stomach.

Damn! There's nothing more frustrating than getting all excited about something and then that something not happening. Particularly when you don't know the reason why.

Determined not to bore myself with my own bad mood, I phone Jilly and ask her if she wants to come kite-flying with me instead. I'm pleased that she's absolutely thrilled at the invitation.

'Where are you?' I ask.

'In the office.'

'Brilliant. I'll meet you in Cirencester Park in half-an-hour. Ok with you?'

'Perfect. I've had a nightmare day and I don't fancy going home early. But I am desperate to get out of here. See you there.'

★ ★ ★

When I get to the park entrance I see Jilly's Volvo lurking up by the wall. As I swing in through the gates, I toot my horn and she follows me in. We're not really allowed to drive up here, but my father knows the estate manager so we get special privileges, if we're good.

We move in convoy up the long, straight road, the rolling grounds and swaying trees on either side. At the great house, I hang a left and pootle along until we arrive at a gravel car park. In front is a huge area of mown lawn, without any trees, perfect for kite-flying purposes.

I pull up and tug the handbrake on. Jilly stops next to me and we both get out of our cars with the kind of synchronicity choreographers can only dream of.

'How are you doing?' I ask as Jilly's hair blows over her face in the strong wind.

'The fucking bastard is definitely cheating on me, I'm convinced of it!' she shouts.

Oh dear, not again. This isn't turning out to be a fluffy afternoon at all.

'Oh rubbish.'

Like I said, I don't know Jeff very well but I do know this: he works long hours for a stockbroking firm in Cheltenham and is not what you'd call a catch in the looks department. In his early-twenties he had a chubby boyishness about him that was 'winning' but now in his mid-thirties, his features have blurred and his waistline expanded. He's also gone very thin on top. Though the charm remains, it is somehow more difficult to detect. He isn't really affair material.

'What proof do you have that he's cheating?' I ask. 'You can't keep accusing him of playing away without any evidence.'

'I had a look at his mobile call register.'

'Which said?' I open the boot and take the kite out.

'He's been making calls to Spain.'

'And?'

I'm now assembling the kite, putting the carbon fibre struts in place and attaching the lines. And struggling.

I snap the final strut into its plastic housing and turn to look at my friend. I don't know what Jilly's getting at. And I don't think it's worth pursuing any more than it was before.

'I'm sure you shouldn't be worrying about anything.'

'But his ex was Spanish,' Jilly says finally, looking at me triumphantly.

'Oh, so what? So's Seve Ballesteros. Come on. Let's get this thing up in the air.'

★   ★   ★

Flying a kite is something my father taught me to do at the age of seven. He took me into the back field one Boxing Day, wound out the line, told me to toss the thing into the air and from then on I was hooked.

The kite he'd bought me that Christmas had a contraption that made it whizz and buzz as it flew through the air, and it had the longest, brightest red tail I'd ever seen.

But the really great part was its design. It looked like a Peacock butterfly.

That first, frosty morning of piloting will always stay with me. It taught me so much about life: the ups and downs, the freedom to change direction, how you can come crashing down to earth when you make a mistake, how remaining calm is important, how tragedy can strike at any moment but with time can be overcome.

This last observation may seem a little melodramatic, but imagine the scene: a seven-year-old girl flying a kite on a gusty day, the inexpert little hands tussling with the handgrips of the lines, the joy at seeing the kite jink and swoop in the air. And then . . . then the farmer's herd of cattle come roaring around the corner, spooked by the noise.

In a panic the little girl lets go of the lines and the kite spins out of control, twirling back down to earth, directly into the path of the cows.

There follows much mooing and stamped-ing as the herd unwittingly trample the kite and become entangled in the line. The beautiful butterfly struggles to free itself, but dies. One of the cows breaks a leg and the farmer has to be called.

Yes, it taught me a lot that day. More, perhaps, than I wanted to learn.

'So how are things with you anyway?' Jilly asks after I've calmed her fears and we've got the kite in the air.

'Oh, you know. Was supposed to be on a date this evening, but the bastard never showed up.'

'Oh Christ, men!' And that sentence seems to say all that needs to be said on the subject.

'I know.' I tug the lines on the kite right

and left, making it dance to my tune. 'If only men were as easy to control as kites.'

And with that I yank hard on the right line and put the thing into a terrifying nosedive.

Nick

There's something completely decadent about being in bed in an afternoon, isn't there? Even if your bed is only a couple of caravan mattresses with a duvet thrown over them.

Well, not completely thrown over them. As I look down, just poking out above the top of the duvet is one perfectly rounded breast.

I move my hand to cup it, feeling the warmth from it seep into my fingers. It feels so soft and sexy.

I shuffle onto my side and lean over to kiss it, gently, delicately. I then peel back the duvet and administer more kisses, working gently downwards across the sooth curves of her tummy and-

'Stop it, will you!'

Danielle pulls the duvet back over herself playfully.

'That's not what you were saying earlier.'

I raise an eyebrow before making another attempt to start nuzzling her chest. We haven't had sex like this for ages. A whole afternoon of end-to-end shagging of the highest quality. Not the quick bonk before you switch the light out stuff that we'd got into back home. But full-on, totally naked, in full daylight, doing our best to send the other into ecstasy type sex, like the kind that you have when you're first with someone, like I haven't had for four or five years.

She pushes me onto my back and leans into my face and kisses me like I'm the biggest super-stud on the planet.

The kiss goes on for what seems like hours but it still isn't enough. I try to pull her close for another but she frees herself and climbs to her feet.

'Need to use the bathroom.'

She smiles and blows me a sexy little kiss before turning and walking towards the door. I watch her go. The bright daylight is streaming in through the windows. It picks out every curve. God, she's gorgeous. So gorgeous that stirrings under the duvet tell me another round might be on when she returns.

As I roll onto my front I hear a mobile phone ringing from somewhere in the untidy pile of clothes on the floor beside me. I stir around in the crumpled mess of blouse and knickers and eventually find it. Danielle's phone. I answer it.

'Hi, is she there?' It's a male voice and it

doesn't sound very happy. Perhaps it's her new boss or something. Better not give too much away.

'She's dealing with a bit of a crisis at the moment,' I lie, quite convincingly.

Then something new happens to his voice. It kind of cracks and splinters. 'Can you just tell her Neil rang and that he's sorry.' Bloody hell, I think I can hear him sniffing. 'Just tell her . . . tell her that I'm sorry. I didn't mean it. Tell her I need to talk to her as soon as —'

The line goes dead. The room suddenly feels like all the air has been sucked out of it and my insides have gone with it.

'Ok mate, I'll tell her that,' I say to the silent handset before throwing it hard at the wall. How could I have been so fucking stupid?

Danielle watches me from the bathroom door. 'What the fuck are you doing? Who was that?'

'Your boyfriend.' I wrench out the words before getting up to put my clothes back on. 'I can't fucking believe you.'

Cassie

When I get home, I go to bed early and cry. Yesterday was Pooh's funeral. The only thing that kept me going through it was the thought that nature had some cunning plan up her sleeve. She was taking Pooh away, but delivering Nick. I could live with that. That sounded fair.

But when Nick didn't show up this afternoon some of my strength was sapped and having listened to Jilly's woes and trying to be strong for her too, I feel like a little Sunday roast chicken that's had all the stuffing taken out of it — hollow, brittle and on the verge of collapse.

Pooh's funeral was such a struggle. The vet had called me the day before and said the results of the post-mortem revealed Pooh had died from ingesting rat poison, a common occurrence here. If that wasn't bad enough, he said he needed to be buried straight away — I didn't have much time to plan.

I decided I wanted him in my garden so I went and collected his little body and performed a service under the willow tree, before burying him in the far corner where he used to enjoy scrabbling about.

My parents came, so did Daisy and Jilly. Sadly, everyone else had to work, but the most important people in Pooh's little life were there.

After my father lowered him into the hole

he'd dug, and I'd thrown in some bluebells that Pooh always loved sniffing, I read out the following words of wisdom from AA Milne's Christopher Robin.

'Pooh, promise you won't forget about me, ever. Not even when I'm a hundred.'

Pooh thought a little. 'How old shall I be then?'

'Ninety-nine.'

Pooh nodded. 'I promise,' he said.

Still with his eyes on the world, Christopher Robin put out a hand and felt for Pooh's paw.

I wiped away a tear.

'Don't forget about me Pooh. I won't ever forget you.'

I then bowed my head and said a little private prayer.

'Thanks for coming, everyone,' I snivelled when I'd finished. 'Pooh would have loved it.'

My mother then planted seven daffodil bulbs in the soil, one for each year of his life, and we all went inside for drinks.

Snuggling under my duvet tonight I say another prayer for my little friend and whisper, 'Oh Pooh, I miss you so much. You never let me down. I hope you've gone to a better place.'

Nick

I stride down the stairs, stuffing my arms into the sleeves of my shirt as I go.

I can't stand being in the same room as her any longer. I walk out of the front door, without breaking stride, and head across the car park to the restaurant.

'I'm sorry Nick. Come back.' I hear the shrill voice of my ex-girlfriend behind me.

I turn around. I can hardly bear to look at her but I want her to see my face. Just so she knows what she's done. 'Why don't you fuck off, back to your swanky new job and leave me alone.'

The site manager and his two assistants are having a fag just outside the restaurant. They turn to see what's happening. At least someone will find this whole thing entertaining; an angry looking restaurant manager being pursued by a woman who hasn't done her blouse up yet.

'Nick. He means nothing. It's you I want. That's why I came back.'

I look at the semi-clothed figure, standing there with her remaining garments bundled up under her arm. I feel anger surge through me like a searing heat. I hate like I've never hated before. I feel like raising my hand and slapping those fake tears off that pretty little face of hers.

'Bollocks. You came back because you had a row with your boyfriend and you thought the poor bastard deserved to have his heart ripped out just like you ripped out mine.'

'That's not true Nick. I came back because I realised I don't love him. I've never loved anyone like I love you.'

How can she stand there and say that? I'm shaking with anger now. I turn to go again before I do something that she might regret.

'Nick, I love you,' she screeches out in a long hysterical wail behind me.

'Too fucking late!' I call back over my shoulder.

★   ★   ★

I walk into the restaurant and head straight to the far end. I go up the stairs and into my office, locking the door behind me. I don't know if she's following me and I don't care. I just sit down on the floor, my back resting against the door like some naughty little kid who's been sent to his bedroom.

I kick the bottom of the filing cabinet hard with my foot and punch the floor beside me with my hand. How the fuck did I let that happen? What went on in my head to make me open the door and let her in?

I breathe heavily, concentrating on every breath as it goes in and out. I will not cry. I won't give her the satisfaction.

After a few minutes I crawl across the room and pull back the corner of the blind. She's taken the hint then. There's no sign of her car. Hopefully she's fucked off for good.

I flop back into my chair and let the cosy creak of the new leather comfort me. I have an overwhelming desire to go and find a bottle of whisky from somewhere but I remind myself that's exactly what the old Nick would have done. This is the new Nick, the one who doesn't let his life fall apart just because some manipulative little floozy has come back for another go at sticking the knife in. She's not going to wreck this one for me.

I nudge the mouse and deactivate the screen saver. I'm already behind today because of her.

I open my organiser page and my heart sinks. I now feel like kicking myself rather than the filing cabinet. I suppose Danielle can be satisfied that she's fucked up at least one bit of my life.

I click on Cassie's name and open up a new email. She must think I'm the biggest twat on the planet. I could lie and pretend this afternoon never happened but it occurs to me that that would make me as bad as Danielle. No. It's time for some damage limitation. There's no need to suck another person into this mess and fuck up their life too.

Hi Cassie,
You're probably thinking I'm a total tosser right now. I'm not going to make any excuses for missing our date this afternoon. There aren't any, other than I'm a complete wanker.
I won't blame you if you're angry with me. I deserve it.
I just want you to know that I think you're a great girl. I enjoyed our time together the other night more than you probably realise. I just hope that one day you'll get someone who'll look after you properly, the way you deserve.
I'd love it if we could be friends but you probably hate me already.
Sorry for everything,
Nick

I click send, and clasp my face in my hands. I know I've done the right thing, so why do I feel like I've just made the biggest mistake of my life?

Cassie

I have a confession to make. I wasn't only upset about Pooh's funeral and Nick not turning up for our date last night. I was ashamed of my behaviour.

On the way out of Cirencester Park a car flashed it's lights at me and tooted its horn like I was about to lose a wheel or something. I pulled over in the driveway and got out.

'Hi there!' Andrew stuck a hand in the air in greeting. 'I just rang you about an hour ago to see if you wanted to have dinner tonight. I've been practising polo.'

He looked incredibly dashing in his jodhpurs and polo shirt . . . how could I refuse? And why should I refuse?

Jilly pulled up too and was incredibly flirty so we all went for dinner and got very drunk. I ended up getting a taxi home, but not before I'd had a thoroughly decadent snog with Andrew in the Market Place. This would have been fine if I'd been thinking of Andrew and had a future date to look forward to. But I didn't want to go out with Andrew again. I wanted Nick.

Throughout dinner he talked about no one but himself and sounded very arrogant and pompous. I had to drink to get through the whole thing. I only snogged him before lurching into the taxi to get my revenge on Nick. He'd let me down and I didn't like the way it felt.

Getting out of bed, I struggle to the shower, my head feeling muzzy and achy from all the red wine I guzzled. When I'm done, I wrap my hair in a turban and wander into my studio.

Jilly had promised she'd email me the address of a farm that had some puppies for sale. In my drunken state last night I'd wailed on about how I couldn't live without Pooh.

I'm not sure if I want to get another dog straight away, but perhaps it'll help my decision process to go and have a look.

As usual it takes ages to surf out into the net. The tide is clearly against me today. When I eventually make it I find not only the email from Jilly, but also one from Nick. My fingers immediately become jumpy as I rush to find out what he's got to say . . .

The first few times I read it I'm in such a panic that I don't take anything in. But as my heart-rate becomes less frantic I manage to focus on the monitor and read more clearly.

Not that it makes me any the wiser.

With much fiddling about I manage to

210

print off a copy of his note on an ancient printer that my father gave me, and I take it downstairs with me.

Over a breakfast of fresh fruit and muesli, followed by two blueberry muffins (well there's no point in worrying about weight now), I read Nick's email again and again.

After half-an-hour, I decide it still doesn't make any sense. We got along really, really well at The Bug Bear. He was charming and polite and he wanted to get to know me better. I'm not an expert at body language or anything, but I'm not completely blind either. He was flirting with me. He liked me. And I liked him.

So why this?

Hmm. No idea. Well, there's only one way to find out and if there's one thing my parents drummed into me when I was at school, it was, 'If you don't ask, you don't get.' So I scamper up the stairs and go through the whole tortuous process of linking up again and write this in an email:

Nick,
Thanks for your message. I was disappointed not to see you yesterday.
Perhaps this is not the best time for you to get to know someone new, but I would really like to see you again, if possible, just

211

*to make sure you're not angry with me
about anything.*

   Take care,
   Cassie x

I agonise for a good ten minutes over whether or not to put in that single kiss, but in the end decide it's what I do with all the people I care about on cards and letters and stuff, so why not put it to Nick, someone I don't know very well but do definitely care about.

I press the send button and hope I've done it right. The computer doesn't squeak at me or anything so I guess it's gone. Amazing thing technology. Scary too.

Once I've turned the computer off I think I feel better, but of course I won't know for sure until I get a reply.

I look up at my Large Blue butterfly and think again how happy I am with this particular painting. Perhaps it came out so well because I love them so much. I look at the wings and imagine them flapping through the bluebells. Then I think of the logo on my email system and its butterfly, and then my finger is reaching out for the 'on' button on my ancient computer and I'm already looking at my messages to see if Nick has replied . . .

Nick

Dear Cassie,

How could I be angry with you? You're the nicest girl I've ever met.

I've spent the last twenty-four hours moping around here just wishing I'd been brave enough to kiss you the other night. I've imagined what it would be like in my head over and over.

I keep thinking back to the other night and how much fun I had. I haven't felt that happy in ages.

You don't know how much I want to rush round to your house, take you in my arms and hold you. But I can't because I don't deserve to.

The other afternoon when we were supposed to be flying kites I was lying in bed with another woman. I wish I could promise you that I'd never do that to you again but, in all honesty, I can't. I promised myself I'd never go near that poisonous bitch again, but I did.

You see that's how I am. I just blunder through life and let people down. It's my biggest talent: something I can do with unerring accuracy. But I don't want to let you down; you're too good for that. If I did that I'd never forgive myself.

So you see that's why I can't go on seeing you. Not because I don't like you or because I'm angry with you or even because I don't think I could fall head over heels in love with you within minutes (because I could). It's simply because you don't deserve to have your life screwed up by some tosser who just can't get his ex-girlfriend out of his head.

Hope you understand,
Nick X

I read through the email two or three times, feeling every word.

My finger hovers over the mouse, the cursor points at the send button. I take a deep breath.

And then delete the lot.

Cassie,
I'll be in The Bug Bear tomorrow night at about seven-thirty. It would be great to see you.
Nick

I do click send this time.

I stand up from my chair and look out of the window. If I look across the fields, I can see the chimneys of a little cluster of cottages. I think one of them is Cassie's; I know she lives somewhere over there from when I walked her home.

I've looked out of this window many times over the last day or so, gazing over to those chimney pots and wondering what she's doing. Wondering if she's thinking of me or if she's just busily getting on with her life oblivious to the way I feel about her.

I wonder if she's got my email yet? Will she meet me at the pub or will she see sense and stay at home?

I let my eyes wander across the horizon, taking in the beautiful scenery. Even in the dull-grey light of a drizzly July day, this place still looks vibrant and green. It's beautiful here, possibly too beautiful for the likes of me.

But there's something about it. There's an energy here that I've felt since the first morning I woke up in that caravan, an energy that's making me feel alive for the first time in years, an energy that's making me fight back. I've been given another chance to make something of my life here and no one, not even Danielle, is going to make me screw it up.

8

Cassie

Yesterday afternoon's *Richard and Judy* show, which I'm watching this morning, clinging onto a cup of cocoa for dear life, has a feature on testicular cancer. Strangely the show's producers thought it a good idea to have a male model pinching his right ball at the cameras in order to show the male populace how to check for lumps. Though this piqued my interest momentarily, I have to say the sight of a very embarrassed young man pinching his scrotum on national television wasn't the show-stopper I thought it might be. When sex organs are reduced to areas prone to disease, all the fun goes out of it.

Discouraged, but now with men on the brain, I decide to phone Daisy. I need advice and she's usually pretty good at it.

'So are you going?' she asks after a brief bit of back-story.

'Don't know.'

'But you really like him, don't you?'

'Yes, but . . . oh, I don't know.'

'Oh go on, you have to go. You'll never get

into a nice relationship if you don't give men a chance. You know how they like to . . . well . . . fuck about, for want of a better expression.'

'Oh, I suppose. I'll let you know later.'

'You do that. And you go.'

After a quick coffee, I phone Jilly for a second opinion.

'Sounds like damaged goods,' she says. 'Don't waste your time.'

'Thanks.' I hang up.

Now I am totally confused. In desperation I go and lean on the gate at the back garden and tell the whole story from start to finish to Christopher Robin. He stands there patiently listening for twenty minutes while I pour out my heart to him.

'So what do you think?' I ask when I'm finished.

He nods his head and nuzzles at my pockets, hoping for a carrot or a Polo or something.

'Is that a yes?'

As a fly lands on his nose, he shakes his head.

'Christopher Robin. You're giving me confusing signals. I'll ask you again. Should I go out with Nick tonight?'

I accidentally drop a Polo on the floor and his head nods down.

'Right, that's decided then.' I give him a pat. 'Tonight I will meet Nick in the second-chance saloon.'

★ ★ ★

To say I am nervous about going to the pub would be a huge understatement. I'm terrified. It's said that we fear the unknown more than anything. Well, meeting Nick again is a total unknown. And I fear it.

In my mind, as I walk up the lane, three possible scenarios are playing out.

One: he won't show up again.

Two: he'll show up and confess he's back together with his ex-girlfriend.

Three: he'll show up and we end up snogging.

Well, he does show up and our time in the pub goes well. I arrive twenty minutes late to teach him a lesson and also to see how he reacts. He is charming. When I say I'm sorry, I'd got held up, he replies that he was surprised I'd turned up at all.

He then buys me a glass of Champagne to apologise. After a couple of sips, he tells me how beautiful I look. He explains that he hadn't turned up for our date because his ex had phoned and said all sorts of nasty things about him and he'd spent the afternoon feeling wretched and unsociable. (Fine.)

He says he'd really been looking forward to our date. (Brill!) And that he thought I would never want to see him again for letting me down. (How sweet!) He'd have phoned, but he didn't have my number. (True.) He guesses that he's blown it, but it'd be nice for us to be friends.

And this is where I intervene.

'No, no,' I say, 'you had a bad day. I wouldn't want to go out either if I was feeling sad or depressed. I'll tell you what. Why don't we start all over again? Let's say this is our first date.'

He grins at me then and looks almost overjoyed.

'You sure?' he says.

I am.

'One rule, though,' I suggest.

'Yeah?'

'You stand me up again without ringing and I'll set my cats on you.'

He laughs at this and his eyes crinkle up, before looking right at me and I think, 'Yes, I like you. I definitely do.'

★   ★   ★

Nick and I are now standing outside my cottage and, as we have walked very slowly

219

back from the pub, my eyes are now used to the dark and I can see his face clearly in the moonlight. He looks shy and vulnerable.

'Well, thanks for . . . tonight.' I move ever so slightly closer to him.

'I'm pleased that we . . . you know, cleared a few things up.'

'Me too.' His hand is resting on the gatepost, a single finger tapping at a splinter. 'I'd really like to go kite-flying you know.' We both burst out laughing, breaking the tension. He leans in a little closer. I put my right hand on his shoulder and say very quietly, 'Do you want to kiss me?'

He smiles and his head moves slowly down until his mouth is an inch away from mine. I can smell his aftershave, a hint of tobacco and beer. It's a heady combination. My heart begins to race.

'Do you want me to?'

The tension in the air is palpable. Our eyes lock together. I put my hand on his waist and move it gently up his back to his neck. Slowly I move my palm round onto his cheek and bring my lips up to his. I kiss him ever so gently, pulling away to look at his face again.

'Yes,' I breathe, and this time I put my lips against his more hungrily and he kisses me back, his tongue sliding between my lips. Now I have both arms round his neck and he is drawing me in with his powerful arms and for a moment I feel like I'm being totally consumed. But it's a comforting feeling, not a scary one.

When we are finished kissing, I relax on my heels and put my head against his chest. I'm happy to hear his heart beating as quickly as mine.

'We can go kite-flying tomorrow, if you want . . . '

I hear the laugh come from deep inside his chest.

'We could too,' he says. 'We could too.'

This time I know he'll show up.

9

Nick

When I see the signs for Junction 33 of the M1, my stomach starts to tighten a little. It feels strange heading back to Sheffield. Although I've only been away a few weeks it feels like a whole lifetime since I was last here. It's a bit like meeting up with an old school friend and wondering if they'll remember you or if you'll still get on with them like you used to.

I glance across at Cassie in the passenger seat. My stomach tightens even more. I'm not sure how I ended up bringing her with me. Don't get me wrong, the more time I can spend in this girl's company the happier I am, and three hours or so in the car go much faster when you've got someone to talk to, but it just feels a little soon to be bringing her home to meet the relatives.

I didn't intend to. When I rang to cancel our Saturday night out at the pub and explained I had to come back here to sort some stuff out with the estate agent, she interpreted it as an invite to come with me. I couldn't say no, could I? Not after stuffing up the other week.

I'm not ashamed of who I am or where I come from. But things are so different up here; I'm not sure how she's going to react. It feels like I'm parading myself naked in front of her. Well no, actually I'd probably prefer that. I can't wait to get into some situations of extreme nakedness with her. I've been well-behaved so far. I haven't pushed it. I've contented myself with Olympic-standard snogging. I'm determined I'm not going to blow it by coming on too strong. Easier said than done.

'Are we nearly there?' Cassie asks, as I flick the indicator on.

'Nearly.' That knot in my stomach isn't getting any looser as we pause at the traffic lights at the top of the slip road. 'Just another mile or two.'

Eventually red turns to green and we head off down the Parkway.

'We're nearly there, Rooney.' From the tone in which she addresses her furry travelling companion I can tell Cassie's excited. She's never been to Yorkshire. I hope she's not going to be disappointed.

As we cruise round the final bend of the Parkway the city comes into view in front of us.

'Welcome to Sheffield,' I say, tour-guide fashion.

From the small squeal I hear from the passenger seat I guess Rooney has administered a welcoming lick as well. At least that's one member of the family she seems to like. She's been cuddling him since we left, lucky little sod. Mind you, I did get a pretty cracking session of tonsil tennis when we stopped for petrol so I can't complain.

As we pull up to the Park Square roundabout I notice all is ominously silent in the passenger seat so I decide to point out a few landmarks: Ponds Forge and Hallam Uni on the right, the railway station on our left. All riveting stuff. Perhaps I missed my vocation in life as a tour-guide.

'What's that thing there?'

'Big, silver, looks like four giant kettles have just landed from outer space?'

'Yes, that.' She's giggling. I suppose that's a good sign.

'That was The National Centre for Popular Music and now I think they've turned it into the Student Union Bar.'

She's definitely enjoying herself. No sign of an allergic reaction to the north or a plea to turn the car around and head home yet.

'Is that where you go to watch the football?'

I shake my head and allow myself a little smile. 'No my dear, that's where the subordinate species known as 'The Blades' hang out.'

Confused silence fills the car. I'm flattered she's bothered to remember I like football but I think we need to go through a few basics.

'There are two teams in Sheffield: one red, one blue. The red one, Sheffield United, play there and we hate them. The blue one, Sheffield Wednesday, play at a ground called Hillsborough over at the other side of town and we like to think that some day soon they will rise once more from obscurity and come back to spank this lot.'

'Oh. Well, good luck!'

Hmmm. Time for a change of topic I think. Much as she's trying, it's obvious football isn't her thing. Mind you, she can tell the difference between Wayne Rooney and Michael Owen now, so we're making progress.

Eventually we break out of the city centre traffic and turn into the familiar-looking suburb. I turn in, pull on the handbrake, and nudge the gear-stick into neutral before looking out at a three-bedroom terrace with no distinguishing features other than I used to call it home.

We haven't got our bags together before Debs is out of the house hugging me like I've been away for years. Cassie doesn't escape either. She's treated to a mammoth-sized Debs hug too. She doesn't seem to mind.

'Just like you to come back with a bit of southern crumpet.' I look up to see Scotty, one hand resting on the frame of the open front door, the other casually holding a cigarette.

Cassie seems to find it funny. I had spent most of the journey filling her in on my brother-in-law and his antics so she should be well-prepared.

'Come on in,' Debs finally says, after making sure Rooney doesn't miss out on the hugs either. 'I'll put the kettle on.'

★ ★ ★

As I carry the bags upstairs I suddenly notice that I don't feel as nervous as I did. Things are going well. Debs seems to like Cassie and is clucking around her like a mother hen on turbo power. Poor girl's had so many cups of tea and chocolate biscuits thrust at her in the last hour she must wonder whether she's coming or going.

Debs has squashed Scotty into best behaviour mode too. Not a single crude joke since we got here. She must have put sedatives in his tea or something.

'You alright?'

'I'm fine.' Cassie rests a reassuring hand on my arm and gives a little nod just to emphasise the point.

'Right. Which room do you want?' I push open the door to my left, the door to what used to be Debs' room when we were kids.

As it swings open I can see Scotty's been on yet another painting and decorating mission. It's looking swish in there.

'Or there's this one,' I offer as I push open the door to what was my room and realise to my horror that Scotty's still in the process of redecorating. There's no bed. There's just a pair of stepladders and an old wardrobe.

Fuck! Diplomatic minefield ahead. Debs has obviously assumed that I'm going to sleep in the same bed as Cassie. And Cassie must now be assuming this is all a plot master-minded by me to get my leg over.

Fortunately she's quite understanding. 'I don't mind, you know . . . ' she says, looking bashful and blushing furiously. 'I don't want to put your sister to any trouble.'

I look at her and try to read the situation. I fight furiously against the little voice that's attempting to persuade me this is an invite to sleep with her. Oh God, how good would that be? But I manage to find a bit of gallantry from somewhere.

'It's alright, I'll kip on the sofa.' I look at her with what I hope is a sincere and non-lecherous expression. 'I should have said something to Debs on the phone. I'm sorry. I think she just assumed . . . can we just sort of . . . pretend we are though . . . I just don't want her feeling uncomfortable, you know how it is . . . I'll sneak back downstairs when they've gone to bed.' I finish my garbled suggestion and look across at her.

'That's fine. I quite understand.' She comes across and twines her arms gently around my neck, pulling my face towards hers for a kiss, a long slow kiss. The sort of kiss that makes me wish I hadn't just volunteered to spend the night in another room.

Cassie

Usually a nervous type when thrust into unknown situations, I'm happy to say that I feel perfectly relaxed here in Sheffield, in the house where Nick grew up. Perhaps it's the way his sister Debs hugged me when I arrived. Or her husband Scotty saying Nick always went out with girls with pinchable arses! But I feel right at home from the moment I walk through the door, not on edge like I did at Andrew's flat in London.

In true northern-style, the kettle goes on the minute we get into the kitchen and we all stand round sipping tea and chatting. I can see a great affection between Scotty and Nick. They're not scared to take the piss out of each other and laugh good-naturedly when they're the brunt of jokes.

Debs isn't shy about teasing Nick either. I feel quite sorry for him when she starts going on about what a nightmare he was as a child, how stroppy he used to get when he didn't get his own way, and how he'd burst into tears if he lost at anything.

'He still does that now,' Scotty jokes, giving him a dig in the ribs.

Nick just stands there with his head down, muttering, 'Don't believe a word of it. Debs was a much worse loser than me. She threw plates around.'

I put my arm round his waist and give him a squeeze to tell him it doesn't matter. I had my moments as a child too. Anyone who tried to take Crowley, the black family cat, out of my embrace would get screamed at until they backed off. I was an animal lover from birth, hugging anything with fur.

Now I'm older, I hug any human I really like. I guess I'm just a very tactile person. I need to feel the warmth of another body. And Nick's is one of the best I've ever felt. I simply can't stop touching him. Hope he doesn't mind!

After what seems like four packets of biscuits, Nick announces we have to go and meet the estate agent at his flat. Although I love spending time with Nick on his own, I'm almost disappointed to leave Scotty and Debs behind. They're such good fun it's like hanging out with old friends.

'Can I quickly use your loo?' I ask Debs as Nick gathers up his car keys and the inventory he needs for the estate agent.

'Course you can. I'll show you where it is.'

I follow her up the stairs. When we get to the landing she turns and smiles at me.

'You know, Nick phoned me up yesterday and said he was bringing a friend with him. He doesn't usually do this kind of thing. But I can see why he did. You're lovely.'

She gives me another big hug before rubbing my shoulders.

'He's had a really tough time recently.' I can see her eyes filling up. 'And he can be a bit moody, but he's a lovely guy with a heart of gold. And I can tell he's smitten with you.'

'I really like him too,' I assure her. 'Don't worry, I'm not a heart-breaker.'

'I can see that.' Debbie waves a hand in front of her face. 'Oh, I don't know why I'm so emotional. I think I'm just pleased to see two people so happy together.'

'Thanks.' I hug her in return. 'That means a lot.'

'Right, I'll leave you to it. See you back downstairs.'

'Thanks.' I smile again and bolt the bathroom door. All the tea has shot straight through me and I feel like I'm going to burst.

Once I've done what I needed to do (and cripes did I need to!) I wash my hands and glance around the bathroom. I'm pleased to say this one is full of family photos, books and all kinds of clutter that tells the visitor what sort of people live here. But strangely I don't need to look too hard. I feel like I know them already.

Nick

I turn the key in the front door of the flat. I push it open and step back so that Cassie can enter first. It seems strange being here now. Just an empty shell with no furniture.

I squat down and pick up the post that's

231

lying on the floor. So much for it all being redirected. I guess a stroppy phone call to the Post Office is on the cards.

Cassie is now standing in the middle of the desolate living room, her head turning this way and that, taking it all in. I look at my watch: we're early. The estate agent won't be here for a few minutes yet.

In the absence of chairs I wander through to the kitchen and lean against the work surface, leaving Cassie free to wander around and open doors here and there. I can't face looking around myself. I just want to get rid of this place now — it feels like soiled goods. In my pokey little kitchen the walls seem to have too many bad memories oozing out of them. I think of my new, happy home in the Cotswolds and for the first time feel sure of where I now belong, and it isn't here.

Cassie saunters into the kitchen. I lift my head and smile at her. She comes across and curls her arms around my waist. I don't know what it is about the way she holds me but it makes me feel like . . . well, it feels so warm and reassuring I never want her to stop.

I gently push her hair back from her face and kiss her. I don't think I could ever get bored of doing that. She kisses like an angel: so soft, so warm. I don't know what I did to deserve her suddenly walking into my life but boy am I glad she did.

Eventually she releases me and leans against the work surface opposite and flashes me one of those cute little smiles of hers. I smile back before reaching round to start opening the pile of post beside me.

It's mostly junk mail inviting me to take out new credit cards and all that crap. Oh, bizarre! A set of photographs back from the developers. I don't remember sending any off. With great curiosity, I tear off the layer of plastic and read the enclosed letter. It apologises for the delay in processing my pictures and draws my attention to the attached voucher. I'm entitled to a free set of reprints next time.

'What are they of?' Cassie comes across and stands beside me.

I shrug my shoulders to indicate my ignorance and lift up the flap of the little envelope. Oh God. Why? Why did they have to be those photos? Not here, not now.

'What are they?' Cassie asks again. I've obviously not hidden my discomfort very well.

'My engagement party,' I answer as I look down at a picture of myself and Danielle, our arms around each other, smiling like we've won the lottery.

Cassie

On the journey out to Nick's old flat I tell him what a great time I'm having and he almost swerves off the road in shock!

'I thought you'd be bored stiff watching those two take the piss out of me for two hours. I was trying to get us out of there as quick as possible.'

I laugh and give him a nudge. 'Don't be silly. People would pay good money to see that in a comedy club.'

Nick shakes his head and scratches the back of his neck with his hand.

'Your sister's lovely,' I continue. 'And so pretty! Gorgeous hair. Same eyes as you, too.'

'You don't fancy her, do you?'

I ignore this comment, knowing that he's teasing. It's funny, he can be such a laugh sometimes and then, at other moments, he's really quite serious. I wish he hadn't been so diplomatic about the sleeping arrangements. I'm sure he just wanted to be polite, but now I feel a bit rejected. I couldn't think of anything better than snuggling up to him tonight.

Perhaps I'm just naturally nosy, but I want to find out soon if he's a duvet hog, or a sleep talker, or a snuffler or something, so I can reconsider my position before things get too serious.

'I'll show you where the other football ground is when we've finished here,' he offers.

'Have you ever played there?' I tease, knowing he can't possibly have.

'I was never that good.' He sounds all serious. Poor lamb. He's lovely to be with but he does take his football terribly seriously. I don't mind, though. I like men to be passionate about stuff. It shows, well, passion. If he can give me even a little of what he was showing watching England play I should be in for an exciting time.

'If you're a good girl I'll take you out to lunch in Derbyshire. There's some nice pubs out that way.'

'Lovely.' Two northern counties in one day; I'm almost becoming an expert.

'This is it.'

We pull up to the kerb and he yanks on the handbrake. 'No sign of the estate agent. Bet he'll be late again.'

I hop out and wait for Nick to lock the car.

It's a lovely sunny day again, challenging the adage 'it's grim up north'. I've been very impressed with the area. There's some lovely countryside and even though some of the terraced houses could have done with a more imaginative architect back in the early 1900s and the gardens are tiny, the differences

235

between the north and south are far less obvious than I'd been led to believe. I've not seen one whippet, one flat cap or even a snatch and grab robbery.

And it looks like I'm not going to. Don't know whether I'm relieved or disappointed. Perhaps it's true what they say: the whole world is becoming more similar and pretty soon we'll all be living in one giant Birmingham or something. Hmm. The mind boggles.

'So, this was your love nest?'

We wander in the front door and I start doing some furious snooping. It doesn't take long. The flat is cosy, to say the least. One small bedroom, one tiny bathroom and a narrow kitchen. The living room would be cramped with four people in it and the airing cupboard is teeny-weeny. There's just about room for a hanky. And an earwig. (Why do they always end up under the wooden slats?)

'What time was your estate agent supposed to be here?' I ask as I wander back into the kitchen and give him a quick snog before he can answer me.

When I finally give him his mouth back, he looks at his watch and says, 'He should have been here twenty minutes ago.'

'Tut tut. I hope you give him a good spanking when he comes.'

'I'll give you a good spanking when you come,' he replies without missing a beat and then suddenly goes red as he realises what has come out of his mouth and starts fiddling about with the post.

I laugh to myself as I watch him concentrate rather too hard on opening the envelopes. He's so sweet. And he has been thinking about me in a sexy way!

'Ooh, what have you got there?'

He opens a bubble-wrapped package that doesn't look like a boring bill. He then slides out a photo envelope and flips it open. His face seems to go a little redder.

'Just some photos.' He closes it again quickly.

'Of what?'

'Just my engagement party.'

I feel a lurch in my stomach. A shadow being cast over our day by an ex-girlfriend who I've never met and don't want to.

'You don't want to look at those right now, do you?' I take the photos from him and place them on the work surface.

'No,' he agrees.

I move my lips up to his again. He puts his arms round my back and I push my pelvis forward and flick my tongue against his. Moving my hands up to his neck and then back down to his firm bum, I move my lower body from side to side as I feel a certain hardness against my stomach that tells me Nick is a man and, yes, he does fancy me. Quite a lot.

Just as his hands begin to make their way from my back to come round and squeeze my breasts we hear a key turn in the lock and the estate agent's voice saying, 'Mr Ratcliffe? Sorry I'm late. The traffic was awful.'

Nick and I pull apart like naughty school-kids and laugh as he strides into the kitchen, unaware that if he'd arrived five minutes later he may have seen rather more of his client than he wanted to.

'Shall we get straight on with it?' The estate agent says, nodding at me politely. 'I've got another meeting in half-an-hour.'

'Yes,' I cross my arms and smile at him. 'I think Nick is more than ready to get straight on with it.' I wink at Nick as he finishes pulling out his shirt to hide quite how ready he is.

'I'm ready.' He seems slightly more composed. 'Why don't we start in the bedroom . . . '

Nick

'Shhhhhh!' I press my finger to my lips and snigger like a naughty schoolboy as we get

238

back to Debs' house. We've had a great night out and are both fairly inebriated. Cassie giggles and then starts snogging me. Not that I'd ever complain but it's making it difficult to get the key into the door.

Suddenly I'm aware that it's got lighter and the front door that I was jabbing my key against has disappeared.

'Night went well, then?' Scotty is standing there in the doorway.

Cassie releases me quickly and switches to hiding coyly behind my shoulder.

'Where'd you go?' Scotty asks as we both step inside.

'Went up West Street, that way. We didn't wake you up, did we?' I notice Scotty is wearing his pyjama trousers.

'Nah, was just getting a glass of water.' He winks at Cassie. 'We've only just turned in ourselves. I'll leave you two lovebirds to it then.' He winks once more before trotting up the stairs. ''Night mate.'

I wait for him to add the wisecrack but it doesn't come. Debs really must have put the thumbscrews on him this time.

'I'll have to come and get my stuff out of your room,' I say quietly.

'You can stay for a while, if you like,' Cassie whispers, her round eyes looking up at me invitingly.

Oh, I wish she hadn't said that. There are thoughts running through my head that really don't need to be there. Bite your tongue Nick.

'If that's what you want.'

She nods and kisses me full on the lips. I feel her soft body pressing against mine and just pray she can't feel what's going on in my trousers at the moment.

I follow her up the stairs.

'You know where the bathroom is and everything, don't you?' I desperately try and reroute my thoughts to more mundane matters.

She nods and pulls me into the bedroom, planting another divine kiss on my lips. She stops suddenly and looks like she's going to say something, then doesn't and then does, 'You don't have to sleep on the sofa if you don't want to,' she whispers, looking down at the floor instead of at me.

I swallow hard. Every sinew in my body wants to push her back on that bed and take her right now. But that's not what she means is it? Behave Nick. Don't jump to conclusions. Sleeping in the same bed and shagging each other senseless aren't necessarily the same thing.

I look at her, trying to read what it is she wants. I can't tell. Come on Cass, give us a clue.

'I'll just go and use the bathroom,' she

eventually says to break the silence, grabbing some stuff out of her bag and heading off down the landing.

She returns a few minutes later, wearing a rather sexy pair of satin pyjamas and with her hair loose around her shoulders. She looks gorgeous. I feel inadequate standing here in the old pair of pyjama bottoms that I've just plucked from my bag. I hadn't bargained on being seen in them. I don't have a huge selection as I don't usually wear any. I only packed them in case of latenight missions to the bathroom. And that's where I'm heading now before she notices that it isn't my toothbrush stuck down the front.

When I return, she's already tucked in under the duvet, her hair flowing over the pillow and her arms outstretched towards me for a hug.

'Stay here and hold me, Nick,' she whispers in my ear as I cuddle her.

'Are you sure?'

She nods and pulls back the duvet for me to get in.

I willingly oblige.

She reaches over and switches off the lamp before snuggling her face into my chest. 'Goodnight.'

I kiss her hair and place my arm gently over her. 'Goodnight.'

＊ ＊ ＊

What seems like an eternity later, I look over at the illuminated red numbers on the clock on the bedside table. It's just after 2am and I'm still wide-awake. Cassie's lying beside me. She looks so beautiful when she's sleeping.

I can't stand this anymore. I'm going to blow it soon if I'm not careful. If she wakes up I don't think I'll be able to stop myself. The desire to gently wake her and ask if she'd mind awfully if I made mad, passionate love to her is overwhelming. I resolve to do the responsible thing. I slip quietly out from under the duvet and pad across to the door. I step out onto the landing and tug the spare bedding from the airing cupboard before making my way down to the sofa.

Cassie

I've had such a great day that by the time the evening rolls round I'd have been perfectly happy to go to bed after a cheese and pickle sandwich. But Nick, sweetie that he is, insists we go out for dinner.

'We don't have to. I'd be perfectly happy to stay in.'

242

'You might be,' replies Nick, as he washes up the cups from yet more tea we've drunk on our return from his flat, 'but personally I'd rather not have those two taking the piss out of me for the rest of the night.' He nods towards the living room where Debs and Scotty are snuggled up on the sofa.

'Ah, have you had enough of being picked on?' I flick him under the chin. 'Can't you take any more?'

'Frankly, no. Come on. You've got five minutes to get ready or I'm going without you.'

'Oooh, I like it when you get all masterful,' I tease and nip up the stairs.

It's here I agonise over what to do. Should I change or is that going to look too posh? But if I don't make the effort will I look like I don't care? Hmm. After a couple of minutes in the bathroom correcting hair that is tending towards the curly, reglossing my lips and applying a dab more perfume to my wrists and neck, I decide to change my top and wear a jacket, but keep with the same cream jeans.

'You look gorgeous,' says Debs when I wander into the living room. 'I love your silk top. Very Japanese-y.'

'Thanks.'

'What are you wearing?' she asks Nick.

'This.'

'No, you're not. Go and put your white shirt on. The one you left here last time you stayed.'

Nick rolls his eyes and says, 'Yes, Mum,' before getting up and heading for the stairs.

'And don't think you're going out before you've tidied your room, young man!' Scotty calls behind him in a fatherly voice. 'And make sure you're back in before midnight.'

I laugh as Scotty winks at me.

'Have you had a good day then?' he asks.

'It's been great.'

'Yeah, I'll bet. Tea, Sheffield town centre and a couple of hours with a boring estate agent. I tell you, Nick knows how to show a girl a good time. Do you know what you're doing later?'

'No.'

'He's taking you down the dog track, then you'll be supporting him in the Whip and Whippets darts tournament.'

'Oh.' To be honest, after the wonderful afternoon I've spent gadding around in the Peak District, I don't care if we do but I suspect Scotty is trying to wind me up.

'Nah, don't worry. I think he's found a pretty decent restaurant to take you to.'

'What's that?' Nick looks suspiciously at Scotty as he returns looking like he's done something nice to his hair as well as changing.

Scotty holds up his can of Stella. 'Just offering Cassie a swig of my lager.'

Nick shakes his head.

'Right, let's get you out of here, Cass. See you later, guys.'

We take a taxi into the centre of Sheffield as we both want to have a few drinks with our Thai meal in a place called the Green Mango.

I really enjoy my red chicken curry although it's about as spicy as I can handle. Nick, who seems more used to it, has spicy beef with little green chillies, which he tells me are the hottest and keeps getting me to try them, though I keep refusing.

After the dinner we go to a wine bar with a name I don't see when we go in and don't remember when we come out. We find ourselves a table where we can just about hear each other speak over the music and set about agreeing that we've both had a really lovely day, even though nothing we've done was particularly exciting.

'I just like spending time with you, I guess. I don't like doing flash things anyway.'

'So, you've enjoyed your first experience of Sheffield then?' he asks, still seeming to be nervous about everything I've said.

'YES! How many more times? And it

wouldn't have mattered if I hated it here. I didn't come here for a guided tour. I came because you were coming and I didn't want to spend the weekend without you.'

'Ah, you're so sweet.' He takes my wine glass from me and gives me another passionate snog. 'Do you want some more wine?'

I shake my head. 'Let's go home. I'm feeling ready for bed.'

* * *

At two in the morning Nick gets up and leaves to go downstairs and sleep on the sofa. I was pretending to be asleep but as soon as he goes I feel wide-awake.

Having got him into bed, I thought I'd better not seem too pushy by pouncing on him, so I waited for him to make the first move. And it never happened!

I don't know what's wrong with him. Earlier today I felt positive he'd be all over me tonight, but when we got back he seemed to go all shy again and then, after I persuaded him to come and sleep with me, he just lay here right next to me as rigid as a road sign (I mean his body, not his, you know, thing).

At one point I was tempted to pretend that

my hand just moved on its own while I was sleeping, just to see if he had a whopping great erection or not, but decided that he may be so shocked that he'd scream the house down. So, I just lay here hoping and slowly getting more and more disappointed.

I'm ok now, though. I have decided that sex will happen, but only when it's the right time for both of us. I have to remember that Nick has just come out of a serious relationship whereas I've been single for several lifetimes.

There is one thing I have to know, however. Creeping downstairs, holding the empty glass Nick gave me for water, I turn right in the hall and head for the kitchen. I flick on the sub-unit lights and nip over to where Nick left the photo envelope. I open it up with shaking hands and rapidly leaf through the pictures until I get to the shot I was hoping like mad wouldn't exist.

But here it is.

Nick smiling so wide it looks like his mouth is about to tear, hugging a gorgeous girl with poker straight hair, a model smile, a nose that would make even Daisy gasp with envy and (presumably) calves as thin as matchsticks.

'Oh f . . . iddle.' A wave of jealousy hits me. 'This is not good.'

Nick

There's something different about the atmosphere in the car on the way back. Cassie seems glum. I can't remember doing anything to upset her, but I'm never that good at spotting that I've made a monumental cock-up.

Perhaps it's all got serious too soon. I should have said no when she offered to come back home with me. A weekend with my family would be a trial for anyone.

But I can't stand it anymore. Two hours of being trapped in a car with no more than the odd monosyllabic utterance is getting wearing. If I'm about to be dumped, I'd rather get it out of the way.

'You alright?'

'Fine.' Great! More monosyllables from the passenger seat. Even Rooney's shut up and gone to sleep.

'No, you're not.'

I try to keep my tone neutral. I don't want this to sound like a confrontation but I can't cope with being kept in the dark anymore. 'You've hardly said a word since we left, Cass. If I've done something to upset you at least tell me so I can have a crack at putting it right.'

Silence! Fantastic! I can't even see her

expression, well not without putting us in danger of swerving off the road.

'I . . . ' she begins and then stops.

'Go on,' I prompt.

'I thought I'd upset you.'

In the split-second of jaw-dropping confusion that follows this utterance I nearly do swerve off the road. Where the hell did that come from? I try not to sound too exasperated. 'Why would you think that?'

'I just thought . . . you know . . . when you went downstairs in the middle of the night . . . '

Nope. I'm not with this at all. Why do women do this? Does the female brain not include a 'straight answer' facility? 'For God's sake Cass, just spit it out will you? I can't do anything if I don't know what the problem is.'

I can tell from the little sniff that precedes her next comment that we now have tears thrown into the bargain as well. 'I just . . . thought . . . I wondered why you didn't want to sleep with me. I mean, I know I'm not as pretty as your last girlfriend and I know she hurt you and all that, but I thought you fancied me and then when you went off and left me last night I realised I'd been pushing things too far too soon and I'm sorry.'

I jab on the breaks to avoid the blue Astra

that's just slowed down at a queue of traffic in front of us. I run the words through my head again to make sure I'd got it right.

'Oh, I see.'

'Please don't be angry with me Nick.'

'Angry?' I laugh out-loud.

More tears, proper crying now. Oh God. Fortunately, the traffic's moving again and a lay-by appears just ahead. I flick on the indicator and pull the car onto the side of the road.

I undo my seatbelt and turn to face her.

'Cassie, what are you crying for?'

'Because . . . ' she stops as soon as she's started, wrestles a tissue from her handbag and then looks up at me. 'Because I want you to fancy me.'

Now, something has been happening on another frequency here that I've missed out on. Fancy her? Christ!

'Cassie, I fancy you more than I'd ever thought it was possible to fancy a girl and the reason I went downstairs last night was because I didn't trust myself to keep my hands off you.'

'Really?' She looks at me even more intently.

I nod and place what I hope is a reassuring hand on her shoulder.

'You mean you did want to . . . you know.'

'What do you think?' I almost add that I've thought about little else since I saw her bending over at the vet's that first day but it occurs to me we might be getting into dirty old man territory there.

'Oh . . . but what about the photos? The ones of your engagement party?'

'What about them?'

'Well, I thought that you'd . . . ' Her voice trails off. I think I know where her mind is wandering.

'What you're asking me is whether I still have feelings for Danielle, isn't it?'

The way she stares straight into the foot-well and goes silent, tells me I've probably hit the nail on the head.

I reach out with my hand and turn her face gently towards me. 'Cass, I'm not going to pretend that I never loved Danielle or that she's not a beautiful woman, but she's a spiteful, selfish manipulative bitch and that's why those photos are in Scotty's dustbin where they belong. You're worth ten of her, Cass.'

'You don't want her back then?'

I decide to be honest. 'I thought I did. For a little while, but not anymore. It's you I want now Cass, not anyone else.'

We get another wave of tears but this time she holds her arms out to me like a little kid who's just fallen over and wants a kiss better. I hold her tightly, kissing her hair and feeling her wet face against my neck. I gently press my finger underneath her chin and lift her head so I can look at her face. She is beautiful. So beautiful that I lean over and give her a long, slow but extremely intense kiss. Just so that she can be in no doubt about how I feel about her.

10

Cassie

Lying with my head on Nick's chest, my left ear listening in on his slow heartbeat, I feel the most relaxed I've felt in weeks. I don't know what time it is, but it must be the early hours of the morning. There is a vague hint of dawn lurking behind my bedroom curtain.

Nick has been asleep for ages. Earlier, when I snuggled into his strong chest, he put his arm round me and ran his hand gently up and down my arm. His intention was to soothe me gently to sleep. Of course, what happened was he soothed himself all the way to the land of nod and left me stranded. Not that I mind. I want to stay awake to savour the moment for as long as possible. I worry that if I fall asleep the spell will be broken and somehow the world, which last night had developed such a rosy glow, will suddenly seem dark and wintry.

When we got back from Sheffield I knew he was going to stay the night. After everything he'd said to me on the journey home, it seemed the right moment. I could tell he felt the same. He didn't even need to be invited in when we arrived at the cottage. He simply parked the car, got out, took my hand and walked me to the door.

We went straight upstairs and into my bedroom. Thank God I'd decided to change the sheets before going away! Nothing worse than a terribly sexy moment being marred by clammy sheets. No scrunched-up knickers on the floor either, and no Piglet or Roo kipping on the duvet.

So far, so good.

'We'd better close the door.' The last thing we needed was to be interrupted by Tigger quacking in halfway through or some such mood breaker.

Nick turned and flicked the door closed with his right foot. Soccer skills, I suddenly realised, did have their uses.

'Ooh. That was very manly.'

I was feeling nervous and I needed to say something to calm us. Nick flexed his muscles in a mock body-builder way and laughed.

'You better believe it, baby.'

I was overjoyed he'd picked up on my mood. Some of the tension ebbed away.

'Well, you're going to have to show me how much of a man you really are.' I sat myself down on the edge of the bed and looked at him cheekily. 'Come on, take your shirt off.'

'I can't do that. You'll see my nipples.'

I smiled at him.

'Well, come here and give me a kiss then.'

He moved forward, lowered his head to mine and gave me a very tender kiss. Then he put his hands under my armpits and lifted me up so we were standing with our bodies touching. The only light in the room came from the stars outside. A light breeze rippled the open curtains where the window was ajar.

I reached out and began to unbutton his shirt, starting at the top and working my way slowly down. I ran my hands back up over his gorgeous flat stomach to his shoulders and rolled the shirt off his back. It fell to the floor with the smallest sound. To keep things fair, I crossed my arms in front of me, grabbed the bottom of my T-shirt and pulled it off in one clean, scissor movement. He gave me an intense look before putting his arms round my waist and kissing me again.

My heart was hammering like I'd just run a four-hundred-metre race and I felt my face begin to flush. When he pulled away, I was pleased to see he looked equally excited.

'What's the betting I have real trouble getting your bra off?' His voice was quavering ever so slightly.

'Well, you won't know unless you try.'

If he didn't hurry up I was going to take it off anyway. I needed to feel his flesh against mine soon or I'd burst.

Smiling more broadly now, he put his hands round my sides and moved them up from the small of my back. With only the smallest pause for the clip, his hands continued on up to my shoulders where he took hold of the straps and guided the bra down over my arms.

'Very impressive.'

'First-time lucky.' He looked down at my breasts.

We stood there for a few seconds doing nothing, the air thickening. I think he was enjoying looking at me, and his eyes assessing me gave me a real thrill. Yes look, I felt like saying, they're all yours . . . But I kept my mouth shut and, unable to bear the anticipation of what was going to happen next, I closed my eyes.

I felt Nick reach out with his right hand, his left arm circling my waist. Then I felt his lips on my chest, little kisses moving down to my left breast. I gulped hard as his warm mouth enclosed my nipple. I enjoyed the feeling of it stiffening as his tongue teased it. After administering the same luxurious treatment to the other one, he sank to his knees and removed my jeans and knickers. He then stood up, looked down at me, tugged his belt undone and was suddenly, magnificently, naked.

'Ready?'

I blinked a 'yes'. Blimey, his body was better than I'd thought. Well-muscled, well-proportioned and hard in all the right places.

He lay down on the bed and started kissing me, his right hand cupping my face, then my right breast, then gliding down my stomach, and across to my outer thigh.

I pushed my tongue further into his mouth and grabbed him round the back of the neck, parting my legs a little as I did so. Nick took the hint and let his hand wander up my inner thigh. I closed my eyes again and let his gentle but insistent touch kick my heartbeat up another notch. The teasing seemed to go on forever.

'Nick, this feels wonderful, but can we . . . '

He immediately slipped a leg between mine. Then he pushed himself up with his hands so he was looking down at me. He kissed me for another few seconds before moving his other leg into position and gently lowering his full weight onto me.

Just the heat of his body felt terribly exciting. I felt my heartbeat pick up even further. Steady, I said to myself, breathing deeply; now is not the time for a burst pulmonary artery.

I closed my eyes and concentrated on the sensations coming to me from between my thighs. I felt a slight stretching, my body resisting momentarily before opening up and allowing him inside.

Ever so slowly he sank further in until at last our hips were touching.

'How does that feel?' His voice was barely audible.

'It feels . . . heavenly.'

He kissed my mouth as he inched his body further up mine. I wrapped my arms round his muscular back and clung on for dear life. I gasped involuntarily several times and my breathing became so shallow and tremulous he asked me if he should stop.

'No,' I whispered as my body tingled and shuddered under his touch. 'You just . . . feel . . . so . . . good.'

My whole body was tingling. Minutes after we'd finished, waves of pleasure were still rippling through me. Then he said the sweetest thing. He didn't say, 'Wow, that was great, thanks love.' He didn't say, 'Well, that's a relief to have got the first go out of the way.' Nor did he say, 'I love your boobs.' (All of which are comments I have received after previous liaisons with boys.)

What he said was, 'Can we go to sleep hugging?'

And that was when I lay my head on his chest and he started stroking my arm, and the buzzing sensation was replaced with a warm gooey feeling.

For the first time in my adult life I felt truly whole, truly loved and very, very smug.

Nick

Before I open my eyes I'm aware that I'm not alone. I can feel a warm, soft body beside me. A warm soft body that I distinctly remember making love to last night. I let that thought linger for a while.

I can't feel my arm properly. It's all stiff and I obviously haven't moved it for hours, but I can live with that. It's still wrapped tightly around the girl that I think I'm very probably in love with.

I remember thinking it last night. I almost said it. I won't though. Not for a while. It's all happened a bit quickly and I don't want to scare her away.

That's how you tell, isn't it? You know you love someone when the thought of them not being there cuts you in half like a scythe. She's lying here in my arms and I want this to happen again and again. Though I don't want to jeopardise it by coming on too strong too soon.

I open my eyes and see that she's already awake, looking up at my face, her cheek still resting against my chest.

'Good morning.' She smiles and strokes her hand up and down my body.

I shuffle onto my side and tug my numb arm out from underneath her, before brushing her hair from her face and giving her a good morning kiss.

I lift up the duvet, very gently, to have a little peep at that cute little body. It's lighter in here now and I can see everything much more clearly. She curls her knees towards her chest defensively.

'You're so beautiful.' The words come out of their own accord and I see her body loosen a little. She raises her hand to her mouth and lets out a coy giggle. 'Thank you.'

She pulls me in for another kiss and then takes her turn to look down the duvet.

'Time for round two?' Her hand slides down my body and . . . I start running the prospect of long, slow Sunday morning sex through my mind when it suddenly occurs to me that it isn't Sunday. It's Monday and looking at the bedside clock I should have been at work half-an-hour ago. Shit! I reluctantly remove her hand and sit up. 'Cass, I've got to go.'

'I'm sorry, I thought . . . ' Oh God. She looks horrified.

'I've got to go to work,' I explain, hastily, as I leap out of bed and start plucking my crumpled clothes off the floor. 'Pete's arriving today; I've got to be there to let the removal men in and stuff. Oh shit Cass, I'm so sorry.'

It's ok. She's laughing now. That's probably because I've had about four goes at getting my boxers back on and have managed to get them on inside out or back to front every time.

'It's alright.' She finally lets me off the hook and I smile gratefully before wriggling into my jeans and bolting for the door.

'I'll ring you later,' I call out from halfway down the stairs.

'You see that you do,' she calls back, now out of bed and leaning over the banister at the top of the stairs, naked.

I scoop Rooney up, bed and all from the hall floor, and leave quickly before I have the chance to change my mind. I dive into the car and turn the key in the ignition. It doesn't take long for me to get back to Pete's and I can see that I'm there just in time. There's a huge lorry in the car park and two officious-looking men with clipboards scratching their heads, obviously wondering if they're at the right place.

I wrench on the handbrake and jump out. 'Sorry I'm late,' I call as I jog over to them.

'That's alright mate,' one of them answers, looking at me oddly. It's no wonder, I've got my t-shirt on inside out.

Cassie

Even by Tuesday morning I'm still walking around in my newly-created, wondrous universe. It feels like my entire brain has been sprinkled with fairy dust and my body bathed in finest goat's milk.

It's funny how you sometimes don't realise how lonely you've been until someone special comes along. I love my animals to pieces and Jilly is a friend most people would kill for: loyal, supportive, straightforward and great fun. But these relationships can never give you the emotional tenderness a lover can. Just one night spent snuggled up to Nick has boosted my confidence, calmed my nerves, and even allowed me to paint fluidly again.

I've been working on the much-delayed portrait of Digger for a couple of hours so far today and already he's looking much more dog-like. Gone is the strange porcine nose, the legs that would have looked more at home on a deer and the tail that could have made a good job of dusting your sideboard. Hmm. Now he looks like the proud Springer he is, even though his owner is somewhat stuck-up.

'What do you think of the doggy?' I ask Piglet as she hops onto my lap and starts purring. There's something rather peculiar about Piglet's purr. It's a little stuttery, like an engine with a couple of cylinders misfiring. I'm sure she's jealous of Roo, who purrs like a well-oiled Rolls Royce. But I prefer Piglet's staccato rumble. It's an endearing quirk and it makes her stand out.

Nick has a quirk I noticed on Sunday, too. When he gets stressed or embarrassed, he rubs the nail of his thumb on the bridge of his nose, half-hiding his face with a pretend itch. It's terribly cute. I'm almost looking forward to seeing him get embarrassed again. Preferably when he's naked . . .

With this lovely thought in my mind I put my brush into the jam jar of water on the little table I keep next to my easel and pop Piglet onto the floor.

'Sorry darling. I've got to go out for a bit. Why don't you go and snuggle up with Roo in the living room?'

Piglet, still with her strange arrhythmic motor running, wanders out onto the landing and lopes down the stairs, her tail flicking the banister as she goes.

I change out of my green cords and slip into a flowery summer dress Jilly bought me and, she'd kill me for this, my clogs.

Late, as usual, I scramble down the stairs, grab my purse off the kitchen table and bolt for the car. When I arrive at The New Inn I get a bit of a shock. I'd arranged to have lunch with Daisy to have a good gossip about Nick, but sitting next to her is my mother, replete in a straw hat and what looks like a pair of dungarees with a white t-shirt underneath. They spot me and wave furiously. 'Cassie, hi!' they almost scream.

'Hi!' I call. 'How are we all?'

'Daisy's got some exciting news,' Mother says.

'Oh?'

'Yes.' Daisy's eyes are glittering. 'Guy proposed. We're getting married!'

I can hardly contain my excitement. 'Oooh, how wonderful. The summer of love . . . Have you ordered the Verve Cliquot?'

'The waiter's bringing it,' my mother tells me.

And just as she says it, the young man appears with the ice bucket and three flutes.

Nick

'Right, I think I've had enough for one day.' Pete loosens his tie and pulls his fags out of his suit pocket. He offers me one but I put my hand up to refuse. I'm doing well. I haven't had one since I left Scotty's.

'Sorry mate, forgot.' He lights his own and stuffs the packet back into his pocket.

'I'll go and put the kettle on, shall I?' I offer as we both head for the door.

We've been interviewing waiting staff all day. It's not an energetic task, but it's tiring. I don't know why, but I almost get more nervous than when I'm being interviewed. Although it does have its plus points. I've seen enough 'inadvertently' revealed cleavage today to keep me going for a very long time.

I really don't get it sometimes. How are we men meant to keep up? If you dare to look at or, God forbid, pass comment on the wonders of the female form then you instantly have the words 'male chauvinist' screeched at you before getting walloped with the nearest available handbag. Invite a women for a job interview, however, and you get a whole procession of thigh-revealing skirt splits and low-cut blouses.

As we step out of the restaurant I take the time to breathe in a bit of fresh air. It feels like we've been cooped up in there for days. I'm ready to head off and collapse on that nice new bed that arrived with Pete and Carrine.

I wait for Pete to lock the door behind us and we turn to head for the house.

'Uncle Nick!' Harry comes bounding across to us, Rooney at his side — as he has been since they arrived on Monday. 'Uncle Nick, you've got to come in quickly!'

I laugh at the stern look he's giving me and give his hair a quick ruffle. 'Why, what's up, mate?'

'Your girlfriend's here!' he announces like some officious master of ceremonies and then runs back to the house.

'Jesus, hasn't taken you long.' Pete winks playfully at me.

'Well, you know . . . ' I shake my head and smile. 'Anyway, it's your fault.'

He looks at me and waits for the punch line but I just give him a wry smile.

Yes! The look on his face tells me he's curious. 'Remember that girl you gave my card to at the Tate?'

'You are joking?' His jaw almost hits the tarmac as we walk.

'Nope.' Smug smile from me.

'Bloody hell!' He laughs and pats me on the back. 'You never cease to amaze me

Nicholas, I'll give you that.'

Once inside the house I find Cassie has already been seated in the kitchen and given a cup of coffee. She and Carrine are chatting away like old friends.

'Ha, here he is!' Carrine announces as we both enter the scene. 'You dark horse. You've only been here a few days and already you have a secret girlfriend that you don't tell us about.'

I hold my hands up. I know better than to try and defend my corner with Carrine. I'd never win and I've seen what happens to Pete when he dares to argue back.

'The poor girl must think you're ashamed of her or something!' She continues to mutter as she pours two more cups of coffee. I can see Cassie's gone a bit blushy so I wink at her. I'd had every intention of being here to introduce her properly when she arrived but either she's early or I'm late. I look at my watch and decide it's the latter.

'Well, aren't you going to introduce us then?' Pete tries to sound impatient, just to make me squirm.

'Cassie,' I look at her and almost forget to say the rest. I'm suddenly taken by just how pretty she is. There's something about the light in here that's catching her face and making her look even more beautiful than ever. 'You've met Carrine, obviously, and this is Pete, the comedian who goes round giving my business cards to random women. And that,' I add on as a scuffling entourage of dog and four-year-old come bounding in from the back garden with a tennis ball, 'is Harry.'

Cassie does a nervous little wave and says hello. We all chat for a while over coffee. I've enjoyed the space but it's good to have company again.

'I suppose I'd better go and get out of my work things. You can come too if you want,' I say to Cassie and then wish I hadn't. Pete's winking at me and nodding at her. I roll my eyes to show disapproval at Pete's deliberate misinterpretation. I don't mind so much but I can see Cassie's a little embarrassed.

Fortunately Pete notices too and apologises. 'Anyway, it's your room mate, you do what you like in it.' He then laughs as he realises he's probably made matters worse.

'Come on,' I say to Cassie. 'I'll give you the guided tour.'

Once upstairs I open the door and hold my arm out to welcome her in. It's more like a hotel suite than a spare room. I've now got a bed, sofa, TV, bookshelves and my own bathroom. The door even locks with a shiny new brass key. Not that I've ever bothered.

'It's lovely.' Cassie wanders across and sits

down on the edge of the bed.

'Not bad, is it?' I take my jacket off, throw it onto the sofa and start to loosen my tie. 'What?' I suddenly realise she's staring at me intently. Ah. Perhaps she's uncomfortable about my undressing in front of her. Mind you, she's seen it all already so I didn't . . .

'I was just thinking how handsome you looked in your suit.'

I look down at my attire. I suppose I do look quite dapper. She's only ever seen me in jeans and casual clothes. Tie and cufflinks make a bit of a change. I'm just so used to seeing me in them that I don't notice it anymore. It's what I've worn for most of my working life.

'I don't scrub up too badly, do I?'

She gets to her feet and wanders across to me. 'Very well indeed.'

I let myself sink into her kiss and my body loosens. It feels good after a long, stressful day. There's something about being kissed by a beautiful woman that can put everything into perspective. I get the impression my day's work isn't over though as she starts to help me undo my shirt.

'I reckon you're trying to seduce me, you wicked woman,' I say in the short pause before I return the kiss.

'I do like perceptive men. They really turn

me on,' she replies as she continues undoing my shirt.

There's no answer to that, is there? I simply raise my eyebrow quizzically, reach back and turn that key in the lock for the first time.

11

Cassie

Oh God. Just as I'm beginning to think life is perfect, one of the little people brings me back down to ground zero with a bump. For the second time in as many weeks, Wiggy visits me in the afternoon and bursts into tears in my kitchen.

'What's wrong?' I immediately reach for the avocados and elderflower cordial. 'Don't you like your new school?'

'Daddy's gone to live in Cheltenham,' Wiggy wails. 'Mummy doesn't love him anymore.'

Oh God, I think; why hasn't Jilly phoned me about this?

'Oh darling.' I smother Wiggy in a tender hug. 'I'm sure that's not true. Sometimes grown-ups say things they don't mean. Just like boys at school. I'm sure your mummy didn't mean it.'

'I don't want Daddy to go away.' Wiggy has tears pouring down her cheeks.

'Why doesn't Mummy love him anymore?'

'I'm sure she does.'

God, I wish I knew what was going on.

'Where's Mummy now?'

'She's gone to Granny's.'

This doesn't sound good. Jilly only ever runs home in moments of extreme crisis.

'What? Who picked you up from school?'

'Sandra's mum.'

'And she took you home?'

'Yes.'

'And Mummy wasn't there?'

'No.'

'So how do you know she's at Granny's?'

'Sandra's mum told me and then I asked her to drop me off here.'

'And Daddy's in Cheltenham?'

'Yes.'

Sounds like the wheels have well and truly fallen off the wagon.

'Are you ok here for a minute? I'm just going to phone Mummy.'

Wiggy nods silently, her mouth a thin line of distress.

I go into the hall and phone Jilly's mobile but it's turned off, so I hang up and ring her home number. I get the answer phone.

'Jilly,' I say, 'Wiggy's here. I'll hang onto her until you get back. Can you call me the minute you get this message? I need to know what's going on.'

I return to the kitchen where I find Wiggy stroking Piglet who has instinctively visited her. Cats are very good at detecting stress and do their best to soothe it. Good show, Piglet!

'Mummy will come and pick you up soon.' I stroke Wiggy's hair much like she's petting Piglet's fur. 'Would you like an avocado?'

Wiggy shakes her head glumly.

'No thank you, Auntie Cassie.'

'Would you like to go for a little walk?'

'Where's Pooh?' she asks suddenly. 'Can we walk with Pooh?'

Oh dear. Jilly and I had agreed we wouldn't tell Wiggy about Pooh's passing until she was more settled at her new school. It's in situations like these I wish I was able to think on my feet but I can't, so I say, 'Pooh's not with us anymore.'

'Why not?'

'Well, he got very old and went to another place.'

I speak quickly, hoping that Wiggy won't quite hear and drop the subject.

'You mean he's in Heaven?'

'Yes . . . he's in Heaven. And having a lovely time, I expect.'

'So, he can't come walking with us?'

'No, not today.'

For a minute I think she's taken the news philosophically but then her face crumples again.

'Why is everyone going away?' she asks

between sobs. 'I don't understand.'

Her arms shoot up to loop around my neck and I feel her button nose press against my collarbone. I'm absolutely lost for words, so I end up crying too.

Rather than moping in the kitchen I decide we really do have to go for that walk so I pull myself together, put Wiggy in my denim jacket and we go for a wander up the lane.

We don't speak as we trudge along the verge, but I think the fresh early-evening air does us both good. I hold her hand and it feels so tiny and fragile in my grip that I almost can't believe it's real. Goodness, the responsibility of looking after a child . . . I wonder if I'll ever be able to take on the job. Now I've been given another hint. It's bloody tough, but rewarding. I grip Wiggy's hand tighter.

'Are you ok?'

She nods silently.

'I just want to say something,' I start tentatively.

'What?'

I want to say, 'Don't let the world corrupt you. Don't become cynical. Don't let anyone hurt you. Stay innocent. Never stop marvelling at the beautiful things . . . ' But I know Wiggy has already been touched by heartache and ugliness, and there's nothing any of us can do to prevent it. So, as a consolation prize, I say, 'I want you to know that you are the most special, beautiful person in the world. And we all love you.'

Wiggy absorbs this information quietly and we walk in silence for several minutes.

'I love you too,' she says eventually.

I feel myself welling up again. A butterfly then flits across our path and Wiggy saves me from another blubbing by saying excitedly, 'Look it's just like the picture in your house, Auntie Cassie!' And I smile as I realise that she's right. A Large Blue has just proved that miracles do happen, life is full of beauty and we can make it through the difficult times. Against all the odds, it has survived, and so will we.

This is the thought I tell Jilly when we return. We find her under the willow tree, staring into space.

'We'll get through this,' I tell her. 'We'll all look after each other.'

And as the sun begins its descent I put my arms around Jilly and Wiggy and think how lucky I am to have Nick.

Nick

'What shall we do now?' Harry asks as the titles start to roll on *Finding Nemo*.

We've had a good boys' night in front of the TV. I enjoyed the film almost as much as Harry. It was certainly better than the other option, helping Pete to mow his considerable expanse of lawn.

'I think it might be getting on for your bedtime, mate,' I say as he shuffles round on my knee to look at me.

'Awww!'

He makes me laugh when he does that. He just screws his face up and makes no attempt to disguise his disappointment. Kids are like that. What you see is what you get. No silly games or subtexts. They just say and do what they think.

'I tell you what. Why don't we go and fix ourselves a bedtime milkshake?' My attempt to lift his mood obviously works as he throws his arms around my neck and gives me a big hug.

'I love you, Uncle Nick. I'm glad you and Rooney came to live with us.'

If only milkshake had that effect on everyone. 'I love you too, mate,' I reply as I hug him back, rather amazed at how soft and gooey my insides feel at this moment. I must be turning into a right girly.

I'm quite attached to the little fella now. I've never really had a big family of my own and I suppose this is the first time I've ever felt part of one. I do like being Uncle Nick and a bit of child-minding is the least I can do after all Carrine and Pete have done for me.

I sweep him up in my arms and head for the kitchen. 'Chocolate, strawberry or banana?'

He purses his lips, indicating he's thinking hard about it. 'Banana.'

'Good call.' I place him on one of the kitchen chairs and wander over to where the huge supply of assorted Nesquik is stored. Truth is I'm almost as fond of the stuff as he is. Not that I'd ever admit that to another human being. Especially not one who takes the piss as much as Pete does. I'm quite good at pretending I'm drinking the stuff under sufferance.

'You two will be turning into milkshakes soon,' Carrine comments. She's sitting at the kitchen table reading a pile of magazines. No, that's not strictly true. She's not actually sitting at the kitchen table. She's sitting a fair distance away from it owing to the enormous bump that precedes her everywhere.

I wink at Harry. He giggles.

'Will you read me a bedtime story tonight, Uncle Nick?'

'I think it might be time to let Uncle Nick have a rest.' Carrine looks up from her magazine and gives Harry a firm look.

'I don't mind, really.' I come across with the two milkshakes and sit down at the table.

'I can see why Cassie is so taken with you,' Carrine suddenly throws into the conversation from nowhere. 'You're obviously a natural when it comes to children.'

I don't know what to say to that. I'm flattered by the compliment. I'm also intrigued to know what Cassie has said about me. 'Really?'

'Oh, yes. We were discussing you on the phone just now.' Carrine delivers this news quite matter-of-factly, as if she rings my girlfriends without my knowledge all the time. 'I've invited her here for dinner on Saturday.'

Cassie

My excuse to go puppy shopping is that it will cheer up Wiggy to see me with another dog and might even distract Jilly from her misery. But the truth is I'm doing this mostly for myself. And why not?

So far this month I've completed the following paintings:

- Digger (thank God. Nightmare over)
- Horace the tortoise (bit like painting a jelly mould. But sat very nicely, so no

complaints from me).

- Wittgenstein and Schopenhauer, two guinea pigs. (Wit and Pen for short. Much like painting hamsters. So just a slosh of watery gouache with a couple of black dots for eyes.)
- And a snake called John Holmes. ('You've really captured his personality,' said the owner's girlfriend when I took it round. Oh please! A politician has more personality than a snake.)

Been busy, haven't I? And this means I have money in the bank. Sadly, money in the bank can't be cuddled so it needs to be spent on something that can be.

My partner in this endeavour will be the dog anorak, Guy. Apparently, his family have had dogs since he was tall enough to get bitten in the face by one, and they've had quite a variety of them so he knows 'what to look for', whatever that means. I simply go by huggability. I mean, what else is there?

'Ready to pick one out then?' He strides into my kitchen and gives me a kiss on the cheek followed by a rub on my shoulder. I like this about Guy. His tactile nature. It immediately puts me at ease.

'My hands are primed and ready to assess fluffiness, cuddliness and strokeability, yes.'

'Good. You can start on me.'

'And you're about to marry my sister!'

'Well, she did promise me that you were thrown in with the bargain.'

'What a cheek!'

Guy laughs.

'Come on. Let's get cracking. We'll go in my car. Don't think I can handle your driving today. Had a bit of a rough night last night.'

I tut. 'Every night's a rough night for you, Guy.'

We go out to my weedy driveway and I'm confronted by a car that's very definitely a different colour to the one Guy had before. And a different shape.

'Whose is this?'

'It's all mine.'

'It's very smart! Very smart!'

I know boys like their cars to be complimented almost as much as girls revel in being told their thighs look incredibly slim. 'What is it?'

'It's a Ferrari Dino.'

'That sounds nice,' I say vaguely.

Guy shakes his head. 'Of course it isn't a Ferrari Dino. Do I look like a millionaire?'

I don't bother to answer. Guy is dressed in yellow shorts, flip-flops and a grubby sweatshirt that reads: 'REALITY IS FOR THOSE WHO CAN'T HANDLE DRUGS'. Very mature.

'It's a Volkswagen.'

'Black's a bit of a boring colour, isn't it?' I say, getting in.

Guy shakes his head again, only this time a bit more huffily. 'I hope you're not like this with the puppies.'

'What do you mean?'

He starts the engine and we back out. 'I mean, I hope you don't go, 'Have you got this one in brown? I don't like it in white.''

'Oh, don't be ridiculous,' I reply. 'Who wants a plain brown dog?'

The place we go to where the puppies are waiting patiently for their new owners to hurry up and collect them is called Rambling Rose Farm. It's on one of the many back roads east of Burford. We get lost on the way. Well, that's not strictly correct. We pass it twice, convinced it can't be the right place. But it is, even though there isn't a rambler or a rose in sight, just a grubby collection of outhouses overlooked by a large tumbledown house.

The woman who greets us at the door is plump and ruddy-cheeked, just like a farmer's wife should be. Her name's Teri. She also has a great Gloucestershire accent and insists on calling Guy and me, 'Moiy lurve' whenever she refers to us.

As we head out to the barn where the

281

puppies are she asks us if we've been married long! Guy, being the cheeky sod that he is, says, 'About a year. We've got one on the way.'

'Ahh,' Teri replies, giving me a beam. 'Well, the pocket beagle is a great dog with kids. They have a reputation for being affectionate and playful.'

'Just like my wife,' Guy continues, before I dig him in the ribs and give him my severest frown.

'Here they are then,' our plump guide tells us as she opens the barn door and we are confronted by a beagle mum keeping a watchful eye over lots of scampering paws and floppy ears, in-between which there doesn't seem to be much puppy.

'Aaaahhhh,' I squeak. 'How cute!'

I crouch down and watch the babies tumble on the straw-strewn floor. There are five all together.

'Two have been sold already,' Teri tells us. 'A few others wanted one, but I wouldn't sell to them. Didn't seem like proper dog people to me.'

I respect her principles and tell her I am very much a dog person. Always have been, always will be.

'I can see that. Which one would you like?'

Well, she's got that right too. There's no way I can leave this farm without one. But they're all so gorgeous, I can't choose. They score off the scale on cuddleability. I confer with Guy who rustles around with them, checking hips are level, splaying paws and digging about in ears. Eventually, he plucks one out by the scruff of the neck and says, 'This is the little fella for you,' and, as the pup squints at me, I fall instantly in love and say, 'sold' as if he's an antique or painting or something. I hand over the money, cradle him to my chest and rush to the car, thanking Teri as I go.

'Aaaahhh,' I say as we drive home. 'He's just too delicious. My very own pocket beagle!'

'He's not even pocket-size yet. He's more of a teabag.'

'Alright, teabag beagle then.'

'What are you going to call him?'

'Rabbit,' I announce, without pausing for thought.

'Continuing The Hundred Acre Woods theme?'

'Yup. Don't know what I'll do when I run out. Haven't had an 'Owl' yet, though. So I don't need to worry too much.'

Guy laughs and drives in silence for a while as I go all gooey over Rabbit.

Then he says, 'Oh, I knew I meant to say something. I spoke to Jack the other night.

You know, about Andrew. Apparently he's a great bloke. No skeletons in the closet, no ex-girlfriends out to kill him. He's just a bit posh and disorganised, but a lovely bloke.'

'Doesn't matter now, anyway,' I tell him. 'I'm happy with my Nick.'

'Oh yes. How's that going?'

'Like a . . . like a Volkswagen.' I enjoy my own joke.

Nick

'No, I did not streak on school sports day. I think you'll find that was Scotty.'

'Oh yeah, I remember now.' Pete smirks and knocks back another slug of wine. He's determined to embarrass me in front of Cassie somehow. Luckily, if the wine's going to her head like it is to mine she will hardly notice. There are lots of bottles we need to try for the restaurant and she's doing her bit to help, bless her, though her comments don't go much beyond, 'Delicious' or 'Lovely'.

Pete's been doing the cooking tonight. It's normally Carrine who does all the domestic meals. She's a mean cook, but she's so enormous at the moment she can hardly reach the work surfaces and standing up is making her ankles puffy. So Pete's stepped into the breech, as it were. It's obvious he's driving her mad. She keeps telling him to piss off to his own kitchen instead of wrecking hers, but minor squabbles aside this is turning out to be a fantastic evening. Good wine, good food, good company — what more could you ask for?

'So when's the baby due?' Cassie asks. She seems to be getting more comfortable now, not quite the shrinking violet that she was at the start of the evening.

'Yesterday,' Carrine replies matter-of-factly, before biting into the spear of asparagus that she's got on the end of her fork.

'Oh.' It's obvious from Cassie's expression that this isn't the answer she was expecting.

'Takes after her father. Always bloody late.' Carrine doesn't miss the opportunity to have another dig at Pete.

If you walked in and watched as an impartial observer, you'd probably think these two were on the brink of divorce with all the spats and bickering. But it doesn't take long to realise it's just the way they are. There's no malice behind any of it. It's like they have to do it just so they can test the other one is still there in the room somewhere, like bats sending out sonar.

'Could've been worse.' Pete stands up to give everyone's glass a refill. Everyone's except for Carrine, who's been on orange juice for most of the evening. 'We thought he was on his way when we were in the car coming over from London, but it turned out to be just indigestion, didn't it love?'

'He?' Carrine waves her hand dismissively towards him. 'Why are you always saying that? It will be a girl.'

'We'll find out soon enough, won't we?' Pete puts the bottle down on the table and sits back in his seat.

'One of each would be quite nice though, wouldn't it?' Cassie chips in again.

'To be honest, I don't care.' Something in Pete's expression softens as he speaks and a blissful smile erupts across his face. 'It'll be great whatever happens. Honestly, having kids is just the best thing that can happen to anybody.' And then he does something I've never seen him do before. He puts down his knife and reaches across to squeeze Carrine's hand.

The moment brings a lump to my throat. The way they look at each other for that split-second just gave the game away and showed the whole world that, underneath the banter, these are two people who love each other very much.

Perhaps it's just the wine but the mood and the moment suddenly seem to get to me and I feel a bit soppy myself. I can't resist slipping my hand under the table and giving Cassie's leg a little squeeze. She rests her cheek on her hand and looks at me fondly.

I suddenly have to remind myself that we've only been together a couple of weeks. It feels like she's been here forever. I certainly can't imagine going back to life without her.

'Come on *garçon*, stop drooling over the beautiful ladies and get the plates cleared, will you? We've got another four courses to get through yet.' Pete interrupts my reverie. I'd agreed to be headwaiter tonight. He told me I need to get back in practise before we open. Not that there's much to forget about opening a bottle of wine and scooping vegetables onto plates. And not that I have any intention of waiting tables that often. I have a headwaiter and team of assorted minions to take care of all that. I've done my time wielding spoons and forks; I'm rather looking forward to the sanctity of my office.

Cassie seems to be impressed by the full silver service that's being laid on for her though so I'm sure it's worth coming out of retirement this once. I'm probably showing off but it has its advantages. I think back to the effect just wearing a suit had on her. She should be gagging for it after this.

'Sorbet madam?' I place down the delicate

little dish in front of her and can't resist giving her a fleeting kiss before I sit down.

'Oi! We'll have none of that sort of thing with the customers,' Pete calls out across the table.

'I don't know. It might increase the bookings.' Carrine keeps a straight face as she spoons her first taste of sorbet into her mouth.

Cassie and I laugh. She's obviously caught Pete off-guard for once. You can almost hear the rubber bands whirring round as he tries to work out whether that was a dig at him or a pass at me. He wisely decides to leave well alone and turns his concentration towards the sorbet, which is just as delicious as everything else we've eaten so far. For a bloke who used to live on Fray Bentos and Mars bars he's obviously come a long way.

★　★　★

It's nearly midnight now and I seem to have done nothing but eat and drink for hours. Exquisite as it's all been, I feel absolutely stuffed.

'I suppose I'd better walk you home.' I take the hint from Cassie as she yawns and looks at her watch. I don't think she's bored but the evening's reached its natural close.

'Remember your key, mate, 'cause we won't be waiting up.' Pete gets his parting shot in before walking around the table to give Cassie a hug.

'Thank you so much.' Cassie hugs him back, her cheeks slightly pink from all the wine. 'It's been lovely.'

She goes to hug Carrine too, who as she attempts to heave herself out of her chair stops suddenly.

'What's up love?' Pete suddenly looks concerned.

'I think she's coming,' Carrine answers, wincing slightly.

It takes me a moment to realise what she means.

'Are you sure?' Pete asks, going across and squatting down beside her.

'Of course I'm sure,' she snaps at him. 'I can tell when I am about to have a bloody baby for fuck's sake. I thought it was indigestion again, but it's contractions.'

I look at Cassie and she looks at me. Without words we agree that our departure needs to be put on hold for a moment.

Carrine winces again and clasps her hand to her huge stomach.

'Is there anything I can do?' I don't suppose there is but it only seems right to offer.

'You could call us an ambulance, mate.'

Pete looks at me with a certain degree of gratitude. 'I can't drive; I've had a skinful.'

★ ★ ★

'Where is that fucking ambulance?' Pete is now looking worried and I'm back to feeling fairly useless.

'I'll go and try again.' Cassie heads off to the other room to phone.

Carrine's lying on the floor now, propped up by several cushions that we've hoicked out of the living room. I'm kneeling to one side of her and holding her hand. Pete is alternating between crouching beside her, holding the other hand and pacing around the kitchen like a man possessed.

'It's no good. I'm going to have to drive,' he suddenly announces, sounding heroic and decisive.

'It's too late,' Carrine tells him between moans, tightening her grip on my hand. 'She's . . . aghhhhhhh . . . nearly . . . aghhhh!'

The pain of her fingernails slicing into my hand is excruciating but I do my best to put a brave face on it.

'They say it's on the way. Should be here any minute.' Cassie's head appears round the door.

'Well, they'd better hurry up or this baby's

going to beat them to it.'

'Shall I get some towels?' Cassie offers.

She doesn't get an answer as our attention is taken by Carrine's next almighty scream. Jesus. Isn't it Pete's hand she's supposed to be doing this to?

'Oh bollocks!' I'm not sure what the matter is or what Pete's doing down at the other end of Carrine and I'm not sure I want to know.

Suddenly something happens to his demeanour. It's like he's been taken over by some other being. He takes Carrine's hand and looks her in the eyes steadily. 'It's ok love, we can do this.'

And it's at this moment it hits me. She's going to have the baby here and she's going to have it now. I'm not sure how long Cassie has been stood behind me with her pile of towels but she takes one and puts it into Pete's outstretched hand.

The next few minutes are the most surreal of my life as I hold onto Carrine's hand, feeling her body tense up and listen to her cry out and make noises like I've never heard from another human being before.

Her screams are punctuated with Pete's words of encouragement. I can't believe how calm he's being. My stomach is doing somersaults and it's not even my kid that's about to arrive.

'Ok love, we're nearly there.' His voice is soothing but strong at the same time. I'm suddenly very proud of him. This is my mate that's doing this. My mate who I've known since we were eleven. 'That's it love, keep going.'

After another screech, which I'm sure ought to have shattered every window in the house, Carrine's grip on my hand loosens and I look across to Pete, who is laughing with relief.

'That's it girl. We've done it.' His face splits into an enormous grin. 'We've done it,' he repeats, 'and you were right sweetheart, we've got a little girl.'

12

Cassie

I was delighted to be invited to dinner by Carrine. The phone rang on Friday night and she very sweetly said they needed my help in trying the new wines and menu. Even with a new puppy in my life, I was thrilled. I felt like doing a Sally Field in her famous Oscar speech by screaming, 'They like me; they really like me!'

Having spent the day cuddling Rabbit and getting him used to my voice and his new name, I tucked him up in his basket, on which Guy had stencilled 'THE HUTCH', struggled into my slinky silver dress and drove over to their house.

I hadn't seen Nick all day. He and Pete had been working on figures, projected turnovers and 'covers' (thought they went on beds), so I'd been left to fend for myself. But when I arrived he gave me a big hug like we'd been apart for months, which totally made up for it.

'You look gorgeous,' he said as he took my coat. And for the rest of the night, he didn't stop complimenting me.

The dinner was delicious and I was just beginning to feel soporific from all the wine when Carrine let out a groan and said she'd gone into labour.

I haven't been more shocked since seeing a Brit reach the semis at Wimbledon. In a second everyone was rushing around like ball girls and boys. Were the covers coming off? Were we going to see a long drawn out rally or a quick serve and volley game?

Carrine supplied the answer early in the first set. With a deep breath and a huge effort she aced it, and the baby arrived before the umpire! Phew!

Standing ovation! Wild cheering! Baby has all ten fingers and toes!

The ambulance arrived ten minutes after the birth (great timing, boys!) and whisked Pete, Carrine, plus bundle of joy, to Cirencester Hospital.

'Crikey,' I said to Nick once they'd left.

'Yeah. Maybe the baby smelt the food and decided it was time to crash the party.'

He moved forward and gave me a kiss.

'Are you staying the night?' he asked.

'I don't think so. I mean, I haven't come prepared. Why don't you come and stay at mine?'

Nick looked up at the ceiling.

'There's a little guy upstairs who shouldn't be left on his own.'

'Oh, crikey, yes. Sorry, I forgot.'

'I've got a t-shirt you can wear,' Nick said, putting his arms around my waist. 'You can borrow my toothbrush in the morning.'

'It's very tempting, but I should get back and check on Rabbit. He's probably scared in his new home on his own.'

'Well, go and check on him and come back.'

'I'll come back tomorrow,' I replied. 'I'm shattered anyway. All the excitement has killed me.'

'Ok,' Nick agreed reluctantly.

After a quick snog, which perked him up, he opened the front door for me and I scampered out while he waved me off.

When I got home I had a cup of tea watching Rabbit's little body move up and down as he slept. It had been an incredible few days. So much more life has come into mine.

A puppy, a baby, new friends, romance. I'm not sure if I can take it all in.

I wonder briefly how Pete and Carrine are getting on at the hospital with their new baby. They're in for a tough time. I remember seeing how tired Jilly was after the birth of Wiggy, and she wasn't trying to start a new business.

I've never thought about having babies much. With all my animals it feels like I have them already but, now I think about it, I can quite see me and a certain someone oohing and ahhing down at a little face. And I'm not talking about Rabbit.

I wash up my cup, leave it on the draining board and head upstairs.

The minute I get into bed, I wish I'd stayed with Nick. Rabbit is sleeping peacefully downstairs, all my other pets are snoring and snuffling their way through the sweet-smelling night and I'm suddenly wide-awake in a bed that feels terribly empty.

I'm going to phone Nick early tomorrow so I can nip straight over there and lure him back to my lair.

Nick

'Ok, bye then.' I hang up the phone.

I'd been looking forward to cuddling up to Cassie last night, but by the time the ambulance turned up and collected Pete and Carrine and little Leanne or Jasmine (whichever they decide on when they've finished arguing), it was late. Cassie needed to get home to check on her puppy, and I had to stay and look after Harry.

I'm looking forward to spending a more relaxed time with her this morning.

Last night ended up being manic.

I'm only halfway through an article in the Sunday papers when she arrives.

I really like this about Cassie. She doesn't keep me hanging around for hours. She's not trying to play it cool.

'Hi.' She comes in the door, straight into my arms and gives me a long kiss.

'I missed you last night. The bed seemed to be big and . . . '

'Uncle Nick! Where's Mum?' A small figure in pyjamas appears at the top of the stairs and bounds down them towards us.

I look at Cassie and she looks at me. I feel a man-to-man chat coming and I kneel down so I can do it face-to-face. How he slept through all of that last night I'll never know. Pete went up to him before they set off in the ambulance but he was sound asleep.

'Listen mate, your mummy and daddy are at the hospital at the moment. Don't worry, there's nothing wrong. It's just that Mummy's baby arrived last night.'

I want to look at Cassie for a bit of reassurance that I'm doing this right but I can't see her as she's standing right behind me.

'So, the baby's come out of her tummy now?'

'That's right. And your dad's going to ring me when he wants us to go and fetch them all from the hospital.'

'What's his name?'

I suddenly feel like I'm under interrogation by a four-year-old. 'I don't know yet. Besides, it's not a he; it's a she.'

Oh God, I've cocked-up somewhere along the line. I now have a little boy folding his arms tightly around his chest and screwing up his face at me. I feel a slight panic start to rise from my stomach. 'What's the matter?'

'I wanted it to be a boy so he can play football with me.'

I can hear Cassie laughing behind me.

'Don't worry, mate. Girls play football as well these days. Anyway, you've got Rooney until then.'

'But what about when you move in with Auntie Cassie?'

Right, big logic hole here. I feel myself falling into it and feeling distinctly uncomfortable as I do. 'Why do you think I'm going to move in with Auntie Cassie?' I ask, hoping that she isn't reading too much into this conversation.

'Because you love her. I've seen you kissing her and that's what people do when they love each other. They want to kiss all the time, Mum says.'

You know that feeling? The one where you know whatever comes out of your mouth next is going to be the wrong thing.

'Look I promise you, mate; much as I do like kissing Auntie Cassie, I'm not going anywhere for a little while yet. I've only just moved in with you, haven't I? Besides, I don't know if Auntie Cassie wants me to go round kissing her all the time yet. We've got a lot of sorting out to do.'

He scrutinises my face carefully. Just like I'd like to be scrutinising Cassie's at the moment.

'That's alright then,' he says at last. 'Can I have some Coco Pops please?'

Cassie

I find there's only one way to get rid of a squiffy hangover — plenty of fresh air and vigorous walking. I suggest this to Nick as he stirs next to me.

'Walking?' He looks at me as if I've just spoken in Mandarin and doesn't understand a word I'm saying. 'What for?'

'For the joy of it.' I kiss his forehead. 'To soak up a bit of nature. Enjoy the scenery.'

Nick gapes at me. 'Can we talk about it later?'

'Well, if you don't want to go for a walk, what are we going to do? All we've done is laze around in bed all day.'

'That isn't quite true, is it?' A smug grin appears on his face.

After Pete got back from the hospital, we had a coffee, checked everything was ok with Carrine and then came back here. A few kisses later we were in the bedroom, naked. And an hour after that we were both fast asleep.

'Yes, but it's half-past-two now. Come on, we have to do something.'

'Tennis,' comes the reply, before he rolls over and goes straight back to sleep.

I've never worked out how boys do that. After eating, after sex, after virtually anything, they can just close their eyes and in the time it takes to say 'antidisestablishmentarianism' (don't ask me what it means) they are already checked into a cosy little B&B in the land of nod. For me, once I'm awake, I'm awake, so I ease out of the bed, slip downstairs and disturb Rabbit instead.

After twenty minutes of tickling his chin and stroking his head, the poor mite seems exhausted so I leave him alone and go out to the phone in the hall.

Now I know Nick said tennis just to get me off his back, but it just so happens tennis is

300

the one sport I'm actually reasonable at. Feeling slightly devilish, I telephone the sports centre in Fairford and book a court.

After a quick cup of tea and a read of the paper, I nip upstairs, pull the duvet off Nick's feet and give his big toes a twist.

'Come on sleepy,' I say as I pull his legs off the bed. 'We're on court in an hour.'

Nick opens an eye and gives me a withering look.

'You are kidding.'

But I'm not, am I?

★ ★ ★

'Right, shall we stop knocking up and have a proper game?' I call over the net.

Nick walks towards me, already looking sweaty and uncomfortable. 'If you want, but I'm happy just hitting.'

'No, no. Let's play. It'll get boring otherwise.'

Nick shrugs. 'Do you want to serve then?'

He pats me a ball, which I catch and bounce on the tarmac court a few times.

Nick has already admitted he's only played tennis a few times but, rather unwisely, he followed it up by saying a girl had never beaten him at anything. And nor would one. Hmm.

301

I throw the ball up in the air, flick my racket forward and launch the ball over the net. Nick darts forward, shuffles back a step, and then takes an almighty swipe, performing the kind of shot you're more likely to see on a golf course than a tennis court. The only thing he hits is fresh air.

'Was that in?' he calls over the net.

'By a mile.'

'Ok, I'll give it to you.'

He shuffles back to a point just on the baseline and crouches in readiness for my next serve.

'Darling, I'm serving to the other court.'

Nick looks momentarily confused before trudging over. I serve again and this one he returns, but with a woody clunk that drifts the ball right into the centre of my court. I wait for the ball to bob up and topspin it into the corner before Nick can reach it.

'Sorry! Slipped on a bit of gravel.'

By the time we get into our sixth game, I'm four-one in the lead and Nick, footling on his baseline, swatting at the ball like it's a blue-bottle and pirouetting about like a fairy with a wand, is decidedly unhappy.

'It's not easy with the sun in my eyes,' he complains, standing beneath the heavy cloud cover.

'I'm sure it isn't.'

'What say we play one more game after this and finish the other sets another day?'

I want to say, 'What, so you can get some practice in-between?' but I agree and we play the final game where he hits ok, but I still win.

Grudgingly, Nick says I played pretty well. I thank him and we begin packing up the balls. As I slip one back into the aluminium tube, I spot Jeff wandering past, his head down, shirt untucked, an air of total misery hovering above him like a swarm of bees.

'Jeff. Jeff! Can I have a word?' I rush over. 'How are you?'

I don't know why I bother to ask. He looks dreadful, like he hasn't slept in days. Or should that be nights?

'Oh Cassie, hi.' He turns to face me. I think about introducing Nick but on balance decide it's not a good time. A man whose life is in freefall shakes hands with a man who's just been beaten at tennis by a girl . . . No, it won't work. Besides, Nick is studiously checking the strings on his racket, a hint that he's not in a super-sociable mood.

'I guess Jilly told you what's going on, did she?'

'Yes,' I nod.

'That I'm having an affair?'

'Hmm.' I stare down at my pigeon toes.

'Well, it's not true Cassie.'

I look up at him. I don't know what to say.

'It's not true. Jilly just flipped a few days ago and told me to get out, so I'm staying at our flat in Cheltenham. I came up today to have a chat, but she won't let me in the house.'

He stands there looking down at me and not for the first time I think he looks like a fat Lord Percy from *Blackadder*. Sad and out-of-control.

'Oh. So you don't have a girlfriend?'

'No. Why would I? I love Jilly.'

'This sounds very messy.'

'Could you talk to her?' Jeff runs a hand over his thinning hair.

'What do you want me to say?'

'That I'm not having an affair.'

Well that sounds easy enough, even for me. I tell Jeff I'll try.

'I'll go round right now. What are you doing? Going back to Cheltenham?'

'No. I'm going to stick around for a while. Maybe you could phone me with any news?'

'Sure.' Jeff gives me his mobile number. I scribble it on the back of a receipt with his pen. Just as I'm slipping it into my pocket, Nick appears at my side, looking much happier. I think he's overcome the tennis thrashing and is ready to be sociable again.

'Is this a private conversation or can anyone join in?'

I introduce the two men. They shake hands warmly and seem to hit it off straight away. They're talking about football anyway. 'If in doubt, talk sport,' is clearly most men's motto.

'Actually,' I butt in. 'Why don't you two go for a beer or something while I go for a chat with Jilly. Chester's Bar is just round the corner.'

They seem to size each other up a little more seriously before Nick says, 'Sure, why not? Not going to be much use in a girls' chat, am I?'

Jeff looks pleased too. I don't think he was relishing the thought of spending a gloomy Sunday afternoon on his own.

'That's settled then,' I say and, before they can change their minds, add, 'I'll come and pick you up when I'm finished, Nick. I shouldn't be too long.'

I give him a peck on the cheek, tap him on the bum and zip off to the car.

Nick

I turn my key in the front door of the house and push it open as quietly as I can.

'I don't know why we bothered getting you a bed?' Pete is standing in the hall right in front of me and makes me jump out of my skin. 'Jesus, it's like having a randy teenager in the house. Sneaking in and out at all hours of the day and night.' He does one of his hearty laughs.

I have spent quite a lot of time at Cassie's. No willpower I suppose. Every time it comes to the point where I ought to head off home I end up holding her in my arms and I just can't bring myself to let go. I ought to make the effort to use my own bed once in a while. Seems a little ungrateful.

I did think of inviting Cassie back here for the night on the odd occasion. I don't think Pete or Carrine would mind but it doesn't feel right somehow, especially with Harry around. Much as they've all made me feel incredibly welcome, I just feel like that would be taking liberties.

'I'm just making myself a bacon buttie, mate; do you fancy one?' Pete wanders over towards the kitchen and nods his head to indicate that I should follow.

'Be nice.' I walk behind him, finding myself intrigued as to why he has an enormous grin on his face. Oh God, not another practical joke.

'Carrine's just been on the phone,' he tells

me as he drops the rashers of bacon into the frying pan with a satisfying fizz. 'Doc says I can go and fetch them home today.'

Grin explained then. 'That's brilliant.'

'Can I leave you in charge?' he asks, as if he thinks he's giving me a major chore to do. 'Shouldn't be too long; I could well be back in action this afternoon but . . . '

'Take as long as you need.'

'You sure?'

'Least I can do.' I give him a matey smile.

'I just don't want you to feel that I'm dumping it all on you at the last minute.' He flips the bacon and starts carving slices off a delicious white loaf.

The way he talks sometimes, you'd think he saw me as slave labour or something. He pays me wages, gives me rent-free accommodation and then apologises for asking me to do some work. Good job he's not that soft when he gets his chef's whites on or we'd never get any food served in this restaurant.

'Seriously mate, I can handle it. You have a day off and look after Carrine. If I need you I'll shout,' I say, almost feeling like I'm the boss and not him.

Once it's cooked, he flips the bacon onto the bread and brings it across to the table. 'It means a lot to me and Carrine, you know. All the things you've done with the restaurant and . . . well . . . helping out with the baby the other night.'

I look up at him and see that for once his perma-smirk has been replaced by a look that's designed to show me he's serious about what he's just said.

'Any time.' I smile before taking a huge bite from my sandwich. 'Any time.'

Cassie

Nick and I spend Sunday, Monday and Tuesday night together. Tonight I'm on my own. Nick left a few hours ago and I already wish he was back here with me. Rabbit is getting about all the attention he can take. It's difficult to describe what a wonderful time Nick and I have. It's not what we do, it's how comfortable we are together.

Last night we cooked. Just cod fried in a pan with butter and lemon juice and lots of parsley and coriander from the garden, a few new potatoes and some carrots. That was it. No pudding, no gallons of wine. A simple meal with a bit of music playing in the background, and it was perfect.

We chatted about how happy he was to have moved out of Sheffield. How it must have been fate for him to have found Rooney, which led to us meeting again at the vet's. And what had I been doing at the Tate in the first place? I don't even like modern art! And nor does Nick! No, we agreed, it was definitely fate. And we were happy for her hand to have intervened.

I rub Rabbit's bony little head and plop him on the sofa cushion next to me.

'Stay there, Rabbit,' I command. 'I just need to make myself a cup of tea.'

I get up and wander into the kitchen. The surfaces are covered in pots and pans that need washing up, so I have to fight my way to the kettle. 'I'll do them tomorrow,' I tell myself as I pop a herbal teabag into a mug.

On the kitchen table is a half-finished (or half-started) game of Monopoly. A game cut short by wandering hands somewhere around Park Lane.

Nick had laughed his head off when I'd suggested playing.

'Oh come on, it's not so bad. Once you've sorted all the money out, it's fun. Buying up hotels everywhere and charging astronomical rent is what life is all about.'

We both laughed as we fiddled about with the pieces and fake money. As Nick had predicted, the game did turn out to be pretty dull. Two players does not a game of Monopoly make. And that's when his right arm snaked round my shoulders and drew me in for a passionate kiss.

I smile at the memory as I add honey to my tea but then, as I stir away, some of my euphoria ebbs away as I remember my conversation with Jilly.

'Nothing lasts for fucking ever!' she'd said bitterly during our chat.

It'd been hard to see Jilly in this state. She was always so strong.

We were sitting in her conservatory at a glass-topped table, the doors open onto the wonderful rolling countryside. A sprinkler in the garden gave off a whooshing sound. The hot summer had parched the lawn so that it was brown and yellow in areas. Bees bobbed about in the flowerbeds, getting fuzzy on nectar.

Jilly refilled my glass of Pimms and sighed again. Wiggy came racing round the side of the house and into view, peddling frantically on her red bicycle, the stabilisers rocking as she turned.

'Be careful, darling!' Jilly called out. 'The ground's like concrete. You'll hurt yourself if you fall off.'

'I'm ok!' Wiggy called back, before disappearing again.

I looked at Jilly. She looked like a five-year-old whose birthday party had been cancelled. Her face had lost its sparkle.

'Well,' I said. 'At least she's not moping about indoors.'

'Like me you mean?'

'No!'

I stretched out my hand to touch hers.

'I saw Jeff just now,' I said quietly, hoping she wouldn't explode. I hadn't had a chance to mention it yet. Jilly had done all the talking. And not much of it good.

'Coming to you now I've given him the boot, is he?'

'No, of course not. He . . . he wanted me to have a word with you. He wanted you to know he's not having an affair.'

Jilly spat out a 'Ha!' and then laughed bitterly.

'I wasn't born yesterday, Cassie. You know I'm not a fool.'

'Oh God, for sure. But he doesn't even know who you think he's having an affair with.'

'Why? There's more than one is there?'

This wasn't going well. I couldn't seem to say anything right. But I had to keep trying. Jeff's miserable face kept coming into my mind like some terrible apparition.

'You can tell me though,' I said more firmly. 'Who is it?' Jilly took another long swig of her Pimms and refilled her glass. She

311

offered me some, but my glass was still full. I wasn't trying to drink my way through a fast-descending depression. She stared at it intently, as if it was a crystal ball.

'You know, when I first met Jeff,' she said. 'I wasn't immediately attracted to him. But I appraised him like I would a house that's up for sale. I thought, hmm, bit run down, needs some work, some areas a bit pokey, roof needs re-thatching, but has potential. Reasonably priced, offered on a long lease, an ideal place to raise a family . . . So, I made my down payment. I took out a fixed-rate mortgage and I got on with it.'

'And you're still getting on with it.'

'Yes, Cassie. I am. But he isn't. He's given up on the family home and gone and rented a beautiful little penthouse in Spain.'

'She's Spanish?'

'Half-Spanish.'

'And you know he's having an affair with her because . . . '

'Because I just know he is.'

Jilly rubbed her forehead furiously.

'Well, you may as well know. He was mixed up with her before. Before we were married and for a while after.'

This takes a while to sink in. How could Jeff have done this? But I recovered my composure to ask again the question that has remained stubbornly unanswered.

'How do you know he's seeing her again?'

And this time Jilly cracks.

'Oh, I don't have any firm proof. I just know!'

And from outside came the sound of a bike crashing into a wall and the squeal of a young child filled the airwaves.

'Oh hell! Can you have a look for the plasters in the kitchen? I'll go and see which knee she's grazed this time.'

* * *

When I went to the pub in Fairford to collect Nick, I asked Jeff about this Spanish woman. He looked shocked, but admitted it.

'It's true,' he said. 'After I got married she still pursued me and I did see her a few times.'

I didn't look at him while he said this. I didn't want to see his face.

'But I'm not seeing her now. She went back to Spain, oh, two or three years ago. I haven't had any contact with her since. What did Jilly say?' he pleaded. 'Will she talk to me?'

I sat down and told him what we'd talked about. His face got glummer and glummer. Eventually he said, 'Well, I'm going to go round there again and give this another try.

It's ridiculous. We should be together.'

And with that he got up and left the pub.

'Happy days,' said Nick ruefully and gave me a kiss. 'Let's hope we don't end up like that.'

★ ★ ★

I take my tea into the living room and play the same album again, wondering if I should call Jilly to make sure she's ok. After wrestling with the conundrum for several minutes I decide against it. I'd told her to phone me if she needed to talk. So I leave it and simply cross my fingers for them.

'They'll be ok, won't they Rabbit?'

Rabbit, who has curled up on my lap again, doesn't answer.

I take his silence to be positive and sip my tea in relative contentment.

Nick

As I lock up the restaurant and drop the keys into my pocket, I can't help but feel excited. I know Pete and Carrine have been home for several hours now and the temptation to nip across and get another look at little Jasmine has been overwhelming.

I caught a quick glimpse of her as I watched them all climb out of the car, but I haven't seen her properly since they all got carted off in the ambulance on the night of the birth.

I'd resolved to give them a few hours together on their own before I went back to the house. I finished all my jobs for today a while ago so I've spent the last hour messing about on the internet.

Now I think they've had enough time together, I get up, stretch, and head across the drive. I don't get as far as the front door before an excited Harry rushes out to greet me.

'Uncle Nick, Uncle Nick, Mummy's brought our new baby home.'

'Has she?' I let him take my hand and lead me into the house.

'She's in here and she's called Jasmine.'

He pulls me by the hand towards the living room. Obviously the disappointment of his sibling not being up for a game of football has worn off.

'She's having her dinner.'

I suddenly realise what he means as I unwittingly intrude on Carrine doing a spot of breastfeeding.

'Sorry.'

I avert my eyes quickly and feel myself

blushing in an undignified manner.

'It's alright.'

Carrine seems completely unruffled by my entrance and just continues as if I'm not there. Well, French girls all sunbathe topless, don't they?

'I don't know. Anything to get a look at a pair of knockers.'

I hadn't noticed Pete standing by the window behind me.

'Better get used to it, mate.'

He comes across and pats me on the shoulder with one of his sturdy hands. 'There's going to be tits and nappies all over the place for the next few months.'

I slump on the sofa while he goes and makes us all a cup of tea. The tension starts to ease.

Harry comes across and sits on my lap. He surveys the scene carefully and I find myself doing the same: watching little Jasmine rhythmically sucking and twitching her little arms and legs as she feeds. I'm at an angle where I can't see Carrine's breast now, so I feel more comfortable. I've never seen a woman breastfeeding before, not in real life, and it suddenly strikes me what a beautiful, natural thing it is.

'Did you used to feed me like that, Mummy?' Harry calls across from his perch on my knee.

'Yes I did.' Carrine's answer is matter-of-fact. I'm impressed how open they are with Harry. I can remember being told all sorts of crap about where babies came from and what you did with them when I was a kid. I have a vague recollection of being told by one of my aunts that Debbie was found under a gooseberry bush.

'I was in your tummy once as well, wasn't I Mummy?'

'Yes, you were sweetheart.'

Jasmine has obviously had her fill now and the feeding station is being packed away. I watch as Carrine rests the baby against her shoulder and gently starts to rub her back.

Harry seems to have lost interest as he's now playing with my tiepin.

'Can we have some chocolate biscuits with our tea?'

He plops off my lap onto the floor and looks at Carrine intently.

'I don't see why not,' Carrine answers. 'I'll go and see if we've got any.'

She stands up.

'There you go, Uncle Nick, I'll do you a swap.'

I look down at the tiny being that's been placed in my arms and then look frantically up at Carrine. She's on her way to the kitchen, leaving me on my own.

317

A tiny pair of brown eyes stare up at me and little arms and legs move up and down of their own accord. I can't believe how small and fragile she feels. My body turns rigid with the fear of moving and damaging her somehow.

I touch her hand with my finger and observe the tiny fingernails. I feel the warmth from her little body against my arm and for the first time I truly understand why Pete has been wearing that huge grin for the last few days.

She really is the most amazing little thing I've ever held.

13

Cassie

The very next morning I'm lying under my high-tog duvet, all snuggly and warm, when the phone goes. I bolt out of bed, sprint down the stairs and grab the receiver. I'm convinced it's going to be Nick, but it's not. It's a much happier-sounding Jilly.

'Darling, everything's back to normal. Jeff and I are having a party to celebrate. You're coming. It's next Friday. Bring your chap. Bring his friends. Bring everyone, ok? Right, got to dash. Have a viewing to do in ten minutes and I'm half-an-hour away. Bye!'

Phew! And everyone says people in the country live life at a leisurely pace! I put the phone down and sigh. It's great news. I don't know how they managed to patch everything up again so quickly, but I'm thrilled. Not only for them, but also because I now have a valid excuse to phone Nick.

'Yes, it's next Friday. Not this Friday. So we can go, yes? I mean you want to, don't you? And Pete and Carrine have been invited too . . . Yes, of course Harry will be able to come as well. We can set him up with Wiggy.'

'Ok, that should be alright. I'll just check with Pete and get back to you.'

I put the phone down, feeling dizzy with the excitement of going to my first party with my new boyfriend, when it rings again. It's Andrew.

'Hello. Sorry, I've been meaning to call for ages, but have just been frantically busy. How are you?'

Well, wonderful, I think, now I've got a man who actually spends some time with me. But I say, 'Fine. I've been meaning to phone you too. The portrait's ready. When do you want to come and pick it up?'

'Brilliant. Sometime next week? Perhaps we could go for a drink?'

'We could do.'

'I would give you a date now, but I don't have my diary on me. I'll phone you early next week and let you know exactly when I'm going to be down again.'

'Fine.'

There's a bit of a pause.

'This might sound silly. But I've been missing you rather a lot.'

This does come as a surprise.

'Really?'

'Yes . . . well, anyway, I've got to run. I'll call you soon.'

'Bye,' I hang up. What a bizarre phone call. Perhaps it's as they say: men are like buses . . .

Nick

'You're a natural, mate.'

Pete pats me on the back reassuringly as I complete my first-ever nappy change. I don't feel like a natural. I thought you just whipped one off and stuck the next one on. No way. There's a whole array of cleaning and cream application and other stuff I'd never thought about.

It's more complex than changing an oil filter and far smellier. Makes dealing with Rooney's little accidents seem like a doddle.

I pick her up from the changing mat and give her a little cuddle. I feel more comfortable holding her now. I've been puked on a couple of times and managed to cope so I'm quite pleased with my progress. I just have to remember to change into something that doesn't require dry-cleaning before I go near Jasmine again.

'Do you think you and Harry are going to make it tonight?' I ask, as I skilfully pop together the fastenings on the baby-grow Pete has just passed to me.

'Don't know.'

Pete takes over and re-does all the fastenings that I've pressed together in the wrong order.

'Carrine says she'll be alright but I don't know if I want to leave her. You know how it is.'

I give him an understanding smile. 'I'll leave my phone on in case you change your mind. But there's no pressure, mate. I'd better get ready.'

★   ★   ★

I emerge from the bathroom with a towel slung around my hips, hair gelled into place and a healthy whiff of aftershave about my person. I wish I felt as good on the inside. I'm bloody dreading this.

I spent most of the morning being dragged round Cirencester by Cassie, looking for a hairdresser and something to wear. The haircut wasn't too traumatic; I needed one really and haven't got round to it since I left Sheffield. But I hate clothes shopping. And it's no more fun down south.

Apparently, the dress code for tonight is 'smart casual'. Forgive my ignorance here, but what the fuck does that mean? Surely you either dress smartly or you dress casually; I have a range of suits for the first option and jeans and t-shirts for the other.

Cassie informed me that what my wardrobe was lacking was a sports jacket for those in-between occasions. Hence I was carted off to a gentlemen's outfitter and cajoled into spending a ludicrous amount of money on the thing that's now hanging on the outside of my wardrobe door.

Cassie reckons I look sexy in it. I reckon I look a total prat. You could get beaten up for wearing something like this where I come from. (Mind you, at least she didn't make me go for the straw-boater and walking cane. There were some in the shop and I thought I saw her looking at them at one point.)

I can't believe she fancies me in the jacket. I look like one of those upper-class buffoons who mince around, cramming about eight-vowel sounds into every word. (And I'm starting to discover there are plenty of them round these parts.)

I reckon most of the people at this do tonight are going to be exactly like that. I met the bloke whose party it is the other day. Cassie sent me to the pub with him after we'd played tennis. (I let her win obviously.) She had to dash off and deal with some girly crisis, leaving me with him. He was a nice

323

enough bloke but very posh and very down in the dumps. We've all been there at some time or another so I tried to cheer him up, though it wasn't easy.

I was praying Pete would accept his invitation so that I'd at least know there was one normal person going, but he's wussed out. Looks like it's me and a load of toffs then.

I sigh slightly louder than is necessary. Oh well, the things you do for love and all that.

I tug off my towel and reluctantly start to get dressed. I feel like a little kid again. Like when your mum used to take you out and buy you crap shoes and then make you wear them for school because they were 'sensible'.

I stand there in my jeans and shirt, and look at myself in the mirror for a moment. I ponder which tie I'm going to wear and then an idea springs into my head. Maybe if I don't wear a tie she'll let me lose the jacket as well. Hmmm! Worth a try.

I open my wardrobe and pull out a pair of shoes, then stop. I allow myself a little smile and then stuff them back into the bottom of my wardrobe and retrieve a pair of trainers instead. They'll look completely stupid with the jacket so I definitely won't have to wear it. Marvellous. I'm feeling better about the party already.

Cassie

I'm not an avid party-goer these days. I don't spend my evenings worrying when the next invitation is going to plop through the letterbox. But when I do get a chance to go out, I grab it with both hands. There's something about bumbling about on a friend's lawn with a glass of Champagne, talking rubbish, which I thoroughly enjoy. Must have inherited it from my mother.

I am so happy this evening for the many reasons you can probably guess. (Yawn!) But just now I discovered something that's given me an even greater buzz. I haven't been a great fan of the internet, as you know, but all that is fast-changing for I have discovered the joys of the search engine, Google. Not only is Google a great word (being very close to goggle), it also makes finding wondrous things so easy.

So what have I discovered that's put my head in such a spin?

A honey possum!

I feel like a zoologist finding a new species!

The honey possum is the cutest thing I've ever seen. On average it's a teeny 50-millimetres long, it lives off pollen and looks like a squirrel. But cuter.

I want one! I want one! I want one!

I'm tempted to board a plane to Western Australia right now and swoop down on one with my butterfly net before cuddling it until its eyes pop!

Oh, and talking of things I love cuddling . . . I can hear someone knocking.

'Nick, hi!' I say, ripping open the door. 'You'll never guess what I've discovered!'

After five minutes of fiddling about with the computer, I manage to return to the possum page and show him what I've been wittering on about.

'It's a rat,' he says when the picture finally appears. 'Oh and look. The female weighs twice as much as the male. No change there then.'

I squeal in indignation.

'It is certainly not a rat! It is the most gorgeous little creature in the whole world. How dare you!' And I give him a playful slap on the shoulder that skims up and catches him on the jaw.

'Ooops!'

But we're both laughing now and Nick is twirling me round the studio with the easel in danger of being knocked over.

'Nick! Put me down!'

'Rat lover! Rat lover!'

I give him a dig in the ribs, so he plops me back on the carpet and I hurtle down the stairs and out into the garden.

'You horrible man!' I shout at him as he comes out to join me. 'Animal hater!'

When we've both calmed down, Nick asks me how long he's got before he has to face the 'MOST DREADED SOCIAL EVENT OF THE YEAR'.

''Bout half-an-hour. Just enough time for a drink.'

I get him a Heineken from the fridge (some I bought especially for him), pour myself a glass of Merlot and take them outside.

'Can I ask you a question?' he says.

'Shoot.'

He stands up and holds out his arms.

'How do I look?'

'Great. Why?'

'Dunno.'

'Do you feel comfortable?'

He nods, but at the same time looks unsure.

'What are you worried about?'

'The jacket. It's not my style.'

'But you look gorgeous in it.'

'I look like a twat.'

'Just wear it there, so I can show everyone how great you look, and then you can take it off. How's that?'

'Ok, I suppose.'

He's so cute! He looks like an awkward

little boy. He's very nervous about this whole party thing. I tell him Jilly has a pool to cheer him up.

He looks suddenly panicked.

'You're not a good swimmer, are you?'

'I'm ok.'

'Ok, like as in tennis ok?'

Ah, so this is the big question, is it?

'Why? Are you worried you'll get beaten again?'

'You didn't beat me. We haven't finished the match.'

Aha! Clever boy!

Nick sits back on the wooden bench not too far from the weeping willow and Pooh's grave. I still look at it with sadness, but I have so many happy memories of the life we shared together it seems wrong to cry because he's gone. He certainly wouldn't want me to weep every day, so I try my best not to. Even so, I sometimes get emotional.

Nick stretches his legs out and puts an arm over my shoulder.

'It's so beautiful here.' He looks round at the scruffy garden, at the weeds and the animals rustling about everywhere.

'It's not perfect, but it's home, you know.'

I lift my legs up so they're at the same height as my hips and click my ankles together.

'You could live here, too. If you want . . . '

Nick looks at me quizzically.

Oh no! He thinks I'm mad. Why did I blurt that out? It's too soon after only a few weeks together. It just slipped out . . . Agh! Help! I'm mad! I'm mad!

Nick

'You could live here too if you want . . . '

I need to take a pause before I respond. I need to be absolutely sure that I heard that right. Nope. I'm not mistaken. Cassie has just asked me to move in with her. Fucking hell! Cassie has just asked me to move in with her!

My initial urge is to throw my arms around her and say, 'Yes please,' in a very undignified way. I manage to keep my composure, but I can't keep the excited smile off my face. 'Really?'

She looks flustered now. Perhaps she thinks she's overstepped the mark. If you were viewing it objectively you'd say it was a crazy idea. We've only been together a few weeks. But I'm virtually living here anyway and the thought of snuggling up to her every night is mighty appealing. Bonkers as it is, I can't think of anything I've ever wanted more. I'm in danger of getting emotional here. Right, come on Nick, cool façade needed. I put on my suave and non-ruffled face, and say casually, 'Only if you'll move my stuff for me.'

'What? Your other pair of boxer shorts, you mean?'

Cheeky minx! I don't hear her complaining too much when she's dragging me up to the bedroom and ripping them off. 'For a posh girl, you're very rude at times.' I pretend to look all huffy and hurt. 'I've got another shirt too.'

I've made her giggle now. She's so cute when she does that. Like a naughty little schoolgirl. She's got one of the most beautiful smiles I've ever seen.

'Drink up. We've got a party to go to. And if you're going to be staying here for a while, I want you to make friends, not get so drunk you fall in the pool.'

Oh God, reality check. I guess if I'm going to be her live-in lover, I'll have to get used to all this on a regular basis. I half-contemplate dragging her off to bed now as a way of getting out of it, but manage to tell myself the sooner we go, the sooner we can come back and . . . I take a big gulp from the can of lager she gave me earlier. I could do with something a bit stronger and faster-acting.

'Come on then.' I take her hand and lead her back towards the house while my resolve prevails and comfort myself with the thought of seeing her scampering around in a bikini for the next few hours.

14

Cassie

When we arrive at Jilly's party there are already fifty-or-so people milling about on the enormous lawn at the front of their house, the men wearing blazers and ties, the women in exotic summer dresses. To the right of the gates is a large marquee. At its entrance there are young waiters and waitresses offering glasses of Pimms or Champagne. I feel Nick's hand tense on mine.

'Shit, maybe I should have worn a tie.'

'Oh, don't be silly. Everybody will have those off in no time. Come on. Let me introduce you to some people.'

'Exhibit 'A'' Nick breathes. 'I'm going to love this, aren't I?'

The first thing I do is get Nick a beer so he can get a bit tipsy before he starts chatting to people. I don't know what he's so worried about. Everyone here is lovely. I think he just has a slight confidence problem, which I hope won't ruin his evening.

'Just be yourself,' I tell him as we begin to mingle. 'Don't worry, no one here's going to bite. These people are just like your sister and Scotty. They'll make you feel right at home. You'll be fine. Pete's coming later with Harry, isn't he?'

'He said he might. But with the baby and everything —'

'Oh wait. There's Jeff.' I guide Nick over and after a warm handshake they're soon into a full deconstruction of the recent football match and Nick is making friends left right and centre. He's just like a child sometimes. He needs a boot in the bum to get him going.

Now he's settled, I have the perfect opportunity to root out Jilly and find out exactly how she and Jeff managed to save their marriage.

After a good wander round the marquee and a scout through the house, I eventually find her sitting in the back garden at a white, cast-iron table, chatting to Daisy. She spots me and hollers, 'Cassie, darling, we were just talking about you!'

'All good, I hope.' I pull up a chair, having given them both a kiss.

'Yes, we were saying what a lucky charm you are.'

'How?' I immediately spot both Jilly and Daisy are a little worse for wear.

'Well, you were a bridesmaid at my wedding and it went wonderfully. And you were one at, um . . . '

'Yes, Tania's. The friend of mine from Oxford.'

'Yes and that went well, didn't it?'

'Well, it rained. The groom forgot the ring. It wasn't great.'

'But you're going to be a bridesmaid at Daisy's wedding, aren't you?'

'Well, possibly not now that she knows about Tania's.'

Daisy laughs. 'Well, you're my last resort, so you'll have to do.'

'Charming!'

She laughs again. 'I'll be yours, I promise.'

'Could be quite soon from what I hear.' Jilly gives me a meaningful look.

I take a sip of my Champagne and a deep breath.

'Yes, well before we get onto that, can we just clear up how your marriage went from sub-zero to red-hot in the space of three days?' I say this in a jokey way, but somehow it ends up coming out sounding quite harsh.

Jilly looks deep into her glass and seems to sober up a bit.

'Well, Jeff told me he has a client in Spain, which is why he's been calling there. I'm not sure I believe him a hundred percent . . . but I looked at Wiggy, and I looked at our home and everything else, and I just decided I had to give him the benefit of the doubt.'

'Oh right.' I'd been hoping for more of a startling or romantic revelation. Something like, 'I just looked at him and realised there was no one else in the whole world I wanted to be with — no matter what he'd done.' A simple 'I just decided to stick with it' came as a disappointment.

Seeing my look, Jilly says, 'It's all about good years and bad years, Cassie. We can't live our lives in fresh, exciting relationships forever, can we?'

'No.' I feel like I've just been lectured, or even slightly punished for enjoying myself with Nick.

'Hey,' Jilly puts an arm across my shoulders and gives me a hug. 'Sometimes, darling, you just have moments when you realise that all the dreams you had as a kid, they just aren't going to come true. You're not going to ride the winner at Badminton horse trials, you're not going to be district commissioner of the VWH, nor are you going to marry the man of your dreams. You're going to be a middle-aged estate agent with a precocious child and a husband who cheated on you soon after you got married. And it all sounds impossibly grim. But then you look around,' and here she gestures expansively round their walled back garden with its high yew hedges, glittering swimming pool and conservatory, 'and you realise that life is pretty darn good. And that you should knuckle down and stick with it.'

'I know,' I say glumly. 'I understand.'

'Good! Right, have you got your cozzie on under that lovely dress?'

I nod.

'Excellent!'

And with that, she and Daisy unceremoniously hoick my dress clean over my head, grab me by the ankles and armpits and drop me into the pool, still holding my glass of Champagne.

Nick

'You'll have to excuse me,' I smile politely at the buffoon in a blazer who has been boring me rigid for the last half-hour with tales of all the things he's done with horses. Unfortunately, none of the things he has done are terribly exciting — mostly feeding them sugar lumps and sticking rosettes on them from what I can gather.

He keeps talking about people he's met that are big in show jumping or dressage or something and I think I'm meant to be looking impressed.

If it weren't for the huge amount of lager I've managed to throw down my neck already I think I'd be losing the will to live by now. Everyone else has been fine. Just my luck to get stuck with the local bore.

Fortunately, I can feel my phone vibrating in my pocket. Might mean Pete's on his way to rescue me. I nip round the back of the marquee and look down at the display. I'm just about to answer when I notice it's not Pete calling. The display is flashing up another name: 'Danielle'.

I press the reject button quickly. I even think about turning the thing off altogether. In fact I would if it weren't for the vain hope that Pete might need some directions.

Why the bloody hell would she be ringing me? You'd think she'd have got the message by now. Mind you, she never did cope well with having a bruised ego. She can go take a running jump for all I care though. I stuff the phone back into my pocket. I suddenly have an overwhelming desire to go and find Cassie. I could do with a kiss and a cuddle from a real woman. One who's sweet, charming and gentle.

As I get back into the thick of it, I realise I'm going to have to wait a while. I can see Cassie splashing around in the pool with her friends. Being completely unprepared on the swimwear front, however, I can't get in and join her.

'I say.' I feel my heart sink as Mr Show Jumping reappears at my side. What is he, my bloody shadow or something? 'The one in the white bikini's a bit tasty, don't you think?'

I look at him and feel slightly sickened by the smarmy, lecherous expression on his face.

'Yep, she is extremely tasty,' I reply. 'She also happens to be my girlfriend.' I give him an ironic smile and stride off towards the pool. Hopefully, I've offended him enough to stop him following me around for the rest of the evening.

'You not getting in?' A new voice addresses me now, one that I actually recognise. It's Jeff, the bloke who Cassie sent me to the pub with the other week. He's looking a bit happier than he did when we last met.

I take another sip from my drink and give him a friendly look. 'Forgot my bikini.'

'Don't fancy skinny-dipping then?'

I look at him slightly horrified and then realise he's joking. I allow myself a cautious chuckle.

'I've got plenty of spare shorts and stuff inside; I'll get you a pair if you like.'

*   *   *

338

Well, I don't know that they're 'me' but I don't suppose anyone will see them once I'm in the water. Can't look that bad, I suppose — I've already had my bum pinched once on the way back across the garden and not by Cassie. She's still in the pool splashing around. I don't think she's even noticed me.

I lower myself gently into the water. I don't go straight across to her. I just stand and observe for a while. Her hair has gone even more curly now it's wet and she looks ridiculously sexy. I can see the shape of her nipples through the bikini top too and . . . well . . . it's a good job I'm up to my waist in water.

I lean casually against the side of the pool, watching her smiling and laughing and splashing about like a kid. And then it suddenly strikes me, real and clear for the first time. I'm one hundred percent sure and there's absolutely no doubting it: I'm completely and utterly in love with her.

Cassie

My dunking in the pool seems to start a trend. Soon after, I'm surrounded by other bodies, bobbing like ducks. My initial intention to get straight out is calmed by

Daisy following me in and then Guy, who seems to appear from nowhere.

'Come on!' Daisy yells at Jilly. 'You're coming in too!'

'Not until it's dark, darling,' Jilly replies. 'Don't want to scare the horses.'

'Oh rubbish, you have a lovely figure,' my sister yells back and she and Guy drag themselves out and pull Jilly in fully-clothed.

'Honestly,' she moans when she surfaces, 'the hostess of the party should be spared this indignity. If I was a fierce old bat, I'd tell my husband to lock all the Champagne in the garage. Then you'd be sorry!'

'You are a fierce old bat,' a voice says from the deep end.

If he wasn't already in deep water, he is now.

Some kind of sloshing water fight ensues and I'm just starting to fret about my mascara when Nick suddenly appears at my side and gives me a lip-smacking kiss.

'Ooh, hello,' I say. 'I didn't see you slip in, so to speak.'

Nick grins at me and gives my waist a squeeze.

'Thought I better hide the fact I didn't have a tie,' he says.

'Well, you'll be alright when you get out,' I reply. 'There's ties lying around all over the show now.'

★ ★ ★

We stay in the pool until it gets dark and the green underwater lights come on and the white up-lighters on the apple trees cast spooky shapes on the branches.

But before we get out, Nick gives me a wonderfully passionate kiss and says, 'Thanks for inviting me today, Cass. I love you, you know.'

!!!!!!!!!!

I am stunned into silence for a moment. Then I remember how much Nick must have had to drink and I relax a little.

'You soppy old thing,' I say and exit the pool sideways so my bum doesn't look too big thrust in the poor boy's face.

★ ★ ★

Much later we're outside the marquee having a lovely long kiss, the live band thumping out *Satisfaction* inside, and I'm suddenly aware of a ringing in my ears. Thinking I must have developed a severe case of tinnitus in the space of half-an-hour of loud music, I ask Nick if he can hear it too.

He looks blank for a second and then realises it's his phone.

Oh! Mobiles. I'm so pleased I don't have one.

341

He fumbles in his pocket and wanders off in the direction of the house for a quieter environment in which to take the call. I prop myself against one of the struts holding the marquee up, my head spinning ever so slightly. I have no idea how much Champagne I've had to drink, but right now my head feels like a hollowed-out melon someone's emptied a full bottle into.

'Having a good time?' Guy asks me as he comes out of the marquee, looking pretty pissed himself.

'The best!' I yell, giving him a hug that could have easily turned into a snog if I was single and about eight years younger.

'Me too. Just need to bolt inside for a piss.'

'Thanks for letting me know.' I grimace.

'Pleasure,' he winks. 'See you later.'

As Guy strides in through the front door, out comes Nick. He's looking terribly green all of a sudden.

'Is anything wrong?' I ask as he arrives next to me.

'I need to go home.'

'Ok. I'm about ready too.'

'No, I feel terrible. I think I should go back on my own.'

'What? You feel sick?'

'Kind of.'

He kisses me on the cheek.

'I'll phone you tomorrow.'

'Ok.'

I'm completely thrown by this strange turn.

'Are you sure you're ok?'

Nick nods.

''Nother glass of Champagne?' Guy asks me as he barrels up to us, clutching two glasses. 'Come on sister-in-law-to-be. Come and dance with me. I insist.'

I give Nick a questioning look and he nods for me to go ahead with Guy.

'I'll see you later,' he says.

I mouth 'ok' and the next thing I know I'm on the dance floor with Guy yanking me about and soon I feel more relaxed, convinced that Nick has just had too much to drink and needs to lie down.

'You know, if I'd met you first,' Guy shouts at me over The Cure's *Love Cats*, 'I'd have definitely asked you to marry me!'

'Oh bugger off!' I yell back, giving him a friendly knee in the balls. 'I'm way too good for you.'

Nick

I might be imagining things, and that's entirely possible now that I'm leathered, but there's something different about the way

Cassie's kissing me now. It's like there's something more than tongues and lips going on here; it's like something inside us is fusing together and making the world around us feel warm and fuzzy at the edges.

I did it, you know. I told her I loved her.

I'd decided not to at first. I didn't want to freak her out or anything but it just came out all by itself, like it was meant to be or something.

She didn't freak out, fortunately. She seemed pleased. She hasn't said it back yet, but that's cool. I'm not going to push it. I'll make do with this bout of passionate snogging in the meantime.

Oh. No I won't. Snogging has stopped momentarily. It's my phone.

'Back in a second.'

I trundle off to find somewhere quieter to answer it. The band's started up now and it's a bit loud.

I look at the screen. Danielle again!

I've had enough of this now. She's obviously as bad as she ever was at taking a hint. I screw up all my annoyance into one big, powerful ball and press the answer button. 'Just what the fuck do you want?'

The next thing I know the phone call's over and I'm giving Cassie an excuse to leave. I hate myself for lying to her but I can't bring myself to do anything else. I kiss her tenderly on the cheek, savouring it, just in case it's the last time I ever get to do it, and tell her I'll phone her tomorrow.

'Are you sure you're ok?'

I can't bring myself to speak again so I just nod and head off. I sling my jacket over my shoulder and walk down the drive and out of the garden. I set off down the lane, faster and faster, without looking back. I don't know where I'm going and I don't really care. I just need to get out of here. I need to be alone.

It's pretty dark now and my eyes take a while to adjust. Part of me wants to fall in a ditch and die. I keep walking and walking. I don't know why but I don't know what else to do.

Eventually I run out of lane. There's just a rickety old gate leading to a scrubby copse.

I sit down heavily on the grass verge and try to make sense of the last few minutes. I hold my hands out in front of me. They're visibly shaking. 'Be careful what you wish for.' That's what they say, isn't it? For once I obviously wished so hard it came true. Unfortunately, about six months too late.

I rerun the phone call in my mind, analysing every syllable, just to make sure I've got it right. All I can hear are Danielle's words ringing around my head in stereo.

'Nick, I'm pregnant.'

I laughed at first. I thought it was just another one of her stupid games. Told her to go away and stop winding me up, that I wasn't interested anymore.

'You really think I'd lie about a thing like this?' She was crying at the other end. She's capable of turning on the tears for effect, but there was something else in her voice, a desperation that let me know she was telling the truth. I didn't let her say anything else. I hung up. I needed time to think. I needed to get away from the noise and the people.

I swallow hard and take my phone from my pocket. I run my thumb over the buttons, plucking up the courage for what I've got to do.

I snatch a bit of resolve from somewhere and start scrawling through the numbers. I press the call button and put the handset to my ear. It doesn't ring for long before I get an answer.

'Dani, it's Nick,' I say before she has a chance to answer.

'Why did you hang up on me?' Her voice is slicing and petulant.

'Why do you think? You can't expect me to just hear that and —'

'Nick, I've got to see you. We've got to sort this out. I can't do this on my own.'

'And you're sure it's mine?'

The intake of breath at the end of the phone signifies her outrage at me daring to ask that question.

'I don't believe you're asking me that. How can you ask me that?'

'Because I'm well aware of what a conniving little bitch you can be at times, that's how I can ask,' I spit back bitterly.

'You bastard.' I can hear a fresh wave of sobbing at the other end of the line. But it doesn't have the intended effect. I think I'm meant to feel sorry for her and say, 'There, there dear' or something. I don't. I just feel sick.

'You did this on purpose, didn't you?' I feel the anger start to rev up inside me. 'You just thought to yourself, 'I know, Nick's actually getting on quite well without me; I'll just turn up and fuck up his life again.' You selfish, spoilt little cow.'

I don't get any words in return. Just more breathless sobbing.

'I'll ring you tomorrow,' I say and end the call. I can't face listening to any more of that.

I bury my face in my jacket. It still smells of Cassie's perfume. I reach beside myself and pull up a tuft of grass and throw it blade by blade onto the road in front of me. What the fuck am I going to do?

I just keep thinking how it felt to hold Jasmine the other day and wonder if I'll ever get to hold my own kid like that. Should I go back to Danielle and sort stuff out? Or leave her to handle it and spend my whole life wondering?

Whichever way I look at it, it's a mess. A total bloody mess. No matter how many times I push this around my head, I can't find an answer. How could it have all gone so completely wrong?

My phone goes again and the glowing screen tells me that it's Danielle back for another round. I switch it off and get to my feet. Then, I swing my arm back and throw the phone as far as I can over the wall into the trees. Whatever it is I don't want to hear it.

My chest tightens and the feeling of nausea intensifies. There's someone else I need to be talking to now. I'm not looking forward to it, but for once in my life I'm going to have to find the guts to do the right thing.

I take another deep breath before turning to retrace my steps. I could probably forgive Danielle for everything else but I'll never forgive her for making me do this.

15

Cassie

So the night has turned into a complete disaster. My life is in ruins. I don't ever want to speak to another man again.

Way back in 1997, when an email was even more of a mystery to me than it is now, I had a boyfriend. I was nineteen-years-old and impossibly naïve. I'd never slept with a boy, I'd only kissed a few and I had an idealised view of romance.

I thought I'd meet the most gorgeous man, we would fall totally in love, we'd buy a little place in The Cotswolds and have fab dinner parties with our friends, bugger about in the country air, visit our local pub and have a mad menagerie of animals.

The boyfriend I had while I was doing my art foundation course in Oxford was called Tim. He was the man I could see it all happening with. He was the man I wanted it all to happen with. And for a time, I think he wanted it too.

All my friends thought Tim was lovely. He was good-looking in a stocky, farmer way.

He had lovely manners, came from a family that bred racehorses, and complimented me so often I felt like a supermodel, even though I was chubby and gawky.

I suppose it was me thinking that Tim was too good for me which eventually put him off. My constant need to be reassured got boring. So it was no surprise, I suppose, when he started dating a girl who really did look like a supermodel and didn't need to be told she looked like one every five minutes.

It didn't help my heartbreak, however.

The day he dumped me I went from painting wonderful butterflies to dull moths. And I continued with the moths for more than a year after our relationship ended. Every moth I painted represented the hole that had opened up in my life the moment he left.

Moths bumble about in the dark, looking for light. And that's really how I felt. Only I couldn't find any light. The light in my life had been switched off. And it stayed off for years after Tim left me on my own.

Standing in my studio now, the curtains drawn, still in my dress, I take a brush and dip it in the black gouache and carefully apply a stroke to my painting. The picture of the Large Blue butterfly that I was so proud of is soon almost black.

The hope and joy it represented is gone. The vibrant blues and turquoises that I applied with such pleasure a few weeks ago are nearly obliterated. This Large Blue butterfly is a few minutes away from being extinct.

Just like my romance with Nick.

★　★　★

I was dancing with Guy, then with Jeff, then with some guys I don't know that well and then . . . then I got a tap on the shoulder . . . and it was Nick. He'd come back to the party.

Delighted, I went to hug him, but he pushed me away.

His mouth moved and I think he said, 'I've got something I need to tell you.'

He looked extremely drunk. But who was I to tell? I was staggering about myself.

He grabbed my arm and guided me through the dancing couples, out into the fresh air. We had to go a long way from the marquee before we could find a place quiet enough to speak. I can't remember quite where it was, but it was somewhere in the front garden, near the drive.

'I can't see you any more,' he said, looking drunkenly into my eyes. 'My ex-girlfriend's pregnant. I'm so sorry . . . '

After that I think I must have gone into intense shock because I can't remember a thing. I just ran off and kept running until I got back here.

★ ★ ★

Feeling utterly miserable, and totally shattered, I put the brush back into the jam jar of water, give the almost black painting one last look and toddle out to my bedroom. Without even getting out of my dress I flop onto the bed and promptly pass out.

Nick

I'll never forget the look on her face as long as I live. The moment where she registered what I was saying and looked at me like . . . well, like I'd just torn her heart out.

She's better off without me. I knew I'd screw things up, I always do. Just a shame I didn't have the courage of my convictions in the beginning. I should have left her alone and not dragged her into the miserable disaster that has been my life so far.

I tried so hard this time. I was determined

this wasn't going to go wrong. Not with her.

The clock on the dashboard tells me it's nearly 2am. I've no idea where I'm driving to or why I'm going there. I just couldn't face going home to bed so I'm driving far too fast, screeching round bends on dark country lanes, the CD player pounding out music as loud as I can get it. I'm trying to drown out everything: thoughts, feelings, the memory of the last few hours. I'm in the middle of nowhere. The car is bumping and shuddering along the gravel track that took over where the road left off a few hundred yards back.

Suddenly a stone wall appears in front of me. I stamp hard on the brakes and wrench the wheel. The car skids sideways into the verge.

Everything goes silent. I've stalled the engine and the CD player switches off momentarily. I've forgotten to breathe for the last couple of seconds. My initial thought is I could have killed myself. My second thought is that I'm not that sure I care.

The music surges back through the speakers, 'Babe I'm gonna leave you'. How appropriate. I almost find myself amused by my stereo's sense of irony. I don't restart the engine. I just get out into the stuffy night air. I leave the door wide open so that the music booms out and fills the fields and lanes around me.

In the beam of the car headlights I can see all manner of flying insects fluttering and zooming about.

I suddenly feel the urge for more noise. I've got the CD up as loud as it will go but it's not enough. I don't want quiet. That would make me have to think and I don't want to think. I spot a loose hedge stake lying in the long grass by the side of the track. I go over and pick it up.

The splinters from it prickle into my hands but I don't care. I swing the stake up high above my head and bring it crashing down onto the gravel beneath my feet. The ground puts up too much resistance for my liking. Just a dull thud and a shock back through the stake that rattles up my arms. I need something that won't resist, something that will cave in and fracture as I hit it, something that's going to pay for how I feel. An old gate obliges. It's one of those steel tubular ones that usually guard farmers' fields. This one is leaning against the wall, hiding behind a few feet of unkempt grass. It can't escape though. I've seen it and I'm ready.

My elbows and shoulders resonate painfully as I bring the stake down time after time on the metal tubes, making them clang and sing out in pain. My hands are raw and full of splinters but still I carry on smashing and denting.

With every swing I feel the anger tighten inside me. With every impact I feel the tears being jolted nearer and nearer the surface until I can't take anymore.

I throw the stake back into the long weeds and sit down heavily on the stony ground, hurting, sobbing and wondering just what the hell I'm going to do.

★　★　★

It's nearly 3am when I get back to Pete's. I can see a light on upstairs and I guess little Jasmine is interrupting their beauty sleep again.

I pull into the car park and notice a big Mercedes parked next to Pete's car. For a nanosecond I find myself wondering who it belongs to. But I don't care. The bloody Queen could have come to visit and I couldn't give a toss at this moment.

I climb out of the car and slam the door hard behind me.

Then the most bizarre thing happens. I feel a tap on my shoulder and spin round quickly to see who it is.

But there isn't much time to focus. A fist

shoots towards me. There's a loud crack as it connects with my face. I'm on the ground, my head spinning, my lip throbbing, and my mouth full of blood.

Instinctively, I scramble to my feet.

'Oh, you're getting up for some more are you?'

In the darkness I can make out the figure of a man.

I don't get a very good look at him before the next punch flies towards me.

I attempt to dodge it. 'Who the fuck are you?'

'Never mind who I am. It's who *you* are that's important.' The voice is gruff and angry. 'You're the bastard that's got my girlfriend pregnant.'

A series of thoughts attempt to connect in my head as I try to fight back. I bring up my foot, kick it hard into his body, and send him reeling backwards a few feet.

But it doesn't defeat him. He's back within seconds. I feel another punch connect. This time with my ribs.

I swing one back. I think I got him on the side of the head but I'm not sure. The return soon comes, full weight into my stomach, winding me and sending me pole-axed to the ground. I feel the tarmac rip the elbows out of my shirt as I land and skid. I see him bearing down on me as I lay there unable to move. He swings his leg back to kick me. There's nothing else I can do. I screw my eyes shut and wait for it.

It doesn't come. I just hear a scuffling noise and a grunt.

'You move another fucking muscle and I'll break every bone in your body, do you understand?'

If I wasn't still winded I'd get up and kiss Pete.

My attacker is now squirming face down on the tarmac with my friend's knee driven into the back of his neck, pinning him to the floor.

I feel the breath start to seep back into my lungs and I'm about to ask him three billion different questions when another set of headlights appear from nowhere, making us all squint and shield our eyes.

The door of the car flies open and out gets a female figure.

'Nick!' I recognise Danielle's hysterical squeal straight away. 'Nick, I've come to warn you . . . ' Her histrionics stop mid-flow as she notices the struggling body under Pete's knee.

'You came to warn me what? Because I didn't immediately say, 'That's wonderful dear, let's get back together and play happy families,' you've sent your new boyfriend round to work me over?'

'No ... no ... I ... ' For once she seems to be stuck for words. She's not even sure whether to burst into tears. She's not sure at all where her master plan to have every male on the planet running around after her has gone wrong. I can read her face like a book, even in the half-light of the car headlamps.

I use the back of my hand to wipe some of the blood from my lip and stare hard at her.

'Well, as we've got everybody here. Perhaps we can sort this out. All cosy and friendly, you know.'

'Sounds like a good idea to me,' Pete's captive says as he's finally allowed to get to his feet.

All eyes glare at Danielle, waiting for an answer.

'I can't ... I've got to go ... I need time to think.' She lunges back towards her car but I'm faster. I push her to one side and tug the keys out of the ignition.

'Like I said, I think we need to sort this out. Clear up a few things. Like the fact that you didn't actually mention that you'd got a new boyfriend when you came knocking on my door.'

'Don't talk shit! You begged her to come back. She told me everything about what's been going on these last few months. You just couldn't take the fact that she didn't want you and she wanted me.' His voice is angry and bitter and the weird thing is, I actually feel sorry for him.

'Look, I don't know what my scheming bitch of an ex-girlfriend has been telling you, but I assure you that most of it is lies.' I look at her when I say this. Not at him. I want her to look me in the eye but she can't. She just stares at the ground. 'I've slept with her once since we split up. Once. A few weeks ago. And I think you'll remember when it was, as you inadvertently gave me a message to pass on to her on the phone.'

'And you expect me to believe that?' He's pretending to find it amusing now, a cocky laugh and a bit of a swagger. A quick stare from Pete soon checks him.

'Believe what you like. I really don't give a toss.'

'Well, just explain one thing to me then?' He looks like a man who's about to lay the ace of spades on the poker table. 'If what you say is true, then how come she's three months pregnant with your kid?'

I feel myself physically jolt as the wires connect in my brain. It's me who's laughing now. Laughing so much I have to sit down on the bonnet of Danielle's car.

'What's so bloody funny?' He obviously hasn't worked it out. She's frazzled his brain with so many lies that he doesn't know what's real and what isn't.

'Do you want to tell him or shall I?' I look at Danielle who, true to form, is cranking up the waterworks. 'What were you going to do? Try and sneak your way back into my life and hope I didn't notice that it turned up a few months early? Hope I was so pleased about it I wouldn't bother counting?'

'I'm sorry Nick . . . I . . . '

'Go on sweetheart, you have a good sob. You might as well. You've got a lot to be sorry for. You've fucked up my life, you've fucked up his and, for once, you seem to have fucked up your own as well.'

'You mean it is mine?' He looks at her and she manages a pathetic nod. He rushes over and holds her. I feel the urge to puke.

'Aw, isn't that nice; you can now both piss off and stop bothering me.'

'Come on mate, let's get you inside.' Pete puts his arm around my shoulder and steers me towards the house.

We both sit down at the kitchen table. I wipe the blood from my face with the end of my sleeve and take a gulp from the brandy he's just poured for me.

'You want to tell me what the hell that was

all about?' Pete's tone isn't interrogatory. More a mate-like offer to listen. But I've troubled him enough for one night.

'You go to bed mate; I'll tell you all about it in the morning.' I attempt a smile. 'Thanks though, for saving my neck out there.'

'Any time, mate.' He pats my shoulder and dumps the bottle of brandy on the table in front of me. 'Any time.'

★　★　★

I sit there in the kitchen for a while. I don't feel like going to bed. I won't sleep anyway.

So me and the bottle of brandy reconvene in my office. I don't know why. It just feels like the right place to come to.

I've got the blinds open so I can see out of the window. It's starting to get light outside and I can just make out the rooftops against the horizon.

Cassie's rooftop.

I sip the brandy I'm holding. I don't know how many I've had but it's a lot. I thought it might numb this gut-wrenching ache that's going on inside me, but no such luck.

I wish I hadn't panicked. That I'd just kept my mouth shut until I was sure. I'd probably still have her now. I'd be looking forward to more kite-flying and puppy-minding and all those other silly things that she loves to do. I could have been holding her in my arms again tonight, looking down and watching her sleeping against my chest. But I threw it away. I took the most wonderful thing that has ever happened to me and I threw it away.

I can't believe I've been such a prat.

Cassie

Not much later I am woken by my animals.

First I get a quacking Tigger, next the twin cuddliness of Piglet and Roo, and finally little Rabbit. I don't kid myself that they actually understand I'm in a total mess and need attention. They're hungry because I forgot to feed them last night and every time another of them arrives I say to myself that I'll go down and give them something, but I simply can't move. I feel strapped to the bed like Frankenstein's monster.

I'm just about to drag myself up when I hear a knock at the door. My whole being freezes. I'm tempted to ignore it, but am finally driven to see who it is.

I run a comb through my hair so it doesn't look too hideous and rush downstairs.

Yanking open the door the person who greets me gives me a shock, but not an unwelcome one. It's still dark outside, but I can see his face clearly enough.

'I just wanted to check on how you were,' the deep, manly, ever-so-slightly plummy voice says.

'Andrew. That's very sweet of you. Come in.'

I lead him into the kitchen and sit him at the table.

'You seemed terribly upset earlier. I was at the party and saw you rush off. I thought I might just pop in and check you were ok on my way home. I noticed the light on in the kitchen.'

I'd forgotten to turn it off in my inebriated state.

'Oh thanks. That's very . . . kind.'

'It's nothing. I was worried about you. How are you?'

'Still drunk, I think. The whole night's a complete blur.'

Andrew stands up and opens his arms.

'You've had a terribly tough time. Do you need a hug?'

'Yes.'

And I stand up and he takes me in his arms and holds me very tightly.

'You're a lovely person. I wish I could see more of you.' His voice sounds sad.

'Well, perhaps you can . . . '

My words hang in the air. I can hardly believe I've just said them.

'I mean . . . God, I don't know what I mean.'

Andrew puts his arms round me again and I find the warmth of his body very comforting.

Nick

I stumble down the lane, clinging onto the low stone wall beside me for support. My other hand is still clutching Pete's bottle of brandy. I haven't had a drink from it since I left the office but it feels comforting to have my hand clasped around its neck.

I have no idea what I'm going to do or say when I get to the cottage but I need to see Cassie. I have to tell her I'm sorry, even if she just turns round and tells me to piss off.

I attempt to open the small gate that leads to the front of her house, but I don't quite manage it. Somehow my leg gets caught up and I end up awkwardly straddling it before falling face first into the garden.

As I lay there, my legs still on the path, my body on the strip of lawn and my head stuck uncomfortably in a small lavender bush, it occurs to me that I ought to feel like a complete plonker. But as there doesn't seem to be anyone around, I just roll my body across the garden and lay like a starfish on the grass.

I put the bottle of brandy down neatly beside me and let the dew from the grass soak slowly into my clothes. What's left of them. (Note for the future: don't wear best shirt next time you have an evening of girlfriend dumping and car park brawling.) The dampness from the ground is refreshing as it permeates through to my battered body. I look up at the sky. It's got the greenish tint that it always has as the sun is coming up.

After lying here for a few minutes, I decide it's time for action. Unfortunately my legs don't understand and refuse to cooperate. I'm stuck here drunk and paralysed, the house and plants spinning round me.

'Cassie!'

I call out her name as loud as I can manage.

Either she'll come out and help or if not she'll run me through with a pitchfork. But at least I'll know where I stand.

'Cassie!' I holler for a second time.

The lack of response tells me I'm probably wasting my time.

Suddenly I hear a sound, a clunking or rattling noise. Like a key being turned in a lock. She's coming. She's heard me.

I manage to hoist myself up onto my elbows to look. 'Cass?' I whisper hopefully as a figure emerges from the house.

'No, actually. I'm not.'

It takes a moment for my inebriated brain to process this bit but soon I come to realise that, unless Cassie has undergone some spectacular metamorphosis in the last six hours or so, this isn't her.

'Who the bloody hell are you?' I ask, aware that I'm slurring my words.

'I'm a friend of Cassie's.'

Probably one of her posh friends from the party. I suddenly get it. This is my punishment being dished out. I dump her; she comes home with a posh bloke and shags him bandy. Fair cop I suppose. Except I think I'd have preferred the pitchfork treatment. The stabbing feeling in my guts right now is pretty much as I'd imagine that to be.

I curl my fingers into my hands and clench my fists tightly as the thought of her in bed with him becomes 3D and real in my head. Just because I deserve it doesn't make it any easier to swallow.

'Good was it?' I ask, petulantly lying back down on the ground.

'Sorry?'

I'm about to enlighten him when a second

voice enters the arena — the one that I've been desperate to hear.

'Nick? Oh my God, what happened to you?'

I hear the soft scuffle of feet across the gravel path and then I feel a soft hand touch my forehead.

'It's alright Cass.' I look up into her eyes and laugh. 'It's alright. It's not mine.'

Cassie

I seem to have been in Andrew's arms for hours when we hear someone calling my name from outside. I peer out of the window. I can't see anyone. Then my name is shouted again. A strangled, desperate cry that has a familiar northern twang to it.

I feel like I've been hit by a cattle prod. A zing of electricity bolts through me. Panicked, I shove Andrew towards the door, instructing him to see what Nick wants, wherever he is.

Andrew nods solemnly and strides down the corridor with a purposeful step. As he opens the door I strain my head around him to try to catch a glimpse of Nick, but I can't see anything.

My heart is pounding, my fingertips are pounding and I find, suddenly, that I'm not breathing properly. I'm not breathing at all.

I rush past Andrew, not feeling any pain as my bare feet fly across the gravel, and find Nick spread out like a, well, like a road accident really, half in and half out of my flowerbed.

I crouch down next to him, putting my hand on his head.

It's as hot as the side of a kettle.

'Andrew!' I call over my shoulder. 'Can you give me a hand getting him inside. I think he's really sick.'

Andrew crouches down next to me and peers at Nick's face.

'I think he's just had too much to drink.'

'But look at his hands! They're all bleeding and covered in splinters.'

Andrew looks down, agreeing they look pretty grisly.

'And his lip is split. It looks like he's been in a fight.'

'He could have just fallen over.'

'But he needs help.'

I look at Andrew pleadingly.

'Alright.'

He pulls Nick to his feet by his forearms. 'Come on inside and we'll get you cleaned up.'

With a weird new dance, we manage to pirouette Nick through the door, down the corridor and onto the saggy sofa in the living room. I put an extra cushion under his head to keep him from lying right back and ask Andrew to get a bowl of warm, salty water from the kitchen.

I look down at Nick. He's having great difficulty keeping his eyes open. His skin looks awfully pale, almost grey. His chin is covered in blood.

'Nick,' I whisper. 'How do you feel? Where have you been?'

'The baby's not mine.'

He manages to look right at me with his bloodshot eyes.

'It's not?'

'No.'

His voice sounds blurred by the booze and his split lip.

'She was just being a bitch.'

Andrew comes in with the warm water and some kitchen roll and I begin to bathe Nick's ruined face. He winces as I rub away the blood.

'Andrew. Would you mind nipping upstairs and getting me some cotton pads. They're in the bathroom, in the cupboard underneath the sink.'

'Of course,' he replies, but I can tell he's not happy with all the attention I'm lavishing on Nick.

After he's gone, I say to Nick, 'So you didn't sleep with her?'

He shakes his head.

'What does that mean? You did, or you didn't?'

'I'm sorry, I did. But only a few days after we met. I realised straight after that I didn't want to do it ever again, and . . . '

And here his face screws up and tears begin to roll down his cheeks, mingling with the blood on his chin. I wipe them away with my thumb but, after a moment of restraint where I think he's going to stop, the tears suddenly surge out of him with such force that his whole body shakes with the sobbing.

'I just want us to be together. I never want to see that bitch again . . . but now I've screwed everything up.'

I look up to see Andrew standing in the doorway.

I wave my hand at him to leave us alone for a bit and he recedes, but not before throwing the cotton pads onto the sofa next to me and nodding resignedly.

My mind is racing now. On autopilot I start bathing Nick's hands, easing the splinters from his palms.

'I'm sorry,' Nick keeps saying. 'I'm sorry.'

I finish cleaning up his left hand without saying anything. Nick just stares up at me with his glassy eyes.

I start working on his other hand, with more force than before, and he cries out.

'Oh, don't be such a girl,' I snap. 'You've only got a few cuts.'

He closes his eyes and winces as I scrub at his palms, but he doesn't dare moan.

Andrew reappears in the doorway with two cups of coffee.

'Thought you guys could use a drink to sober you up.'

God! Now Andrew's being so charming and sweet. And he looks incredibly dashing in his shirtsleeves with his hair a bit of a mess.

He puts the coffees on the table and tells me he'll be in the garden if we need anything.

'Who's he?' Nick asks a few moments after Andrew has retreated to the great outdoors with a cigarette.

'A friend.'

'He seems really . . . nice.'

'He is.'

I can see Nick trying to work out what the situation is.

'Are we going to get back together?'

'I don't know.'

'You're not going to go out with him, are you?'

'I don't know. I don't think so.'

'So there's a chance we can get back together?'

'There's a chance. Yes.'

Nick attempts a smile, but his lips are too broken for it to work.

I lean forward and kiss his forehead.

'You need some rest. I'm going to get you a blanket. You're going to sleep off the booze and then we'll talk some more, ok?'

'Ok,' Nick agrees. 'Thanks.'

By the time I return with the blanket Nick has passed out and Andrew is back in the kitchen. I tuck Nick up on the sofa, take a sip of my coffee and ask Andrew if he wants to go for a walk.

'That would be lovely.'

I put a jacket on, quickly check all the animals, and then we stride out into the pink early-morning light and trudge up the lane.

16

Nick

'You've got everything that you need?' Carrine looks at me intently. I think she senses just how nervous I really am.

I run the mental checklist through my head.

'Starters are in the fridge, main course will be ready in about half-an-hour and all I've got to do is whip the cream and garnish the desserts when we need them.'

'I will make a cook of you yet.' Carrine smiles and gives me a hug. 'If she doesn't appreciate this then she doesn't deserve you. I will leave you now.'

She smiles at me, gives me a final good luck hug then strides off through the back door and across to the house.

I watch out of the window as she departs. She waves to someone and I'm pleased to see it's Cassie.

I watch them hug each other, both smiling. Although I'm pleased to see Cassie giggling, it doesn't diminish the nervous anticipation that's been mounting up inside me all day.

The pressure to get this right has been turning me inside out.

Cassie looks so beautiful as she stands there chatting. She's wearing her hair down and it flutters slightly around her face in the breeze.

At last the girlie chat is over. Carrine goes towards the house and Cassie heads in my direction.

'Hi.' She smiles sweetly at me as she steps into the kitchen. 'Gosh, this is amazing, isn't it?'

I'd forgotten this was the first time she'd ever been inside the restaurant. It's impressive now it's all finished and the builders and plastic covers have gone.

'Let me show you the rest of it.'

I sound really formal, but it seems appropriate somehow. It's like it puts us at a comfortable distance from each other, a place from where we can start again.

'Thank you.'

She steps towards me and hooks her arm through mine like we're a Victorian lady and gentleman. I guide her through to the main restaurant, now fully decked out with tables and chairs. Just one table has a cloth on it, and a candle and a single white rose in a small crystal vase.

'Oh Nick.' She clasps her hands to her mouth

as she beholds the view. So far, so good.

I wander over to the array of switches behind the bar and dim the lights slightly.

'Would madam care to be seated?' I ask above the sound of the music I've got playing softly in the background.

'Madam would quite like a hug first if that's alright.'

I feel like pulling my shirt over my head and doing a celebratory lap of the restaurant. The thought of touching her again makes me tremble.

I stretch my arms out in front of me and then pull her tightly into my body. I can't believe how good it feels.

I wrap my arms around her, enjoying the sensation of my cheek against her hair. It feels like an eternity since I last held her.

I'm suddenly aware I might be squeezing her a little too hard so I loosen my grip slightly.

She looks up into my face and smiles.

'So. How have you been?' I ask, my voice quavering.

Cassie

About a week after the garden party, having had numerous conversations with Jilly, Daisy, my mother(!) and even my father(!!) about the perils of dating a complex man, I decide I have to call Nick to find out how he is.

When he answers the phone and realises it's me, he seems to turn into a gibbering wreck and has trouble getting his words out, though he does manage to very sweetly ask me for dinner. Tonight.

I accept without hesitation and then kick myself as I remember Jilly's words, 'Play hard to get. Don't make it easy for him.'

Drat!

Now I'm standing in my kitchen, dressed in my little black dress and strappy black shoes. I'm doing some deep breathing exercises in between glugs of wine, but my hands are still shaking.

I want to touch one of my lovely animals before I go, but I can't because I'll get hair all over my dress. So instead, I lick my fingers and pat all those present on the head, hoping they think I've kissed them.

I then take one final hit of wine and dash out of the door before I have a chance to chicken out.

After a brief chat with Carrine, who sweetly tells me Nick is more nervous than I could ever be about tonight, I walk into the restaurant. As Nick greets me I feel my heart hammering at the back of my throat, but I think I manage to look reasonably composed.

He looks gorgeous with his hair tousled and, as he shows me round the restaurant, I can't seem to take anything in apart from him. He looks so smart in his suit and he smells divine!

I think we're onto the main course before I'm calm enough to start thinking straight again.

'I've missed you so much this week,' Nick tells me, playing with rather than eating his guinea fowl.

'I've missed you too,' I blurt.

Oh drat, drat! Play it cool, Cassie. Play it cool.

'I mean. It's been good to have some time apart. Some space to think things over.'

Nick nods.

'I'm so sorry about what I did. It won't ever happen again.'

'Yes, but how do I know that?'

Wow! I've done it! I've asked a proper question.

Nick's eyes fill with sadness and then a little sparkle comes into them.

'Because I love you. I truly love you.'

And that's when all Jilly's advice goes out of the window and I revert to Daisy's approach: go with the flow.

I put my hand over Nick's and give it a squeeze.

'I love you too, you silly boy.'

'Really?'

Nick looks shocked.

'Really. I haven't been able to think about anything else all week. I went for a walk with Andrew after you passed out on my sofa. I thought maybe I could forget about you if I was talking to him. But I couldn't. Even when he was looking gorgeous and you were looking like a riding accident, I still couldn't get you out of my head.'

His face cracks into a huge grin.

'So we can forget all that crap from before?'

'I've forgotten it already.'

'Can I hug you?' Nick asks, getting up.

I stand up next to him and he draws me in. Before long the hug has turned into a full-on snog and I'm going all light-headed again.

When we break off I feel such a sense of euphoria that my brain goes onto blurt mode and I say something Jilly would spank me for, 'So, when are you moving in then?'

Nick hugs me tighter, telling me it might even be tonight. And, despite everything, I know we're going to be very happy and I'm just slipping into a romantic reverie when Pete comes rushing into the restaurant, shouting, 'Wednesday won! Wednesday won!'

'But it's Tuesday, isn't it?' I bleat, all confused.

And the boys roar with laughter and tell me it's their football team and I feel foolish but with an accompanying warm glow.

Sheffield Wednesday, I note. Not Sheffield Tuesday.

See? I'm getting into the swing of my new life already!

I am and I love it!

We do hope that you have enjoyed reading this large print book.

Did you know that all of our titles are available for purchase?

We publish a wide range of high quality large print books including:
Romances, Mysteries, Classics
General Fiction
Non Fiction and Westerns

Special interest titles available in large print are:
The Little Oxford Dictionary
Music Book
Song Book
Hymn Book
Service Book

Also available from us courtesy of Oxford University Press:
Young Readers' Dictionary
(large print edition)
Young Readers' Thesaurus
(large print edition)

For further information or a free brochure, please contact us at:
Ulverscroft Large Print Books Ltd.,
The Green, Bradgate Road, Anstey,
Leicester, LE7 7FU, England.
Tel: (00 44) 0116 236 4325
Fax: (00 44) 0116 234 0205

Other titles published by
The House of Ulverscroft:

SPIRIT WILLING, FLESH WEAK

Julie Cohen

Rosie Fox is a really good liar. But when you're a stage psychic who's not actually psychic, you have to be. One night, while pretending to commune with the dead relatives of her audience, Rosie makes a startling prediction — which tragically comes true. Suddenly she's trapped in a media frenzy, spearheaded by the handsome journalist Harry Blake, a man intent on kick-starting his stalled career by exposing Rosie as a fraud. Yet when his interest in her goes from professional to personal, she thinks she can trust him not to blow her cover — but maybe she's making a huge mistake.

THE SCENT OF WATER

Alison Hoblyn

History repeats itself, so they say. Perhaps it has to because no-one listens? Ellie, an artist in her middle age, needs to live her life in a new way after the death of her husband. She enrols on a garden course in Tuscany one spring. Here she begins relationships with fellow students Nerine, an eccentric character in her seventies, and the younger Max. Through the teaching of Salvatore — the owner of an ancient palazzo — who runs the course, Ellie finds that the universal truths, expressed in the Renaissance painting *Primavera* and the philosophy of Marsilo Ficino, are still potently relevant.

HE LOVES LUCY

Susan Donovan

Most women would *kill* to have access to personal trainer Theo Redmond. But Lucy Cunningham's starting to wish she'd never met him! Marketing exec Lucy's original idea for a reality TV show, in which Theo transformed someone from flabby to fabulous, hadn't featured *her* being the star . . . Balancing the need to lose weight against being watched by the whole of Miami, Lucy sweats her way into a new life. And as things also heat up between them, could chocoholic Lucy and Gym Bunny Theo be about to discover that true love lies somewhere between pizza and Pilates?

THE EX-WIFE'S SURVIVAL GUIDE

Debby Holt

Sarah Stagg thought she had it all: a lovely husband, twin teenage sons, a cottage in the country. Then her husband, an amateur thespian, leaves her for his leading lady, her sons go off to India, and Sarah is left alone and single. The path of a discarded wife is strewn with hazards and humiliations, and Sarah needs to acquire survival skills. Help (and hindrance) is at hand in the form of well-meaning neighbours, a psychopathic mongrel, an unassuming plumber — and an unwelcome role as Mrs de Winter in the forthcoming Ambercross Players' production of *Rebecca*.

1	26	51	76	101	126	151	176	201	355
2	27	52	77	102	127	152	177	202	357
3	28	53	78	103	128	153	178	203	363
4	29	54	79	104	129	154	179	204	375
5	30	55	80	105	130	155	180	205	380
6	31	56	81	106	131	156	181	206	383
7	32	57	82	107	132	157	182	208	400
8	33	58	83	108	133	158	183	212	451
9	34	59	84	109	134	159	184	227	453
10	35	60	85	110	135	160	185	233	460
11	36	61	86	111	136	161	186	234	461
12	37	62	87	112	137	162	187	237	478
13	38	63	88	113	138	163	188	238	486
14	39	64	89	114	139	164	189	241	488
15	40	65	90	115	140	165	190	242	509
16	41	66	91	116	141	166	191	243	511
17	42	67	92	117	142	167	192	262	519
18	43	68	93	118	143	168	193	269	523
19	44	69	94	119	144	169	194	279	534
20	45	70	95	120	145	170	195	288	552
21	46	71	96	121	146	171	196	299	570
22	47	72	97	122	147	172	197	310	575
23	48	73	98	123	148	173	198	312	583
24	49	74	99	124	149	174	199	331	619
25	50	75	100	125	150	175	200	341	624